Owen

AN **UNDERCOVER BILLIONAIRE** NOVEL

MELODY ANNE

Montlake
Romance

Text copyright © 2018 by Melody Anne
All rights reserved.

Published by Montlake Romance, Seattle

www.apub.com

Amazon, the Amazon logo, and Montlake Romance are trademarks of Amazon.com, Inc., or its affiliates.

ISBN-13: 9781503905153
ISBN-10: 1503905152

Cover design by Letitia Hasser

Cover photography by Wander Aguiar

Printed in the United States of America

This is dedicated to my father. I miss you so much. Daniel Franklin Beecher, January 19, 1949, to January 25, 2018

Prologue

"Do you promise it'll be like this forever?" Eden asked as she ran her fingers across Owen's smooth chest.

The sun was bright, the air was warm, and it was a perfect August afternoon. At this moment, Eden Skultz didn't think her life could get any more perfect. She hadn't had the easiest childhood, but that had all changed the moment Owen Forbes had walked into her life.

They were young—she was seventeen, he was nineteen—and they were utterly in love. She couldn't imagine her life without him. He sighed while caressing her back, the sound reverberating through her.

They were naked, out in the middle of the mountains in the back of Owen's truck on a pile of blankets. They'd just made love, and all was right with the world.

"I can't imagine anything more perfect than what we have," Owen told her. She giggled when he suddenly sprang up, then flipped her over so she was on her back, lying beneath him. His young-but-solid body felt right pressed against hers.

She smiled as he leaned down and kissed her cheeks, then her lips. She felt him hardening against her, and she laughed again.

"You're insatiable," she told him.

"You make me this way," he assured her.

They made love again.

This was a typical day for them. They were inseparable. Nothing could possibly tear them apart. They lived in their own little bubble, and though trust wasn't easy for Eden, she knew Owen wouldn't hurt her. She felt it in her bones.

They didn't leave the mountain until the sun was lowering in the sky. They finally made their way back down the logging roads, ready to join the rest of civilization. She sat next to him on his bench seat, one of his hands on the steering wheel, the other on her thigh.

When they got to her house, Owen kissed her for long moments, both of them feeling an ache because they had to say goodbye for the night. It didn't matter how much they were together; it was never enough.

Eden's porch light flashed, and Owen let her go, a chuckle escaping him as he looked at her front door.

"I think your father's telling us it's time to stop," he said.

"One more kiss," she begged.

Owen didn't hesitate. He held her close and kissed her long and hard. They were both breathless when they pulled apart. She was glad to see his reluctance as he walked away from her. Their eyes connected one last time as he took a moment, gazing at her through his front windshield before he backed up his truck.

She watched him turn around, not moving until his taillights disappeared. Only then did she walk into the house, finding her father seated in his favorite easy chair with a book in his hands, his worn reading glasses hanging low on his nose. He looked up and smiled.

"You could at least try to be a bit more discreet," her dad told her.

She giggled. "I love him," she said with a shrug.

"I know you do, Baby Girl, but remember you're both young," he said.

She frowned. "I hate hearing that. I know we're young, but the heart knows what the heart wants."

"That's very true. But you haven't seen the world yet. I don't want you to live someone else's dreams. I want you to live your own," her dad said.

"I'm living my dreams," she said. Not that she truly knew what her dreams were.

"There's more to life than a boyfriend," he told her.

"I have friends, too," she reminded him.

"I just don't want you to get hurt," her dad said.

"Why would I get hurt? Owen loves me." It was a simple statement.

"Yes, I believe he does," he agreed.

"I love you, too," she said. She walked over and gave him a kiss on the cheek before she went to her room. Right now, in this moment, life was perfect. She couldn't imagine that would all change in the blink of an eye.

Owen was singing at the top of his lungs, enjoying a Garth Brooks song about rivers and dreams. His cell phone rang, and he thought about ignoring it, but then he thought it could be Eden. He picked it up and answered.

He might not have done so if he'd realized that call was about to change his entire destiny . . .

Chapter One

"Are you going to let me in?"

A person could only resist temptation for so long before they were no longer responsible for their actions. The more Eden Skultz said this to herself, the better she felt—and the more she believed it was true.

Owen Forbes!

Yes, she was thinking his name like it was a curse word. She figured that would help her hate the man who'd broken her heart. Actually, *broken* wasn't the correct term.

Mangled.

Shattered.

Obliterated.

Those were more accurate words.

She hadn't thought it possible to love a man as much as she'd loved him. But Owen Forbes had been her entire world. And then he'd left her without a goodbye. It didn't matter that it had been ten years ago. No one had ever hurt her as much as he had. Because he'd left without so much as a backward glance. One day they'd been fine. He'd been telling her how much she meant to him. She'd been secure. And then the next—he was gone.

At first she'd been worried, devastated to think something might have happened to him. She'd sought out his family, and then she'd known. They'd been tripping over themselves to apologize to her, saying they weren't sure what had happened. He'd left—and it had been on his own. No one had forced him. He'd left her.

And she'd stayed in Edmonds, Washington.

Stayed with her father.

Stayed with her friends.

Stayed put.

Maybe she hated him because she hadn't done anything with her life. And maybe she hated him for breaking her heart. But whatever the reason, she hated him—or she desperately wanted to.

Now she found herself gazing at him as she waited at his front door, asking to come inside his home. She wasn't sure how she'd ended up on his doorstep. He'd come back to town—and it seemed to be permanent.

It had been ten years. He'd visited, and every time he had, it had broken her heart a little bit more. But now he was officially back. And it was killing her. She wanted to not care, wanted the old feelings for him to go away, but it was nearly impossible for her when he was pursuing her, when he wouldn't leave her alone.

Over the past few years, he'd ridden into town with his same flirty smile, his same can-do attitude. He'd made it clear he wanted her. She'd made it even more clear she wasn't his for the taking. She'd resisted him . . . until now. Something had drawn her to him on this night; something had pulled her to his house.

Some people called it fate, called their lives destiny in the making. She wasn't sure that was the case. All she knew was she'd been driving, planning on going home; then she'd found herself turning up his driveway.

As she stood on his front step looking at him—at his tall, muscular frame, at his perfectly tanned skin, at the way he filled an entire doorway as he stood staring at her—she knew the truth. She knew she could never hate this man.

Yes, she knew she could look in the mirror at her own sun-kissed complexion, at the way her eyes were slightly slanted, at how her cheekbones rested high, and her plump lips were more often turned up than down, and she could admit she wasn't hideous. But Owen—oh, Owen—he was in a class of his very own, and when he'd walked away from her, he'd made her feel as if she wasn't good enough for him.

And she hated him for causing her to feel that way. Somewhere deep inside she knew no one could *make* her feel anything. But the people who said that—they hadn't met Owen Forbes.

Eden continued standing at the entrance to Owen's home, looking at him like a deer caught in the headlights. She wanted to have the strength to turn around and walk away. But she didn't.

His lips twisted up, making the rugged planes of his face that much more attractive, though that seemed impossible and irritated her all that much more. She scowled, admitting to herself she probably wouldn't let someone inside her place who was looking at her the way she was looking at him.

But he moved to the side, his wide frame no longer blocking the doorway. "Come in," he said, the words a purr—an invitation.

She knew with every ounce of her being that she should flee—she should turn around and run for her life. This was a road she shouldn't go down. But even as she had this thought, she found herself stepping forward, entering the lion's den.

"Thirsty?" he asked after shutting the door, his large home suddenly closing in on her.

"Screwdriver," she answered quickly. "Strong."

She could've sworn she heard a chuckle escape him as he led the way into his kitchen. The lights were dim, making this scene even more intimate than it should've been. He pulled out a chair at the kitchen island, and she sat, neither of them saying anything. Words had never needed to be spoken between the two of them. It appeared time hadn't changed that.

He was quick as he pulled down a bottle of vodka and some orange juice, the clink of ice in her glass sounding like a shotgun blast in the quiet kitchen. Her body trembled as he handed over the cool glass, and she had to clutch it tight so she didn't drop it.

Eden didn't taste a thing as she downed half the glass in a single swallow. Owen's brows rose, but he didn't say a word as she tipped the glass and polished off the rest. The bite of the good liquor was an instant salve to her frayed nerves.

What was she doing?

When her phone rang, the sound nearly made her fall from her stool. Owen chuckled as he took her glass and made her a second drink. She realized that might not be the best idea. But even knowing that, she didn't stop him.

She picked up her phone, grimaced when she saw it was her dad. A flash of guilt ran through her, as if her dad knew exactly what was on her mind. Then she put the phone on silent and stashed it away in her purse.

Owen gazed at her, making her shift on the stool. She took a moment, closed her eyes, inhaled deeply, and tried to talk herself out of what she was about to do. This was a mistake. It was always a mistake.

It didn't matter.

All that seemed to matter was how handsome and charming this man before her was. He'd always owned a piece of her heart. Even when he'd tried giving it back to her, he hadn't been able to. It was a gift she hadn't wanted back. Yes, it hurt loving this man so much, but love wasn't something a person got to choose.

The stubble on his strong jawline and the twinkle in his deep-blue eyes brought that familiar tingle of awareness alive deep inside her. She was fighting herself, even though she knew it was a losing battle. Maybe it made her feel better to think she had a choice in all of this.

Owen walked around the island and stood next to her, his scent subtle yet intoxicating. He didn't make a move, but the look in his eyes clearly told her he was hers for the taking. A frustrated sigh escaped her lips before she reached out to him, her fingers fisting in his tight T-shirt. It didn't take any effort at all to tug him forward.

That first sensation of his lips pressed against hers was exactly what she'd been waiting for. He instantly devoured her mouth. He'd waited for her to make the first move, but that was obviously the end of his patience because he took control.

No one had ever kissed her like Owen did—with an all-consuming passion that made her feel as if there was no one else on this earth but the two of them. She couldn't even remember her own name when she was wrapped in Owen's sweet embrace.

Owen's arms tightened around her as his stubble rubbed against her jaw, leaving evidence of their passionate encounter. She knew she'd look in the mirror later, run her fingers over her marred skin, and relive this moment again and again.

There was an urgency in Eden she couldn't understand. But thoughts were pushed from her muddled brain as the solid wall of his chest pressed against her aching breasts, the strength of his fingers moving up and down her back, the feel of his lips possessing her. His skin was hot to the touch, increasing her core temperature to dangerous levels.

A groan escaped her as he broke his lips from hers, trailing his sweet kisses across her jaw and down the side of her neck, sucking the skin where her pulse was beating out of control. He pressed his hips forward, his thick erection now against her hot core, making her ache in ways she'd only ever felt with this one man.

Owen turned them, her back now pressed against the granite island as he gripped her hips, then lifted, setting her on the counter before moving forward and aligning their bodies so he was in the cradle of her thighs. She barely felt her shirt come off as he continued trailing his lips down her collarbone and over the tops of her breasts.

His hot breath whispered across her nipples before his tongue flicked out, licking her through the lace of her bra. She cried out as her core pulsed. He released the catch of her bra, the weight of her breasts spilling into his waiting hands. Then his rough tongue swept over her hard nipples, and she moaned as she gripped his hair, begging for more.

Owen didn't move his mouth as he trailed his fingers down her quivering stomach, undoing her pants, lifting her up, then sweeping away the rest of her clothes. Her head was thrown back as she leaned away from him, supporting herself on the countertop. Her body shook as he plunged a finger inside her wet heat.

Owen pumped his finger in and out of her body, building her pleasure up and up as he sucked first one nipple, then the other.

"More, Owen. I want more," she told him.

His fingers stilled for a moment before pulling from her body, making her feel empty. But that sensation didn't last too long because she didn't have a chance to open her eyes before she felt his body pressed against hers, this time with both of them naked.

"I always want you," Owen told her, his voice fierce with possession.

"Then take me," she offered.

She didn't need to say more. With utter confidence, Owen gripped her hips and thrust forward, burying his thick erection deep inside her. The impact was too much, taking her breath away as she adjusted to his girth.

He gave her a few moments to wiggle around him before he lifted her, bringing her to the edge of the counter as he began moving in and out. His tongue danced across her lips, slipping inside her mouth and relearning every hiding place she didn't know she had, while his hips rubbed against her, his speed growing more urgent as both their bodies drew closer to completion.

When the orgasm came, it was sudden and fierce, making her shake as she felt him pump his release. Their hearts beat out of control as he held her tight, her head buried in that sweet spot at his neck. She gently kissed him, fighting back tears.

This moment right here, this moment when they simply held each other as they processed the powerful emotion of what they'd just shared—this was the moment when she'd truly fallen in love with him at the tender age of seventeen.

The words were on the tip of her tongue, but she managed to hold them back. He was no longer hers—just as she was no longer his. She wouldn't regret this night. It had been exactly what she'd needed. But it was time to go.

With reluctance, she lifted her head, not looking Owen in the eyes as she shoved against his chest. He hesitated before pulling back, their bodies separating. Eden felt extreme sadness at the loss.

She didn't say a word as she gathered her clothes, then walked naked into his bathroom. She refused to look at her image in the mirror as she dressed. She pressed her forehead against the bathroom door and took a few breaths before walking out. Owen was right where she'd left him. He'd at least put his pants back on. However, his chest was bare, and she wasn't surprised to feel desire tighten once more in her stomach.

"I need to go," she told him, her voice composed. He didn't say anything, so she finally looked up. His eyes were burning.

"You'll be back," he told her with confidence.

She feared he was right. Instead of arguing, she turned and walked from his house.

Chapter Two

Eden made it home before she remembered she'd put her phone on silent. She decided to check whether her father had left her a message. She was surprised when she saw eight missed calls—all from her dad.

Panic immediately set in as she backed her car from her driveway and sped toward her father's place. She didn't take the time to check the messages. Something had to be wrong for him to call her that many times. And she'd been ignoring him so she could be with Owen.

She saw the flashing red-and-blue lights before she turned the corner to his driveway. Her panic escalated. She suddenly felt as if she couldn't breathe. Slamming her foot on the gas pedal, she drove the last block to his place in about one second. She screeched to a halt, tears welling in her eyes at the sight of an ambulance.

Jumping from her vehicle, she ran up the walkway and was halted at the doorway by two officers.

"What's happening?" she shouted. "Let me inside."

"They're working on him, Eden," Officer Jenkins said, his voice calm.

"Why are they working on him? What's happening?" she asked.

"The neighbor called it in. She was taking a walk and heard a crash inside the house and knocked, and there wasn't an answer. The paramedics are here. Let them work," Jenkins told her.

"I want to see my dad. Let me in," she yelled. They didn't move. "Dad! Dad, I'm here," she cried. There wasn't a response. "I'm here," she said again, her voice choked. "I'm here," she repeated.

"Eden . . ." She turned. Owen was there.

"What?" she practically snarled. "Why are you here?"

"Eden, come here. I'll wait with you," he told her. He held out a hand, standing a few feet back.

"No!" She took a step away from him. "I was with you. He called and I was with *you*," she sobbed. "I ignored his calls when he needed me."

"Eden, let's just wait together. Good people are with him," Owen told her.

"No. I should have answered. I should've been here," she sobbed. She turned back to Jenkins. "Please let me see my dad."

Jenkins looked as if he was going to cry. "There are several people in there, Eden. Just let them work, please," he replied.

Owen's arm wrapped around her, and she lost the will to fight him. She let him pull her aside, and she crumpled against him. Minutes passed. People moved in and out of the house; medical terms were spoken. But no one told her what was happening. After at least twenty minutes, she turned back to Jenkins, hope in her voice.

"If they're working this long, it means he's okay, right? They wouldn't still be working if he wasn't okay." She was begging him to agree with her.

"They're doing all they can," Jenkins said noncommittally. It wasn't what she wanted to hear.

More time passed. She didn't hear Owen's words, didn't hear anything. She just gazed toward the house, toward the back where she knew they were working on her father. Then one of the paramedics stepped out, his face composed, but she knew . . .

"Eden . . ." He paused, and she sobbed. "Eden, I'm sorry. We did all we could. He didn't make it."

Eden felt faint as she tried processing those words. She couldn't speak. She only stared at him. No. This couldn't be happening. There was no way this was happening.

"But he's healthy. He's okay. He's always been okay," she said, pleading with him to be wrong.

"I'm sorry, Eden. I'm so sorry."

Owen tried to hold her, but she pushed him away. She couldn't stand to be touched right then. She gazed at the house as several men walked from the back of it holding bags and medical equipment. Each person who passed her apologized for her loss, then looked toward the floor while they respectfully left.

Eden stood there in complete shock. There was ringing in her ears. This wasn't happening. This couldn't be happening.

"The medical examiner will be here shortly; then they'll take your dad to the funeral home," Jenkins told her.

She nodded as if she could understand him. He moved, allowing her to step inside. She finally did so. Jenkins and his partner stood by the door, waiting.

"Do you want me with you?" Owen asked. His voice sounded as if it was coming to her through a long tunnel. She shook her head. She couldn't speak.

She moved through her father's house. It was where she'd spent most of her childhood. She knew every inch of it. Her dad's bedroom door was open, a light spilling through it. She stopped a few feet away and stared.

Her father was in there. She'd never believe he was gone if she didn't go inside. Her feet felt as if they were encased in cement blocks. But she pushed herself forward. Finally, she made it to the door.

And there he was.

A blanket was pulled up to his chin; his eyes were closed. His skin was white.

He looked as if he were simply sleeping. Maybe they were wrong. Maybe he was just sleeping. Eden moved forward and fell to the floor beside him. She reached out and ran a finger across his cheek.

His skin was cold. But beyond that she didn't feel him. He wasn't sleeping. He was no longer there. Her dad was gone. "Dad?" There was no answer. "Daddy, please." There was no answer.

She wasn't sure how she managed to find the strength to rise to her feet, but she did. She looked at him one final time and walked from the room. That was no longer her father, and she couldn't stand to be there even one second more.

She kept on walking right out of the house. And then she ran, her heart broken, her mind desperately wanting to shut down. She ran faster until she tripped and fell, her body crashing hard to the ground.

She felt no pain.

In life there were days filled with joy . . . and days filled with sorrow. Never before had Eden been consumed with this much pain. It felt as if the world had stopped.

Pain.

Sorrow.

Unbearable agony.

That's what Eden felt. She couldn't breathe, couldn't focus, couldn't see a reason for anything anymore. She wondered if there was a purpose to life, a reason for living.

Rage overtook her sorrow as she lifted her head and gazed at the sky, gazed at the endless expanse before her. There was nothing there. Nothing! It was just empty space. Sure, clouds could fill it, and birds might soar by. At night, little lights that twinkled were visible to the eyes.

They called those lights stars. But in her broken mind, did she believe what these people said—that those twinkling lights really were stars? Had anyone touched them? Had anyone verified that they were burning masses resting in an endless expanse of darkness? No. People were simply supposed to take it on faith that they were stars . . . and that they were beautiful.

They were to take it on faith that the universe wasn't out to get them. Maybe life was nothing more than a cosmic joke. Maybe they were all in a glass enclosure where little green men were watching them, laughing at them, looking at them as if they were nothing more important than a terrarium filled with ants. And they were all so stupid; they continued making their trails, thinking about how smart they were as they lugged ten times more weight on their shoulders than they could handle.

And all the while, they were nothing more than entertainment for something a hell of a lot smarter than they were. Yeah, something in the universe had to be laughing at all of them, but especially at her. The pain was so real she couldn't fathom any other explanation for what she was feeling.

"Why him?" she pled, the sound a gut-wrenching cry that felt as if it were coming from the pit of her stomach. Her soul felt as if it were being torn from her. "Why? What did he ever do? He was a good man. Why?"

She said these same words over and over again. There was no response. No answer. She cradled her head in her hands and sobbed. The sounds coming from her would've stopped people in their tracks if they'd heard. They would have thought someone was dying for sure.

But someone *had* died. Her father had died. He'd tried calling her, and she'd ignored him because she'd been with Owen. Maybe she could have saved him. If only she'd answered her phone, he might still be alive. But she'd been foolish and selfish. And her father was dead because of it.

And he'd never come back to her. He couldn't come back. Fate was a bitch that wouldn't be messed with. Fate liked to play with her little toys, liked to make them dance before her. And when she grew bored, she cut the silver thread that represented a person's life.

"You've taken enough from me," Eden yelled, the words cut off by another sob.

She stayed where she was for so long her legs went numb. When the sobs finally died within her, she simply collapsed, curling up as those deceptive stars twinkled.

She drifted in and out of consciousness, not sure when she was awake or wasn't. But at least there were blessed moments of peace, hallowed moments where for a single second she forgot how truly alone she was.

Finally, she rose. Her mind was blank as she looked around her, wondering where she should go. She was utterly numb. She prayed she'd stay that way.

With no clue where she was heading, she began to move.

"Come find me now," she said, a humorless laugh escaping. She wasn't even sure the sound had come from her. "You think you hold my life in your hands. Well, you don't," she continued. "Fate. Everyone always said *it's in the hands of fate*. Well, screw you!" she screamed. "I create my own fate. You don't get to plan my life."

With that, Eden walked on with no destination in mind. She didn't care about anything anymore. The one person who'd sworn to never leave her had done just that. He might not have chosen to leave, but he'd indeed left her. And she wasn't sure she could forgive him for it. She wasn't sure she could forgive herself. And she certainly wouldn't rely on fate or what it thought it might have in store for her.

The funny thing about fate, though, was no matter how much you yelled, no matter what plans you tried to make, she truly was a bitch, and she had her own ways of making things happen . . .

He chuckled to himself as he slowly sang the nursery rhyme while he lit the first flame.

"Ring around the rosy,
A pocketful of posies,
Ashes, ashes,
We all fall down!

"Let's see you catch me now." His laughter rang through the woods as the dry brush quickly went up in flames, immediately beginning to lick up the walls of the old barn in beautiful shades of orange and red. There'd be nothing left of their operation. For that matter, there might be nothing left of the entire town.

It didn't matter to him. They'd messed in his business, and now they'd all pay . . .

Chapter Three

How could one action turn into something so deadly? How could a tiny spark become a massive flame? How could a foolish mistake end in death?

These were questions firefighters asked themselves each time they rushed into deadly firestorms, praying they weren't too late. These were questions that would never get satisfactory answers.

Don't play with fire, or you might get burned.

Owen Forbes grimaced as this thought flashed through his mind. Raising his gloved hand, he swiped across his cheek, smearing soot and sweat more deeply into his skin, but at least relieving the itch.

"Break's over!" someone yelled.

Looking up, Owen caught the eye of John, a longtime friend and coworker who was currently swinging his ax as he mowed down dry brush, trying to clear a path to gain even a smidgen of control over the massive wildfire they were trying to stop.

Owen flipped off his friend before getting back to work creating a fire line. Though the hotshots were out in force battling this blaze, Owen wasn't going to sit back and do nothing as the forests too close to his home burned nearly out of control.

With the unusually warm Washington summer, the town of Edmonds was on the verge of feeling more heat than it was prepared for. Owen refused to let that happen. A series of fires set throughout the woods surrounding Edmonds, Washington, beginning six months earlier had been obvious arson. This last one had gotten out of control, and they'd yet to get a handle on it . . . or who was causing so much destruction.

"No, thanks," John called out with a chuckle. It took a moment for Owen's tired brain to compute what he was saying. Guess he didn't like the offer of Owen's hand gesture.

Owen sighed, glad for a momentary reprieve when it felt as if the world was coming to an end. Of course, every fire he fought made it feel as if they were in the pits of hell. Even feeling that way, it didn't matter. He loved his job, loved the thrill of it, and loved the lives he was saving, both human and the creatures that inhabited this world with them.

The forest he was in was rugged, beautiful, and in serious jeopardy. It was an all-hands-on-deck situation, and no one was shying away. For the past ten years, Owen had been fighting fires. He'd left home needing to be a hero for one person. Then he'd decided that wasn't enough. He'd become a firefighter at the age of nineteen and hadn't ever looked back.

But he was home now, and he had a lot to atone for. He was confident he could do just that, but confidence could only take a person so far. He needed a damn miracle to pay for his sins, and he wasn't thinking about the blaze at the moment of that thought.

A fire was like a woman. It was mysterious, had no logical explanation for the path it took, and consumed you from the outside in. Sometimes a splash of cold water was necessary to douse the flames, and at other times, a damn ocean wasn't enough to fix the problem. But eventually, the fire *would* be soothed, *would* be extinguished. That's where the similarities ended.

A woman wasn't something to be toyed with, wasn't something to be extinguished. A woman was to be cherished, and when a man was foolish enough to forget that lesson for even a moment, the fire in her might be quenched for good—and there was nothing that would bring the blaze back into her eyes.

Owen hoped like hell he hadn't permanently put out the blaze with the love of his life. She hadn't been too thrilled by his return to town. It was a good thing he was as confident as he was, because when he wanted something, he didn't give up, no matter how futile the situation might seem.

Inhaling a deep breath, Owen felt faint. He'd just sucked in something, but it certainly wasn't fresh air. Throwing down his ax, he picked up his water bottle and took a long swig. That's when he looked around and saw how bad the situation had become.

A fire could turn on you in seconds, and it appeared luck wasn't going to be with him on this day. This blaze was pissed off, and she was coming for him and the other men. She wanted to embrace them, and it wasn't a warm hug they'd get, but a fiery burn they wouldn't recover from.

"John, we're getting boxed in," Owen called.

John looked up from what he was doing, his body going still. They'd both been lost in their thoughts, which was a foolish rookie mistake they shouldn't be making.

"What the fu—" John's words were cut off when Trevor screamed. Both men turned in the newbie's direction.

"Let's go," Owen cried as he and John raced downhill toward the twenty-two-year-old kid whose coat was on fire. In a panic, the kid waved his arm, making the blaze travel across his back. He spun in a circle.

"Stop," John yelled as they quickly approached. They pushed the kid to the ground, rolling him in the hot dirt. The fire was still coming for them. A spark must have landed on Trevor, and just that quickly he'd caught fire.

Part of the flesh of his face was deeply burned, and he was moaning, only half-conscious, his uniform smoldering, his flesh scorched too badly for him to remain awake. Only blackness could extinguish the pain he must be feeling.

"We need to get him help now," Owen shouted. The roar of the blaze was deafening. They'd gotten themselves trapped on this mountain, and if they didn't get out now, none of them were going to see their families again.

Sweat poured off Owen, but he ignored the heat. He'd take a hot sauna of steam any day over the scorching flames of the fire. He and John each wrapped an arm around Trevor's still body and ran for their lives.

They'd all get out together, or they'd go up in flames as one. There was no other choice.

Chapter Four

Eden sighed as she sat in traffic, looking out at the scenic view of the Olympic Mountains. She'd been born and raised in Edmonds, Washington, and she loved the town, loved every square mile of the place. It was nestled in the foothills of the Cascade Range with a spectacular view of Puget Sound. Seattle was close, but there was still a small-town feel to the place.

The security she'd once felt here had been ripped away from her. It hadn't happened in a single instant. No, the wound had been opened slowly, and a little bit more and a little bit more of her had been sliced away as time marched forward.

Six months ago, the biggest chunk of all had been ripped out of her.

Some might say six months was plenty of time for a person to get their act together—they might say if a person was still dwelling on events from half a year before, they needed help. Some might say a lot of things. But those who'd say that had obviously never experienced a traumatic event.

Six months was nothing. It was the blink of an eye. It was less than that. Six months barely scratched the surface of time.

Eden had lost so much in her life—her mother, her lover . . . and her father.

She could do nothing about the loss of her mom, whom she didn't remember, or her father, whom she missed so much it made her heart bleed with the pain. But Owen she could do something about.

She'd managed to avoid him for a long time—since the night her father had been taken from her. She'd been with Owen when her father had needed her the most, and she couldn't forgive herself for it. Owen had taken so much from her. And though he'd come back to Edmonds, it wasn't enough.

She was no longer that naive teenage girl in love with the boy she was never meant to have. He'd left her ten years earlier, and she'd thought her heart would never be the same. He'd been gone a long time before his first visit back home. But as the years passed, him being gone had become easier for her.

That is, until he'd decided to make his visits closer together—making sure she knew he was around. It was a game. She knew it was a game. She just wasn't sure what he thought the winner got at the end of it. She wasn't sure what he wanted.

If she could figure out the purpose of her life, she'd be content again. But it seemed once a person's world flipped upside down, there was nothing that could turn it upright again. There was one thing she knew for sure, and that was that the universe had little minions up above, clasping their hands together and laughing in glee at the misery of these petty humans below.

It seemed there were only two things on her mind these days: the death of her father and her inability to get over Owen Forbes. Maybe she should just leave, start over somewhere else. She knew for sure that her father had loved her with all he had, knew he wouldn't want her to be in despair like she was.

Her father had also loved Owen.

She pushed that thought straight from her mind. Her dad had called her the night she'd been with Owen. He'd called, needing her, and she hadn't answered. The guilt of that would bear down on her for the rest of her life.

Shaking her head, Eden jumped when a car horn beeped. The light had turned green, and it was time to move. She looked ahead at the smoke-filled skies. The wildfire was burning more out of control with each new day. And she needed to go straight for the fire, instead of being smart and running away from it like a sane person.

But since Eden worked for the only law office in town, and since there was an arson investigation going on, she had to do her job. She couldn't lose the one lifeline she was holding on to these days. She needed to work, needed to think of something other than the constant misery she was in.

The people investigating the fire believed it was an inside job, believed it was a local firefighter who'd lit the blaze. Everything within Eden rebelled at such an accusation. She'd grown up in this town and didn't believe anyone living here was capable of such a destructive act.

One name on that list had taken her breath away—Owen Forbes.

She might be furious with him, might be blaming him for all of her woes, but she would never have thought him capable of such an act. But even as she had this thought, she realized she didn't know him anymore—not the adult version of him. The people investigating this fire were strangers. They didn't have any biases against this town or its residents. And Owen had barely settled into his new home before the fires had begun.

What did she really know about her first love?

She knew the boy, knew his family, but did she know the man?

She wanted to tell herself that of course she did, but she also had lost faith in herself this past year, faith that she could make a right choice. Someone had deliberately started this fire, just as they'd been starting fires for months.

Could it have been Owen?

She'd certainly find out.

She pulled off to the side of the road and took some deep breaths. The higher into the mountains she traveled, the worse the air quality became. But she still needed what little oxygen there was in the air she took in.

She picked up the stack of folders on her passenger seat and focused on only one—Owen's. He'd been a hero time and time again, saving countless lives and properties. He definitely was a man who took risks, especially with his own life, but from everything she'd read at least ten times, she didn't see what the fire investigators were seeing. She didn't see any motivation for starting such a deadly fire.

Of course, weren't all firefighters risk-takers? Didn't they get a thrill from rushing in while everyone else was fleeing? It took a special person to don that uniform. Would one of them intentionally light a fire just so they could be the hero who then put it out? Had they been doing that over the past six months only to lose control with this latest one?

Eden shook her head. It seemed so impossible, even with the proof of numerous cases where firefighters had done just that and had been caught. How many of them got away with their deadly acts? She shuddered to even think about such a thing.

And out of all the men listed, she had no doubt Owen was addicted to the thrill of it. Adrenaline was a drug he didn't want to give up. He wasn't even a wildland firefighter, but he'd been fighting this current blaze for two weeks straight, not a thought in his head for his own safety. He was one of only a few local firefighters in Edmonds who was wildland trained and able to fight the blaze alongside the hotshots.

Eden didn't want to be a part of this case. Yes, she needed to work, and yes, she needed to have her mind set on anything other than the death of her father and the guilt she placed on her own shoulders over that. But how was she supposed to do that when this case left her no choice other than to talk to Owen, to be around him?

Her life was a hot mess, and it didn't appear it was going to get easier for her anytime soon. She had two choices. She was either going to embrace her job and her task, or she was going to let despair pull her under.

Eden had never been one to give up. It felt as if she was ready to surrender, but at the end of the day, that wasn't who she was. She'd allow herself moments of grief and self-pity, but she wouldn't wallow in them. It was time to lift her chin and do what she needed to do.

Laying the folder back down, Eden looked up at the smoke-filled sky. She pulled back onto the road, found the turnoff onto the logging road, and began the climb, the visibility growing weaker the closer she came to the blaze.

Her job was her life now, but at times like this, it really sucked.

The temperature increased as she neared the hastily set-up rest station where the fire crews could refill their water packs and supplies, grab a quick bite to eat, and maybe even catch a few minutes of shut-eye. This station would most likely be relocated, as the wildfire was overtaking the land at a rapid rate. They weren't getting it contained as they'd hoped.

She found the station and pulled over, climbing from her car and wiping her brow, which was now beaded with sweat. Pulling her hand away, she saw the soot there, the air contaminated by the burn she was too close to.

When a fire decided to let loose, it consumed everything in its path, including people. But a fire gave the average person a chance, gave them little warning signs, such as ash floating to them through the air, extreme heat waves, and a roaring sound that had a normal person's heart accelerating.

Those foolish enough to play chicken with a deadly fire should be aware of their probable fate. Eden looked around, seeing nothing but destruction and death. It was beyond depressing to see these beautiful trees turned to ash, to see the lush ground blackened.

Eden approached a group of men in a large tent. She heard their frantic voices, and it instantly put her on edge. There were men out fighting the blaze, and the white-haired fire chief speaking into a radio seemed visibly upset. Something was wrong.

"Owen, you damn well better answer," the man said. Eden felt her gut clench as a wave of nausea traveled through her.

There was only static on the radio, and Eden couldn't have moved if her life depended on it. As she looked out across the blazing hills, she realized her life very much *could* depend on it. Usually it wasn't the flames that killed a person, she tried assuring herself. No, normally it was smoke filling your lungs that ended your life. That was at least the less painful way to go. Though that offered little comfort at this moment.

She glanced into the hills and didn't see anyone or anything running toward them. That only made her sicker. Where was Owen, or the other men the chief was trying to reach?

There was silence as several men gathered around the man with the radio. They were waiting for a reply. When minutes passed with nothing, she saw sorrow in their eyes. It looked to her as if they'd lost three of their own up there. With the way the flames were leaping, it could very well be the case.

Eden's entire body felt numb. She'd been praying to get over Owen, to move on with her life, but this was something she'd never wanted. The thought of life continuing on as if nothing had happened in a world where Owen wasn't present was so incomprehensible to Eden—she couldn't even imagine it.

Even not having him in her life, she still got glimpses of him, still watched as he lived his life. She didn't want to watch, didn't want to need to know what he was doing, but it gave her an odd sort of comfort. She couldn't suffer another loss of this magnitude, not so soon after losing her father. Tears streaked down her dirty cheeks without her being aware.

It took several moments for Eden to process the joyous shouts escaping the crew of firefighters as they began running forward. Eden shook her head as she lifted it, the weight of her skull feeling too heavy to move. But as she gazed forward, she saw two men carrying a third out of the dangerous trail that seemed to be getting eaten by flames at their heels.

It appeared as if they had a bubble around them, protecting them from impending doom. The firefighters who'd been at the tent took over carrying the unconscious man, rushing him forward to where they had medical beds set up. It would take an ambulance at least twenty minutes to reach this point. It would probably be faster to drive the man to town even if it wouldn't be the most comfortable ride.

As they moved closer, Eden saw the singed flesh on the man and realized he wouldn't be waking up for any ride. He was going to be lucky to survive his injuries. She had to fight back the urge to throw up. There was too much going on, and she needed to help where she could, not be a burden in this dangerous situation.

As the group of firefighters drew closer, she saw that the other two men who'd come out of the flames were limping. It appeared as if all three of these men had been caught unaware, had been in serious danger, barely making it back.

Though the temperature at this camp had to be more than one hundred degrees, Eden felt her skin grow cold as she laid eyes on one of the men, his face covered in black soot, making it impossible for her to know how injured he was.

Shouts could be heard as the men barked orders, and one firefighter took off for his station wagon. The legs of a bed were hastily cut off as the men put the injured fireman, who was now groaning, on it. They rushed him to the car, carefully placing him inside.

One of the men climbed in next to him, making sure he wouldn't get too jostled as they rushed down the mountain. She prayed he'd be okay, prayed the men had gotten him out in time. She hated herself a little bit for being grateful it wasn't Owen on that bed.

As she had that thought, her gaze came back up, and she looked at one of the other men who'd emerged. He was wobbling on his feet, and another of the firefighters grabbed him before he could fall. Her stomach dropped again. It was Owen Forbes, and he wasn't doing well.

"Let's go, Owen. You both need medical attention," the chief said.

"I'm fine, Eric. I just need water," Owen replied, his voice unrecognizable, it was so raspy.

"Shut up," Eric replied.

Owen sagged as he was led to a truck and practically stuffed inside.

And just that quickly, he was gone. Eden's knees gave out as she sank to the ground. Not one person noticed her, and she was grateful.

She'd come to question these men, to try to figure out who had started this fire. Though it seemed impossible it could have been any of these men, especially Owen, she'd much rather see one of them behind bars than six feet below the ground.

Her wounds, which were nowhere near close to being healed, felt as if they were being ripped wide open again. She should quit this job . . . but she knew she wouldn't.

Her town was about to go up in flames, and she was determined to stop it.

Chapter Five

Owen lay on the bed in the ER, his body twitchy now that he'd worn an oxygen mask for the past hour and was finally able to take in deep, healing breaths. But he was done lying around. The damn hospital staff wouldn't release him until he was signed out by a doctor.

There was a fire that was currently kicking all their asses, and he needed to get back to work. His toes twitched as he cursed beneath his breath . . . waiting . . . and waiting . . . and more waiting. He was about to explode.

The door to his room opened, and Owen let out a groan as the doctor walked in, a big smile on his face. *Dammit!* He was never getting out of this room now. Payback was a bitch, and currently his big brother Kian was heading his way, looking as if he had nothing at all pressing on his agenda.

There was no greeting as Owen looked at Kian. "Can you sign my damn form so I can get back to work?" Owen demanded. "I don't need this IV drip or all of these stupid tests."

Kian grinned as he picked up Owen's chart and carefully looked it over. Though the smile stayed in place, Owen was aware of the concern in his brother's eyes as he looked back up at him.

"You came pretty damn close this time, didn't you?" Kian asked, the words clearly a chastisement.

"You can't fight a fire without getting close," Owen pointed out.

"That's not what I meant," Kian said. "You have some minor burns, but it took nearly an hour to get your oxygen levels stable, and you're still dehydrated."

"I feel fine," Owen insisted. "I've been through worse."

A shudder passed through Kian as he gave Owen that older-brother stare that had always driven him bonkers.

"You can be the tough guy when you're out in your element," Kian told him. "But right now you're in *my* world, and you don't go anywhere until I feel it's safe for that to happen."

There was zero room for argument in his brother's voice. Owen knew when it was time to back down. This wasn't just a brother thing, either; this was probably the first time Owen had really looked at his sibling like the top-notch doctor he was. *Dang.* That was a strange feeling. He was actually proud of him, even if he was currently being a huge pain in the ass.

"It got pretty sketchy out there," Owen admitted. He didn't want to talk about this. If he talked about it, then it became more real. The more real it became, the easier it was to allow fear to set in. The worst enemy for a firefighter was fear. If you second-guessed yourself, it could easily be your life.

"Your buddy isn't doing as well as you," Kian said with a wince. "That's why it took me so long to get in here."

"Dammit!" Owen thundered. He'd known Trevor was in for a painful recovery, but that look in his brother's eyes told him Trevor wasn't going to get better. "Don't tell me you can't fix him."

Kian shook his head. "It isn't over yet, but if he does make it, he's going to have moments where he wishes he was dead."

"How much of his body is burned?" Owen asked.

"Seventy percent," Kian said.

"I thought we were getting a handle on this thing. But today the winds shifted, and the fire exploded. It happened so damn fast," Owen said, his voice quiet.

"I've been seeing too many firemen this week," Kian told him. "I should put away the scrubs and head for the hills. We need more people out there."

Owen smiled for the first time in so long he didn't know when his lips had last turned up. "As much as I trust you with my life and like having you by my side, I think you're needed here a hell of a lot more than up there."

Kian sat down next to Owen, giving him a clear view of his face. His brother had circles beneath his eyes, and Owen had no doubt the man was working double and triple shifts to keep up with all the injuries. Kian didn't need to do that, but none of the brothers could look the other way when they were needed. It was why Owen had so much respect for his family.

"Yeah, I wouldn't know what in the hell I'm doing out there, anyway," Kian said. "Did any other firefighters get shipped to the ER in Seattle?"

"I don't think so," Owen said. "I think it's just John, Trevor, and me causing trouble today. I knew better than to let that bitch surround us like that." Guilt was consuming him.

"For one thing, you're trained for wildland fighting; it's not your primary job," Kian scolded. "For another, you're definitely not responsible for what happened today. Whoever set the fire is responsible. The weather's responsible, and the damn flames of hell are responsible, but *you* are not."

Owen knew his brother was right, and he shouldn't need to hear it, but he had needed to. He was now grateful it was his brother who'd come in, grateful to have him there. As much as he wanted to get back to work, maybe it was better that he was getting a break.

"You know, you lecture a little bit like Dad," Owen said when he felt a slight sting in his eyes. There was no way he was allowing this moment to get emotional. He blamed it on a severe lack of sleep and whatever drugs the hospital had given him. He'd been fighting this fire for two weeks straight with a maximum of five hours' sleep a night. His body was breaking down.

"Considering I'm a father now, I'll take that as a compliment," Kian said. "You've barely moved back home, less than a year now. I'd like to spend some quality time with you before you play chicken with a wildfire."

"If you release me from this bed, I'll get back out there to the fire, extinguish those flames, save the day, and then we can have a round of golf," Owen promised.

His brother smiled again. "I do have your life in my hands right now," Kian said, looking at ease as he leaned back in his chair.

"Is this revenge for that time I locked you in the bathroom?" Owen asked. "'Cause it's time you got over that."

Kian's smile faded as he glared at his brother. "You nailed a damn two-by-four to the door. I was stuck in there for three hours," Kian said. Then he smiled again. "I'd actually forgotten about that."

"Crap," Own muttered. "Can we forget I brought that up?" He didn't see his brother forgetting anything.

"Yeah, that's not going to happen." He glanced down at his watch before looking back at his brother. "You've been in here a little over an hour." He stood up and moved toward the door.

"Where are you going?" Owen called.

Kian turned and grinned at him, and Owen swore under his breath . . . and waited. "Looks like you have two hours to go before I sign anything."

And with that, Kian left the room. Owen shouted a few curses at his brother; then he flopped back in the bed, glaring at the empty doorway. He stayed that way for about five minutes, hoping his brother was going to be a little more professional since he *was* a doctor.

Nope.

Not gonna happen.

With a sigh, Owen picked up his television remote. Since it appeared he wasn't going anywhere for another two hours, he might as well catch up on the news. Brothers were definitely a pain in the ass. But he loved them, anyway.

◆ ◆ ◆

A large man stood looking in the room at Trevor's prone body. Letting out a sigh, he glanced behind him and saw a couple of nurses coming down the hallway. The man left the room and made his way to the staircase. He didn't want anyone to see him at the bank of elevators.

Trevor hadn't been his target . . . Owen had.

Originally, death hadn't been the objective of the fire—that was just an added bonus. But as soon as he'd realized how out of control the fire was getting, he'd been quite pleased to realize Owen could be eliminated.

The Forbes family had been messing in his business for long enough. It was time they felt the burn of the anguish they bestowed on so many—especially him.

He chuckled as he stepped from the staircase, exiting the hospital.

Today hadn't been a loss. The fire was burning strong, and Owen was scared. A frightened firefighter was a dead man walking.

Chapter Six

Eden was good at standing back and observing people and situations. She knew how to go undetected. She'd always liked seeing how things happened, how people interacted, and what decisions they came to. It was so much more fun to stand in the shadows and watch how people behaved than to be a part of the puppet show people tended to act out on a daily basis.

As she watched Owen loaded into a truck and saw the tires peel out as the vehicle made a sharp U-turn and headed out of sight, she was well aware that no one was the wiser to her kneeling on the ground.

But once the excitement died down, they were sure to notice her. She wanted to be long gone before that happened. With a strength she wasn't even sure she had at the moment, she picked herself up and slowly made her way to her vehicle.

One fireman stopped her, his face perplexed as he asked if there was anything he could help with. Eden simply shook her head and got into her car, taking a moment before she started it.

When she began turning her vehicle around, she was aware of the tremble in her fingertips. She just gripped the wheel that much tighter, willing herself to calm down. There were things in life that were beyond a person's control. That didn't give anyone the right to act the fool. It just meant you had to work that much harder to keep it together.

But as she made the long drive down the mountain, she couldn't help but have flashbacks of Owen's face covered in soot, of the way his legs had barely been able to keep him standing. Of how close he'd come to death. And that made her think of her father, of that horrible moment she'd stood next to his lifeless body, knowing he'd never be with her again.

Owen had been close to death, so close the scythe had been slicing through the air, its sharp blade aimed straight at his throat. He'd managed to duck the fatal blow by mere inches. Her father hadn't been so lucky.

Eden's fingers were white. They began tingling, and she had to pull to a stop at the bottom of the mountain and shake out her hands. She wasn't going to endanger other drivers because she wasn't in control of herself. She took in some air and forced back the tears that needed to fall.

"Focus, Eden," she muttered. "You're working a job. You have questions to ask, people to investigate. Don't make this personal. Just do your job." She didn't find it at all odd that she was sitting in her car talking to herself.

She did find it horrible that one of the people she had to question was none other than Owen Forbes. The man she'd always loved, the man who'd nearly died right before her helpless gaze.

She was in no way stable enough to do her job right now, so instead of going to the hospital, she made her way home. A hot shower and a bite to eat were just what the doctor was prescribing. She'd be in a much better place to do what needed to be done if she wasn't shaking so badly.

Her body still trembled as she went inside her home, the quiet almost eerie after being around so much noise for the past hour or so. Why didn't she have a dog? Wouldn't it be so much wiser for her to have a pet, a companion? Maybe she'd get on that. No. She definitely would get on that. She'd go to a shelter. She knew a person could find their soul mate in a pet. She'd know which animal was meant to be hers by looking in its eyes.

Eden was relieved to find that her shaking had stopped when she climbed from the shower. Good. It was better than medicine.

Her nerves were frayed at the thought of seeing Owen for the first time in a bit over six months. She wasn't sure how she'd managed to avoid him, but she was certain he'd allowed it. She figured she'd managed it partly because he hadn't been around, and partly because she just didn't go out much these days, not even with Roxie, her best friend.

It wasn't that she didn't love her friend; it was just that Roxie was married to Owen's brother Kian. The risk of seeing Owen if she was with Roxie was too high, in her opinion. Forcing herself to stop thinking about the past, she gazed in a mirror and tried to decide what she needed to do next.

She needed to look professional when she saw Owen—professional and aloof. But she didn't want to appear as if she'd put too much time or effort into it. With that in mind, it took her three times as long as normal to do her makeup and choose her clothes. She must have changed at least a dozen times. By the time she got to her kitchen, her stomach was making sounds she'd never heard before. At least it took no effort to pick out food.

She made a cup of coffee while toasting a bagel. She sat down and finished the coffee before the bagel popped out of the toaster. She barely tasted it as she filled her stomach. She'd been procrastinating long enough. It was time to find Owen.

She called the hospital, surprised when she discovered he was still there. She'd expected them to tell her he'd been released. Her stomach tightened as she began to fear the worst. What if something terrible had happened to him? She tried telling herself he meant nothing to her. She knew she was a liar.

It took her three tries to start her car, then twice as long to get to the hospital as it should have. She'd had to take the back roads and go slowly, as she was having a hell of a time focusing on driving.

When she finally arrived, she stepped from the vehicle, wondering if Owen was going to notice the changes in her. He liked to tell her she hadn't changed a bit from seventeen, but she knew that was a lie, especially in the last six months. Her appetite still hadn't fully returned, and she'd lost more weight than she could afford to lose, leaving her cheeks too gaunt and her hips too bony.

She almost laughed at the thought. She'd been on a fitness journey just last year, determined to lose ten pounds and build muscle. She'd even hired a personal trainer to help her reach her goals.

But everything had changed when she'd lost her father. She'd somehow lost her joy in life. He'd been the one to raise her, the one to tuck her in each night. He'd been her knight in shining armor and her superhero all rolled into one. She'd always thought her dad was invincible, that nothing could happen to him.

She'd been wrong.

And with his loss, she'd changed. This thought made her even sadder as she moved into the cool hospital corridor. If Owen truly was okay, she was glad their meeting would be in this place. It was easier, more sterile. There was no history between them at the hospital, no memories. It seemed she couldn't look at very many areas in Edmonds without connecting one memory or another with Owen. Why did life have to be so dang complicated?

Eden approached the nurses' station, grateful when she saw April sitting behind the large desk. She pasted a false smile on her lips as she waited for the woman to stop typing. Finally, April did, then smiled when she noticed Eden.

"What are you doing here?" April asked.

"I want to see Owen," Eden said. April's grin widened.

"Are you guys back together?" she asked. People in this town seemed to believe that conclusion was inevitable.

"That was just a kid thing," Eden said, though it hurt her heart to say it. The wild abandon and passion she'd felt for Owen had nothing to do with childish emotion. But she didn't want people to realize how broken she'd become when he'd left her.

"Mmm-hmm," April said with a chuckle that was worse than nails on a chalkboard. "He's in room 306," she finished.

"Thanks, April," Eden said, turning and walking away before the snoopy girl could ask anything else. As it was, Eden feared April would be blabbing all over town about how Eden had rushed to Owen's bedside. She sort of *was* doing that, but she assured herself it was simply because she had questions to ask, not because she was worried.

Eden didn't realize she was only taking shallow breaths as she approached room 306. She didn't take her first full breath until she pushed open the door, not bothering to knock, and saw Owen fully dressed, sitting on the edge of the bed, a grumpy expression plastered on his face.

When he looked up, for just a moment his lips curved, and a sparkle entered his eyes. Too quickly, his expression changed, and she wondered what it was he saw in her expression. Was it relief? Anger? Fear? She honestly didn't know.

"Hello, Owen," she said quietly, feeling almost stupid at the lame greeting.

"Eden," he replied with a tilt to his head. It was such a polite way to answer. His eyes flashed a million questions at her, but he was silent as he waited to see what she had to say, why she was there. Maybe he was just a tad bit guarded himself.

He'd tried calling her a few dozen times after their night together, after her father had died. She hadn't been able to talk to him. So he had to be wondering why she was there now. She should just spit it all out—planned on doing just that if she could stop her brain from firing all of these thoughts at her.

"How are you feeling?" she asked.

He gave her a mirthless smile as he shrugged. "I'm fine. I should've been out of here hours ago, but since my brother is getting his retribution . . ." His voice trailed off as he obviously waited for the small talk to end.

Kian must've had someone bring Owen clothes, because he'd showered and was wearing a black T-shirt that looked painted on him and a pair of jeans that molded perfectly to his legs. She didn't want to think that way, but she couldn't seem to help it when he was right there in front of her.

She closed her eyes for the briefest of moments, and that was a huge mistake, because then she was picturing the last time they'd been together, the way his tongue had circled her nipples, the long, hard thrust of him deep inside her . . .

Eden's eyes snapped open, and she looked guiltily back at Owen, who seemed to be wearing a knowing expression on his beautiful face. There was no way he could've read her thoughts. She was sure of that— sure it was nothing more than her guilt over having them.

And since that wasn't going to happen ever again, it wasn't a place she needed to go, not even in her imagination. Her self-lecture finished, Eden squared her shoulders and gave Owen the most professional look she could manage.

"That's good to hear," she told him, barely remembering she'd asked him how he was doing. "How are the other two firefighters?"

Owen winced and Eden knew it wasn't good. She wasn't sure about one of the guys, but the younger one had appeared to be in pretty bad shape.

"John's fine, but I don't know if Trevor's going to make it," he said after a long pause.

"I'm sorry," she told him, meaning the words. She found her fingers twitching with the need to reach out and touch him, not only to comfort him but also to assure herself he was truly okay.

She might be mental, she decided. She might actually have a disorder that only appeared when she was in the presence of this one human being. Her emotions were all over the place in a matter of minutes—hell, seconds—when she was around him. She'd be so much happier if she could feel nothing other than aloof indifference.

"Why are you here, Eden? It's not that I'm unhappy to see you," he added when she visibly winced. "But you've managed to avoid me like I've got the plague since our last night together."

Once again an image of the two of them locked tightly together played across her memories. But following that was the sight of her father's lifeless body. She'd never forgive herself for her desires, for how she'd ignored her father so she could think only of herself.

"I shouldn't have been at your house that night, Owen," she said. She was trying for coldness, but the quiver in her voice gave away her vulnerability. She hated him a little for making her feel so weak. "We both knew from the moment you opened the door it was a big mistake."

"Us together is never a mistake," Owen countered. "Me leaving was the only error in judgment."

She shuddered as he said those words. "I guess we'll never know," she told him. Maybe they would've stayed together. Probably not, though. How many high school romances actually ended in marriage? Or in lasting marriages? People changed so much in their early twenties. She knew she'd changed a lot from that seventeen-year-old girl. She was sure Owen had changed, as well.

"We could try to figure it out," Owen told her.

She shook her head. "I'm not here to reminisce about the past," she told him. It was time to get to the subject at hand.

"What are you here for, then?" he asked. It wasn't a rude question, just curious. But it still stung how he was all business. Even though that had been what she'd been telling herself she wanted.

"I'm helping with the investigation of the origin of the fire," she said.

His eyes narrowed the slightest bit.

"Why do you need to talk to me about that? I'm just out there fighting the damn thing. I don't know how it got started, and I don't care all that much. I just want it stopped."

"Our firm was hired . . . ," she began, but her words fell off as suspicion entered his gaze. She hated that he was looking at her like that.

"Again, what does this have to do with me?" he asked. He wasn't glaring at her, but he didn't appear particularly friendly at the moment.

"The arson investigator came to our office." She stopped again.

"Do we know for sure it's arson?" he asked. He seemed upset by that. Of course, that could be an act, she told herself.

"Yes, we're sure," she said.

"Then you better find the person before they burn up the entire state of Washington," he said with such conviction she wanted to stamp his name "free and clear" and be on her way.

"You're being investigated," she told him. The shock followed by anger in his eyes made her take a slight step away from him. She didn't remember Owen ever being a great actor, and the look burning in his gaze right now was most definitely rage.

"Men have been killed in this fire," Owen said after several tense seconds. She nodded, feeling on the verge of tears. "And you think I could have any part in taking lives?" His tone was now filled with disbelief. She wanted to assure him that no, she didn't think that in any way.

"I have to follow all leads," she said, a lump in her throat.

"Of course you do. Because this isn't personal at all, is it?" he said. There was barely any sarcasm in his tone, but yes, it was there.

"No, this isn't personal," she told him. They both knew she was lying. If she were to admit it to herself, she *knew* beyond a shadow of a doubt he was innocent. But her job was to investigate who they told her to.

Owen didn't say anything as he stood and began moving toward her. Panic filled her as she took a step back, but there was determination on his face as he backed her into the wall, his body pressed up against hers, his heat scorching her.

She hated how her body responded to him, instantly wanting their clothes gone, instantly wanting that connection she could find only with this one man. Instead of admitting that to him or herself, she glared up at him, trying to keep her cool even as she trembled against him.

"Do you honestly believe I could ever hurt anyone?" he said before lifting his hand, running a rough finger down her cheek before resting it at her throat where her pulse was thumping madly. "That these fingers could take a life?" he went on, his hand going lower, rubbing over the top of her breasts, making her nipples ache at how close he was to them.

"I know you can hurt people," she said, too much emotion in her tone. She had to take a deep breath, which was a mistake. She inhaled his musky scent, and it nearly made her faint. This was too much. It was all too much. She wanted to push away from him, but she wasn't going to show him how much his touch was affecting her.

Instead of trying to get away, she pressed closer, surprising him. "I *definitely* know how much you can hurt people, but that doesn't matter. I'm just doing my job, and you're on the list," she said. "And the investigator wants you suspended until you're either convicted or cleared." His eyes narrowed. "Now back away."

She was proud of the command in her tone. She even thought it might have worked—that was, until she watched his lips turn up. The expression reminded her so much of the boy she'd fallen in love with that it took her breath away. She was seventeen again, and he was just her Owen.

Just the way it was always supposed to be. Just the way it had been for so long.

Chapter Seven

Owen wasn't sure what he'd felt when he'd made the decision to pin Eden against the wall. All he knew for sure was that he hadn't been able to stop himself as he'd moved forward. Yes, there was a need to touch her, feel her, have her in his arms again. But there was also a feral part of him that wanted to prove to her she wasn't as icy as she wanted him to believe.

He'd known her for fifteen years, had been friends with her long before they'd decided to make it more. Then they'd dated for three years, and he'd never been so in love. That had frightened him. He'd wanted so much more than to be that small-town guy who never left—who thought life was complete with the girl next door.

A twinge of guilt stabbed through him at such a horrible thought. The thing was, life had been complete with her. He hadn't needed to traipse across the country to find himself. He'd left who he truly was back home—in this woman's arms. And he'd royally screwed it all up. He had wanted to beg her to come back to him, but his pride had prevented him from doing just that. Besides, he'd figured all she'd need was time to realize he was a new man.

But she was doing her best to keep him at arm's length, even when he showed up to events she attended. But somehow, even with all of that between them, they always managed to end up right back here—with his body pressed against hers, their hearts beating as one.

And now this woman, who he had no doubt he still loved, was investigating him for setting a fire that had killed innocent people, including some firefighters he'd known his entire life. He wanted to strangle her as much as he wanted to kiss her. He was sure he knew which way he'd decide to go. He'd hurt her once—he'd never do it again.

"I told you to back off," Eden said, her voice still a little shaky but filled with resolve.

"I love it when you get all commanding," he told her, making sure there was a smirk on his lips. He knew how much that infuriated her. And right now it was much wiser for both of them to feel anger instead of lust. Of course, lust and anger went hand in hand, he thought a second too late. Damn, his neglected body was hard as a rock.

Owen slowly stepped back, his body calling him a fool for letting her go, his mind telling him this was a much saner move. Once he took that first step, he managed to put a bit of distance between them. He was sure his brother was going to pop his head into the room at any minute, and then he'd never hear the end of this argument. His brothers might all love each other fiercely, but they also enjoyed poking one another as much as possible. That's what family was for.

Once he was a safe distance from Eden, she pulled out a file she'd had stuffed in a cute lime-green bag. She always had loved bright colors. It suited her, he decided. When he glanced down and saw his name on the file, his nostalgia for her likes and dislikes evaporated quicker than the smoke from a cigar.

She pulled out a letter and handed it to him. He quickly scanned it, his irritation growing again. This was a suspension. She hadn't been lying. He knew she wasn't in charge of this, knew she was just the messenger, but he was still pissed enough to punch a hole in a wall. Wasn't there a saying about not shooting the messenger? He wasn't sure, but if there was, it was one hell of a stupid saying. It would feel damn good to lay into just about anyone in this moment.

"This is bullshit and you know it," Owen finally said, the paper crumpling in his fingers.

She looked away, not willing to meet his eyes. He wasn't sure if that was a good or bad sign. Right now there wasn't a whole lot he was certain of. He'd once been more than confident in their relationship, and now he really wasn't sure what his chances were with this woman.

"If you truly are innocent, then don't fight me on this," she practically begged. "Let's get the investigation over with, and then both of us can happily go back to our . . . lives," she told him.

She'd paused for a moment before saying *lives*. He wondered what adjective she'd been wanting to insert there. *Boring? Happy? Fulfilled? Miserable?* He'd felt all those emotions since the day he'd left Edmonds. He was still feeling them now. He knew he wouldn't feel better until he had her at his side . . . permanently.

"What can you investigate, Eden?" he asked. The anger was completely gone now. He knew he was innocent. He also knew she knew it. If they needed to play these games, he was willing to. He just didn't have time to do too much of it because there was a fire that needed to be doused.

"I have to follow all leads," she told him.

"And how did they get this lead that I'm the person you're looking for?" he asked her.

"I didn't ask them that," she admitted.

"So don't you find it odd that one of the key players in trying to get this fire put out is now on suspension?" he asked.

"What are you trying to say?" she replied.

"I'm just saying that if this is arson, then someone out there started it. And that someone might just have a lot of power," he told her.

Her forehead crinkled as if she was deep in thought. Good. That made him feel a lot better. His name might be on a list, but he had no doubt she was just doing her job. He knew that even with their roller-coaster history together, somewhere deep inside her, she did know him, knew he would never do something so heinous. Knowing that made him realize he could get through anything.

"Are you going to fight me?" she asked wearily.

He was quiet for a moment, then decided not to answer her question but to ask one of his own. "Do the powers that be know we have history together?"

She visibly stiffened as she looked up, this time meeting his gaze. "Our relationship is in the past. It's not relevant to what's happening now," she assured him.

"We're never in the past, baby," he told her. His eyes caressed her from the tips of her toes to her sexy hair. Though she looked as if she could stand to put on a few pounds, she was even more beautiful today than she'd been the first time he'd seen her as more than a friend. After that moment, it had all changed.

And now ten more years had passed. Age had ripened her, had improved her in ways the cosmetic industry had no chance of doing. She was stunning.

"Look, Owen, distracting me isn't going to work. Like it or not, I'm a part of this investigation. I want it over as much as you do," she told him. "I'd hoped you could act in a professional manner. You are a Forbes, after all."

He hated that reminder. Though her voice didn't change in the least, he knew that last sentence was meant to offend him. He'd known from the time he was a preteen that he was going to make it on his own. He'd refused to be considered someone special just because of his last name. He wanted to make his mark on the world, and while firefighters were sadly underappreciated, he knew he'd made a difference. He didn't need his name in lights. He just needed to be a hero to one person at a time.

"That's a low blow, Eden," he said. He advanced on her again. This time he was going to do more than push her against a wall.

He was stopped when there was a light tapping on the door, right before it was thrust open. A nurse walked in, pulling Owen's attention away from Eden. He was impatient as he asked what the woman needed.

"Dr. Forbes signed off on your discharge papers," the nurse said, oblivious to the tension in the room. "Here are your take-home instructions. You have a couple of minor burns, so keep salve on them, and you'll be a hundred percent in a couple of days."

"Thank you," Owen told her, his voice dismissive.

She finally seemed to understand she'd walked in on something. She shifted on her feet before handing him the papers and quickly turning to flee. Owen turned back to where Eden had been—and found her gone.

She'd slipped away like a thief in the night. He wanted to be frustrated but instead found a light chuckle escaping him.

"You can run . . . ," he whispered. *But you can't hide,* he added silently.

Chapter Eight

Eden knew the moment she'd slunk out of Owen's hospital room that she was acting the coward, but she'd seen that look in his eyes, knew beyond a shadow of a doubt what was on his mind. Though they'd been apart for a long time, her body reacted to his. If they hadn't been interrupted, the two of them just might have ended up in that small hospital bed.

A shudder passed through her. She could tell herself time and time again that wasn't what she wanted, but Eden knew it would be heaven, knew only Owen could make her body sing, could make her forget all her sorrows.

Instead, she found herself driving along the roads of Edmonds, wondering where she was going next. She pulled over and took a few moments to compose herself. She had a job to do, and the only way to do it was to either confirm Owen was a lunatic arsonist or to clear his name. She had to remind herself she wasn't biased in this.

But, of course, she was.

Declan. She needed to see Declan.

Of all Owen's brothers, he was by far the most clearheaded. To tell the truth, the man scared her a little. He was so large and foreboding. He rarely smiled, and he was some supersecret spy or something. It was downright intimidating, even if she'd known him most of her life.

Still, she had to cast aside her fears and go visit the man. She'd probably have to interview all the siblings, but Declan was the hardest, so it was best to get that one over with. She had no doubt the brothers would lay down their lives for Owen, but they were moral. And if their brother had been responsible for the deaths of others, they wouldn't stand idly by, protecting him. She was pretty sure of that.

As she pulled back onto the road, changing directions to head toward Declan's home and hoping he was there, she couldn't help but think about that small room with her and Owen in it together.

The two of them had never had an issue with sexual compatibility. But their relationship had been so much more than that. They'd laughed together, shared everything, and had been so connected she'd been sure they were soul mates. Maybe they were. It didn't seem to matter anymore, though. In this world of temptation, love was often cast aside for momentary lust.

That was too depressing to even think about. She thought instead of how badly she'd wanted Owen to close that small distance between them, of how she'd wanted his lips caressing hers, his hands to smooth down the straight line of her back. It was so easy being with Owen that when she was, she forgot about all the bad.

Eden was so locked in her own thoughts, she nearly missed the unmarked driveway that led to Declan's private residence. She only knew where it was because she'd been with Roxie and Keera one day when they'd been dropping off food for their brother-in-law. Keera shared a bond with Declan that Eden had never seen anyone share with him. It was very sweet to see the normally stoic man so gentle with his sister-in-law.

She slowly made her way down his driveway, feeling her heart lodge in her throat. She tried telling herself she had nothing to fear, that she'd known this man before he'd been so scary, but that wasn't helping.

She stopped her car and turned off the motor. Then she sat there for several moments. She wasn't sure how to approach this situation.

Should she tell him exactly what was going on? Yes. That would be best. Declan wasn't a fool, and to be honest, she'd be surprised if he didn't already know. He took it upon himself to watch out for his family and those few friends he allowed in. If she tried for even a second to deceive the man, he wouldn't listen to a word she said.

Declan's home was surrounded by western red cedars, red alders, and big-leaf maple trees. The consistently fresh smell in the air was what had made growing up in this region as close to perfect as possible. However, even though Declan's home wasn't in danger from the fire—at least for now—the overpowering smell of smoke was overtaking the other luscious scents of the forest.

Being out in the woods like this sent another pang through Eden's heart. She could close her eyes and picture her father and her traipsing through these woods as he pointed out different types of plant life and animals. Her dad had definitely enjoyed the beauty of nature and had taught her to respect the land they were so blessed to live upon.

She was nowhere near as humble as her father had been, but maybe that was something he was going to leave her. Maybe she'd gain a better appreciation for this land, and for life in general. Damn, she missed him. She missed him so much she wondered if the ache would ever diminish.

Shaking her head, she looked at Declan's house and squared her shoulders. She couldn't keep going back to that sorrowful place that made it hard for her to even get out of bed. She again had to remind herself that wasn't at all what her father would have wanted.

"But you aren't here anymore, are you?" she whispered quietly. "So if I want to have a pity party and curse the heavens, that's my right. You left me behind without warning, and I'm ticked about it, Dad." She waited for a response.

She wasn't surprised when she didn't get one. She'd said at least a few words to her dad every day since he'd passed on. That thought made her scoff. *Passed on.* Who in the heck had come up with that term? Was it better for everyone to believe a person hadn't died, but they'd simply *passed on*? She couldn't even think those two words without a hint of sarcasm in her tone.

Since her dad had died, she'd begged him to visit her, to show her he was indeed out there in the universe. And all she'd gotten was silence. She'd read books on the afterlife, had looked up mediums, had done everything she could think of to communicate with her father. And nothing had worked. Maybe he was just gone. Gone forever. But if that was the case, then what was the purpose of life? Why should anyone ever lay their heart bare for the world to take a stab at if love wasn't eternal?

She still hadn't found answers to those questions. So instead of trying to find the meaning of life, she was focusing on the here and now. The present was something she could grasp, and at least sort of control. The past was what had shaped her into who she was, and the future . . . well, the future wasn't up to her. She hated to admit that, but it was a reality she knew she couldn't escape.

Once again shaking away her gloomy thoughts, Eden took action and walked up the front steps of Declan's massive home. She had no doubt he already knew she was there. She had a feeling he had cameras everywhere. That thought made her want to look around, but she didn't want to appear nervous, especially if he *was* watching. She needed to be the confident professional.

She rang his doorbell, hearing nothing from the outside, wondering if it had worked. She highly doubted anything on this home wasn't top-of-the-line. The doorbell had worked. She stood there and waited, wondering if he was zooming in a camera on her face. She tried to leave her expression neutral.

The door swung open with no warning, making Eden jump, though she'd been telling herself to stay composed. The man who opened it was larger than life, his shoulders so massive they practically took up the entirety of the doorframe, his height intimidating, and his face showing nothing of his thoughts.

"Hello, Declan," she said, hating the slight squeak to her tone. She'd spoken to this man her entire life. There was nothing to be afraid of, she repeated in her head.

"Eden," he replied, his tone giving away nothing of what he thought about this visit. "I've been expecting you."

The way he said those words sent a shiver down her spine, and everything within her told her to run away. Run far and fast. This man was deadly, and there was nothing she could learn from him. He wouldn't give up his brother even if Owen was guilty, even if the man had lit five hundred fires. This was pointless.

And then a thought entered her mind that frightened her even more. She shivered as she stared at this huge man—this man she had no chance of beating in a fight. What if the arson investigators were *very* wrong? What if it wasn't a firefighter? What if it was someone so set on catching a drug ring that he was willing to do anything to flush them out?

What if it was Declan?

Declan moved aside, welcoming her in. She really had no other choice but to move forward. It was either that or hang her head in shame at what a coward she was. She stepped forward, feeling as if she were being locked in a tomb the second Declan closed his front door.

He didn't say anything as he led her down a long hallway, then moved easily through a set of double doors into an inviting den. This room had more light to it, with oversize uncovered windows and cream-colored furniture. She was sure Declan hadn't decorated it. There was too much of a feminine touch to the room. All it really needed was a couple of vases of fresh flowers, and it would be downright beautiful.

"My sister decorated most of the house," Declan said, as if reading her mind. Her gaze fastened on his, and another shiver went down her spine. He was scary, all right, and she was an idiot for being there. This was beyond her job description, and she was so far out of her league she wasn't sure what she was doing.

"I was thinking this room had a woman's touch," she offered. Then she wanted to kick herself. It was none of her business. And it could have been a girlfriend who'd done the decorating. But her tone had sounded so disbelieving. It was strange to think of Declan in a relationship. Eden was afraid he'd consume anyone he dated. That only made her realize there was a real possibility he could be guilty.

"If you've been expecting me, you know I'm here to talk about Owen," she said. There was no way she was telling him he was now on her suspect list. The tiniest smirk rose to his lips, and she was suddenly defensive. "About the fire," she added. "I'm part of the investigation team." She tried to see if he gave away anything at her words.

His expression didn't change. The smirk didn't leave his lips, and she found her fingers grasping at each other as she picked at a nail that was already too short. She hated becoming a child again, especially around men. She'd been raised by her father, and she'd been a tomboy most of her life. Men didn't and *shouldn't* intimidate her. But Declan wasn't an average guy, so she figured she could give herself the slightest of breaks.

"You and my little brother have had quite the number of ups and downs, haven't you?" Declan finally asked.

Though she hated that it was happening, Eden felt hot color rise in her cheeks. "That's not what this is about," she assured him.

"Oh, Eden, if you truly think that, you aren't as smart as I've always known you to be," Declan told her. "You can think this isn't personal all you want, but at the end of the day, it's always going to be personal between you and Owen."

There was such truth in his words, as if he didn't doubt for a second what he was saying. There was also something about his voice that made a person want to fall in line, to do exactly what he told them to do.

He truly was a dangerous man.

But was he a guilty one?

"Honestly, Declan, I'm not here to talk about Owen and me. I'm trying to do my job, and I think you're trying to distract me," she said, proud of the firmness in her tone, choosing to ignore the shake that accompanied it.

"What do you expect to get from this visit?" Declan asked. He moved over to a grouping of couches and held out his hand, waiting for her to sit before he took his own seat. She wondered if that was a gentleman thing or an advantage thing. She was pretty sure Declan wasn't the sort of man to ever be the first one down.

"I won't waste your time. I have a list of people who are being investigated for this fire. Owen's name is at the top." She didn't look away from Declan as she said this. His expression didn't change. He appeared relaxed.

She wondered if she could ask questions that would make him slip. She'd come here wanting to question him about his brother, and she now found she wanted to ask him what he did all day.

She waited for him to say something, and it took all she had not to fidget in her seat. Was this an intimidation tactic of his? If so, it was highly effective. She waited . . . and waited. It felt like hours, but she knew it was only seconds—less than a minute, surely.

Finally, he spoke. "We both know Owen wouldn't ever do anything that would endanger lives, let alone destroy the land he loves so much," Declan told her.

But would you? She barely managed to keep the words in.

"He left his home. I think you're overestimating his love for it," she said, her voice a little too bitter. Her mind was racing, and she wasn't sure which direction she should go.

"He left this land . . . or he left you?" Declan asked. There was no taunt in his voice, but his words stung. He was definitely good at his job. If he was guilty, she had a feeling he'd never be caught.

"I don't matter in this," she assured him. "Owen left this land. Maybe he has some bad memories here. Maybe he wants it destroyed." She paused for a moment, meeting Declan's cool gaze. "Or maybe it's someone else who's responsible. Can you think of who that might be?" The last word was spoken quietly as she lost some of her bravado.

Declan laughed, actually laughed. The sound was so shocking to her, Eden found her mouth hanging open as she stared at him in awe. She searched her memory, *really* searched it, and there wasn't a single time she could ever remember hearing this man's laughter. It was almost surreal.

"Excuse me," he said as one more chuckle escaped before his lips closed and his expression went neutral again. "I know you aren't out to get Owen. That's the only reason you're in this house." The words weren't a threat or a warning, but they carried a thread of steel so strong she'd be a fool not to listen to what he had to say. "And because I know you care about Owen, I'll tell you this much." He stopped and she found herself holding her breath.

"He had to leave this town. It's not my story to share with you, it's his, but he had to leave. But don't ever doubt for a single second how much he loves this land, how much he loves his family . . ." He paused again, looking at her as if deciding if he could trust her or not. Then his lips parted. "Or how much he loves you."

Those final six words hung in the air between them. Eden's heart was thundering as she looked at Declan. He wasn't a liar, had always been known for his unbendable integrity. But a person could change. She knew that more than anyone.

Him talking about Owen and his supposed love for her could easily be a distraction. He could very well be aware she was suspicious of him, as he seemed to have an uncanny ability to read people.

Still, his words swirled in her brain. Did he believe that Owen did love her? Should she even care about that? Was Declan distracting her on purpose? She hated that she cared. At the end of the day, she knew Owen wouldn't have left her if he'd loved her. A person didn't do that to another person they loved.

But none of that mattered, anyway. She'd gone to Owen, gone to him and made love to him, had been one with him . . . and she'd let her father die because of it. She and Owen together might feel right, but no matter what, it always ended in disaster.

"Why did Owen leave?" she found herself asking.

"I told you, that's his story to tell," Declan said. Eden knew she could beg and plead with this man to tell her the story, but there would never be any cracking Declan. He could be tortured to death, and he wouldn't crack. Some men had that quality about them—very few men. Declan was certainly one of a kind.

"I'm going to enjoy watching a woman take you down," Eden said, shocked when she realized she'd spoken those words out loud. She felt her cheeks heat with embarrassment. She hadn't meant to say that.

Declan smiled at her, not a friendly, heartwarming smile, but the smile of a tiger, of a predator, of nature's most vicious creature who'd just spotted his prey. She found herself scooting back in her seat, instinctively trying to protect herself. This wasn't a man you challenged . . . or tried to get in the last word with.

"I look forward to someone trying," Declan said after a long pause. A shiver passed through her. Before she could say a single word, he looked at something behind her; then his smile grew. It was so odd to see this man grin. It was disconcerting.

"It appears as if we have a visitor," he told her.

Eden didn't need to ask who was there. Her body knew without needing to see or hear him. She refused to give Declan the satisfaction of seeing her stress. She simply sat back and waited. At least Declan had given her a few seconds to prepare herself. She was sure that hadn't been his intention.

She was sure he didn't want to answer any more questions. Did that make him guilty? The chances were so slim she knew it was a wasted road.

However, right now, all she could do was sit and wait . . .

Wait for Owen. Wait for answers. Wait . . . and wait. That's what her life had been reduced to.

Chapter Nine

The room was so quiet a cricket could be heard rubbing its legs together as Owen walked in, looking none too happy. Eden glanced at him, refusing to feel as if she was doing something wrong. Yes, Declan was Owen's brother, and yes, he might feel she was overstepping her bounds, but this was her job, and she was doing what she was supposed to do.

She shook off her irrational guilt as she looked at her former lover and waited for him to say the first words. It appeared as if Declan was waiting, too. Of course, that was just the way Declan was. He was never in a hurry to fill silence. Maybe he enjoyed how uncomfortable it made most people.

"I see you ran away from me and came straight to my brother," Owen finally said, moving closer to her. She could practically feel the heat radiating from his body. If she hadn't personally seen him almost get consumed by flames chasing after him, she'd never have guessed his life had almost ended just a few short hours earlier.

"I had questions for him," she answered calmly, doing her best to maintain her composure. "He's been a *big* help," she said with a bit of a smirk. Declan had, in fact, been no help at all, had given her far more questions than answers, but she wanted to see Owen squirm. Her words did the trick, as Owen looked at his brother in a "What the hell" way.

Declan seemed to enjoy this game, too, 'cause all he did was shrug and give his brother that smirk of the lips that was impossible to read.

"We weren't quite finished, if you want to go away," Eden told Owen before he could say something else. They had gotten nowhere, but again, she didn't seem capable of controlling the words escaping her tight throat.

"I think you're more than finished here," Owen said, the words a definite threat. He didn't like her speaking to his family. Was it because he had something to hide? Did he suspect his brother, too? If he did, she had no doubt he'd protect him.

"Do you two lovebirds need privacy?" Declan asked, finally entering the tense conversation. Eden turned and glared at him, forgetting for a moment how intimidated by him she was.

"We're not anything to each other, so no, we *definitely* don't need privacy," she stated. Declan chuckled. Eden caught the surprise in Owen's eyes. At least she knew it wasn't just her who was shocked when that foreign sound came out of Declan's mouth.

The difference between her and the two brothers was how quickly they could compose themselves. Unlike them, she wasn't able to turn on a dime and shift directions.

Owen decided he was done speaking as he marched over to her, grabbed her hand, and hauled her to her feet. She was so shocked by this he-man tactic that she nearly floated into the air as her body was propelled upward. She looked at him in surprise. Owen had always been a gentle man, sweet and kind. He wasn't the caveman type. Of course, that was the man she used to know. This new guy she wasn't sure about.

"We're leaving," he said to both her and Declan.

"Have fun," Declan called out as Owen swiftly dragged her from the room. She was so shocked by this she found herself following him, offering no resistance. She wasn't sure what in the heck to do.

They nearly made it to the front door before she got her wits back and yanked her hand from his, taking a step away. He stood there looking like a linebacker as he waited for her tirade to begin. Because she knew he expected her to yell, she took a calming breath and spoke in the iciest voice she could manage.

"I don't know who you think you are, but you can't go around manhandling people," she said. "I wasn't finished speaking with your brother, and I don't appreciate you interfering in my investigation."

To her surprise, Owen didn't look the least bit upset as he let her finish. He smiled, confusing her that much more. She wasn't able to adjust so quickly to his shifting moods.

"You do realize Declan wouldn't tell you anything even if I was guilty. There's a thing called loyalty among family and friends," he finally said. That's what she feared. If any of the Forbes men were guilty, she didn't think it would ever be discovered. That didn't mean she was willing to give up.

"Are you confessing?" she asked. Her stomach clenched. When she'd been handed this case, she'd honestly believed she wanted him to be guilty, but she'd known from the moment she'd seen his name that it wasn't true. Owen wasn't perfect, and he'd hurt her, but arson was a vindictive crime. It was done with purpose. Owen wasn't the type who could do it.

"Sugar, if I wanted to confess to something, it most certainly wouldn't be arson," he said with a wink. He then took her hand and moved to the door. This time she allowed him to take her outside. It was useless to fight. And she was confused about Declan. She needed to gather her thoughts before talking to him again.

When they made it outside, Eden was irritated to find her car blocked by Owen's massive truck. She was sure that had been a planned maneuver on his part. She was once again ticked off.

"Are you so childish you're now blocking my car?" she asked in her best disciplinary voice.

"Just parking, darling," he told her, leading the way to her car. He even opened her door for her. "I'll back up, then follow you out. This road can get a little treacherous in the evening."

"I've been driving here since I was sixteen. I'll be fine," she assured him. He opened her car door.

Eden got inside, relieved when Owen moved back to his truck. She was going to wait for him to leave, but he backed away just enough to allow her out and then stopped. He was waiting for her. He wasn't going anywhere until he was assured she was long gone. It wasn't as if she couldn't circle back to his brother's house if she wanted to.

She turned her key . . . and nothing. There was no click, nothing. She tried again . . . and nothing. Allowing a momentary lapse in judgment, she slammed her palms into her steering wheel, which normally would've made the horn go off. But again . . . nothing.

This just wasn't shaping up to be her day.

Her door came open, and Owen was standing there. She glared at him. "What did you do to my car?" she demanded.

He looked confused. "I didn't touch your car," he assured her.

"Then why won't it start?" she asked.

"Let me try," he said almost indulgently, as if he could do something she couldn't.

"Be my guest," she offered, stepping out of the car. He sat down and tried the key. She almost expected it to start. Owen was now the one at the wheel, and nothing would dare defy one of the Forbes men.

But much to her frustration, the car didn't make a sound. Owen reached down and found the latch to her hood. He popped it and stepped from the car, opening it up. He looked for a few moments, then glanced over at her.

"I don't see anything wrong," he said. "I have no idea how these new vehicles work. You're going to have to get it towed and . . ." He stopped as he looked down at his watch. "The towing company is closed for the day."

"Dammit!" she uttered, not looking at him when she heard him chuckle. She wasn't convinced he hadn't done something to her vehicle. But she turned and looked at the house. What if Declan had gotten someone to do something with the car? What if he'd been planning something if Owen hadn't shown? His guilt was firming more and more in her mind, and she couldn't stop a shiver of dread from rolling down her spine.

"Looks like you're either taking a ride from me or hiking back to town," he said, as if it didn't matter to him which choice she made. Her pride at full force, she was tempted to tell him to stick it where the sun didn't shine, then hike back to town. But Declan lived out a ways; she figured it was at least five miles, and the sun had already set, leaving the area a little too spooky for her tastes. And with her probably ridiculous suspicions of Declan, the last thing she wanted was to be caught out in his neck of the woods . . . utterly defenseless.

If she made it back home in one piece, it would be a miracle. As much as she hated being indebted to Owen, she was left with no choice but to accept his offer.

"I guess I'll take a ride back to my house," she finally said, so quietly the words barely managed to drift through the small distance between them.

Much to Owen's credit, he didn't seem to gloat. That was a positive in his favor. He had many more marks in the negative column at the moment, though. She grabbed the rest of her files, not willing to leave them in her car. She wasn't taking any chances right now. "I should let Declan know I'll get my car out of here tomorrow morning." She in no way wanted to look Declan in the eyes again right now, not when she was so suspicious of him.

"I'll call him," Owen assured her.

She could do it herself but was glad not to have to. She just nodded as she allowed Owen to lead her to his truck. He once again opened the door and stood there while she climbed inside.

The scent of Owen invaded her as he closed the truck door. It was a mixture of leather, smoke, pine, and . . . and that thing she never could identify, but whenever she managed to smell it, it made her think of making love on a hot summer day down at the mudhole. She clenched her thighs together as heat overtook her. She was grateful this was a short drive, because she didn't think she could manage a long one without finding herself sliding closer to this man who took her breath away.

There was no way she'd be able to stand this drive in silence, so as soon as Owen climbed into the cab, she hit him with a question.

"Declan said you had to leave town. Why?" she asked.

He didn't turn to look at her, but she noticed his shoulders tensed. Declan hadn't been lying to her—at least about that. There'd been something going on that had made him leave. She desperately wanted to know what that was.

"I had my reasons," he told her, his voice not giving away what he was thinking or feeling.

"Didn't you think I had the right to know?" she asked, hating that she needed to say those words.

"Yes, you did," he answered. But he didn't elaborate.

"So why not just tell me?"

"I don't know," he admitted. But he didn't give her more than that. She let out a frustrated sigh as she turned and studied him. He was staring straight ahead, but she had no doubt he was aware of her gaze.

He'd always taken her breath away with his beauty. Men certainly didn't want to be described as beautiful, but he was. He had such a strong profile—with his solid jaw, straight nose, and full lips. He'd always been quick to smile, and she adored the lines next to his eyes that attested to many years of laughter. Had he been happy without her? She'd been happy . . . eventually. It had taken her a while to adjust, but she hadn't let her sorrow from a lost love define her entire life.

It was just that having him back around, and having him pursue her, had sent her world into a tailspin. Then going to him . . . and losing her dad on the same night had made her crash so hard she hadn't been able to pick herself up off the ground quite yet.

She'd always been attracted to Owen. But their relationship had been about so much more than that. She'd loved him with every fiber of her being. She feared she was still in love with him.

"Why did you come back?" she asked. He didn't seem willing to answer her questions, but she had so many of them.

"I finally realized I shouldn't have left the way I did, or for as long as I did," he told her. This time he turned and briefly glanced at her. The look was so intense she felt scorched from the inside out. She had to break the look. She stared out her window instead. "I shouldn't have left you," he added.

"You did leave, and you're unwilling to tell me why. So I'd much rather you didn't make comments like that unless you're willing to explain yourself."

He was quiet for a moment, then he sighed. "We'll talk about it all eventually."

"When it's convenient for you?" she asked.

"Is a conversation like this one ever convenient?" he countered.

"It's necessary," she told him. "We live in a small town, and there are definitely hard feelings. It's not like we can avoid each other, so maybe if you give me closure, I won't hate you so much."

He looked at her with such sorrow she wondered if he was acting or if he really did have feelings for her, if he truly did care that he'd hurt her.

"Do you remember that time we went to the Seattle docks?" he asked, suddenly changing the subject.

She was thrown off-kilter but couldn't help the smile that flowed across her lips at the memory. She closed her eyes and could practically smell the sea air, feel the heat of the sun beating down on her bare shoulders.

"I remember it all," she admitted. What would be the point of lying?

"What did you say to me?" he asked.

She almost laughed. "I didn't want to date you for the longest time because of who you were," she said instead of answering.

"And . . . ," he said, the word drawn out.

"It didn't take me long to see that you didn't act like a millionaire or billionaire or whatever the heck your family is," she said with a shrug. "You like old trucks and worn Levi's. You'd rather swim at a fishing hole than sail at a yacht club."

He laughed. "My fire department in New York didn't have a clue where I came from or what was in my bank account," he told her with fondness.

"That was something you'd always wanted," she said. It was something she'd always loved about him.

"We were down at those docks, and you were making fun of me," he reminded her.

"I know," she said. "I asked you when you were getting one of the big boats to take me sailing around the world." She stopped and gulped. "You said we could go pick one out right then and there if it made me happy." She had to fight tears. "I knew you were just kidding, but after you left, I had many dreams of us doing just that, walking onto one of those big boats and sailing off into the sunset."

"Eden . . . ," he began before his voice trailed off.

"It's fine, Owen. It took me some time, but I got over you. I got over it all," she lied. "And I didn't want you for your money. Just because you can afford any one of those ridiculously priced yachts doesn't mean you should buy one."

"I had the same dream," he admitted. "I pictured us on one particular boat, you topless in the middle of the sea, me providing for us. It was just the two of us without a care in the world."

She wanted to hate him for putting this image in her mind, for reminding her of the past, reminding her of what she could have had. But she was too sad at that moment to hate anyone.

"Well, we were young and stupid," she said with a laugh that had zero humor in it.

"It's never too late to live our dreams," he told her with such intensity she refused to look at him, afraid of what she would see in his eyes. "I will take you straight down there now, and we can sail off into the sunset."

"And run away from all our problems?" she questioned. "Run away from what's happening here now?"

"I'm not trying to run anymore. I just want you to know the door's never shut when it comes to you and me. Your dreams matter to me, and I want to hand you the world."

It was taking all she had not to reach out to him and accept what he was offering. "I have new dreams now . . . and they don't include you." Her voice trailed away. The last words were a lie.

"Have either of us changed that much from the teenagers we were?" he asked.

"Yes, without a doubt," she said without hesitation.

"In some ways," he told her. "But in many others, we're the same people we were then. I'll prove it to you." There was such assurance in his tone that she didn't know how to fight it.

She opened her mouth to say something, anything, to break this spell that seemed to have been woven over the two of them. But then his radio crackled. He automatically reached for it, turning it up.

"There's a fire at . . ." Dispatch listed the address. Both she and Owen went silent as they continued driving. Eden was in shock, all thoughts of the past instantly evaporating.

"That's your place," he said. It wasn't a question. Of course he knew where she lived.

"Yes," she answered anyway. "It appears my place is on fire." The gut-wrenching fear began spreading through her. She lived nowhere near the deadly blaze destroying the forest around them. Why was her place on fire?

Owen sped up as he drove in the direction of her house. They were about to find out what was going on. One thing was for sure, though: Eden didn't believe in coincidence. She scooted a bit farther away from Owen.

It wasn't that she was afraid of him, it was just that . . . it was just that none of this made any sense. Nothing seemed to make sense. She was growing more and more lost, and as much as she wanted to reach out to the man beside her, take the comfort she knew he'd be willing to give, she couldn't.

She was alone in this—utterly alone. Someone was setting fires, and it very well could be someone she'd known all her life—someone who didn't care who got in the way.

Chapter Ten

Owen's throat tightened as he pressed down on his accelerator. He could feel the tension radiating off Eden as they neared her home. Of course they could smell smoke in the air, but the entire area had smelled that way for two weeks straight with the forest fire uncontained and too close to home. How had her house gone up in flames?

Though it panged his heart, he knew she had to be thinking he had something to do with this. If she searched within herself, she'd know he could never start a fire, never destroy these lands or put people's lives in jeopardy. But she was hurt and angry. She had a right to be. What he'd done to her was unacceptable. Yes, he'd had his reasons, and he knew he'd have to share them with her. He just wasn't ready yet. Maybe it was fear that he'd lose her forever.

Hope was something Owen held on to. He had hope that things would work out, hope that his future wasn't destroyed, hope that he'd spend the rest of his life with the only woman he'd ever loved. He'd been young and foolish when he'd set out to see the world . . . when he'd helped a friend. She had to see they were different people now, that they could rise above their pasts.

They neared her house, and he was going slightly insane from her intoxicating scent. It had been six long months since he'd held her. He'd been so close to stripping off their clothes in that hospital room.

She wouldn't have forgiven him if they'd been caught with their pants down.

But when she was near him, he couldn't seem to think of anything other than touching her, holding her, sinking deep within her silken folds. Yes, he'd been with other women in his time away from Edmonds, but none had compared to Eden; none had held his attention longer than the short time they'd given each other mutual pleasure.

But that had ended for him as he'd realized a quick release wasn't what he was searching for. No, what he'd always wanted had been his all along, and he'd risked it all for something foolish.

Owen didn't know if he could make everything right, but his hope had been renewed when she'd shown up on his doorstep six months ago, and the two of them had exploded together.

Then her father had died.

And he knew she blamed him for that, among his many sins. She also blamed herself. Though it had been a heart attack, something unforeseen and freak, she lived with the guilt of ignoring her father's final calls because she'd been with him. Owen wasn't sure if that was something the two of them could get over. That's where hope came back into the picture. She had to forgive herself and him. When she realized neither of them was at fault, the healing process could begin.

Grief was an unpredictable thing, though. It snuck up on a person and held them tightly in its grasp until they either escaped or gave in to the tentacles tightening around them. Eden was too strong to be pulled under. She also wasn't alone. He wouldn't allow her to fade. Even if freeing her from him was what it took, he'd do anything to make it better for her.

They turned a bend in the road, and Owen's gut clenched more. Though they still had about a mile to go, he could see a black plume of smoke rising in the air, see flashes of orange lighting up the night sky. He knew what that meant—everything would be gone.

He heard Eden's soft gasp as she gazed ahead. She'd come to the same conclusion he had. This wasn't a small fire; it was catastrophic. The need to don his uniform and try to salvage what he could was so great his legs were twitching. But he was on a temporary suspension. That made this even worse.

He wanted to offer her comfort, but he knew the best thing for her at this moment was for him to be quiet. She was trying to process what they were about to see, trying to prepare herself. He'd worked many fires where families had lost everything they owned. The impact was devastating.

Though the fire department considered it a success when there was no loss of life, there were some losses that were almost too hard to take. Irreplaceable family heirlooms, photo albums, baby books, wedding dresses, antique furniture. The flames didn't care about a person's sentiment. The fire was hungry, and it fed on everything in its path.

They turned the last corner, and Eden let out a sad cry. Her house was completely engulfed; three fire engines were parked in front of it, their hoses stretched out as commands were shouted.

It was too late. All they could do at this point was prevent the fire from spreading. She had just lost everything.

The three men sat on the hill and looked down, laughing as they watched their handiwork. One turned to his buddy and passed a pipe he was holding. His buddy took it and inhaled, holding his breath before letting out a plume of smoke.

"The boss will be really happy about this," he said.

"There's not a chance they'll figure it out," the other replied.

"It's fun to watch," the third guy said as he grabbed the pipe.

"That bitch is messing where she doesn't belong. Maybe now she'll mind her own business," the first one said as he laughed.

"Quiet. We don't want them to hear," the second guy whispered.

"Hell, they can't hear anything over the roar of the fire," the third one said. "Laugh away."

They sat there as the flames grew. The boss was nowhere near finished. And they'd do whatever he wanted . . . and enjoy every minute of it.

There was work to be done, and they were more than ready. That made the men smile even more. Destruction could be a beautiful thing . . .

Chapter Eleven

Eden stepped from Owen's truck, not waiting for him to come around and open her door. She looked on helplessly as firefighters tried their best to beat the flames taking down her house. They were losing the battle. The place was burning fast and hot, and she'd be surprised if there was anything left by the time they put it out.

She stood there trying to figure out what she was feeling. Was it fear? She didn't think so. Sorrow? Her eyes were dry. Anger? Maybe. She honestly didn't understand what it was she felt. She knew for sure she was in shock. Everything she'd collected her entire life had been within those walls. All of her precious gifts from her father, her photos, her small collection of trinkets that had meant so much to her. And now it was gone. In a matter of minutes, it was all gone.

Owen was one of the suspects in the wilderness fire, but there was no part of her that thought him guilty of setting her house on fire. He wasn't capable of such cruelty. But what did this mean, then? It was too much of a coincidence that she'd been assigned to investigate what was going on in this town, and now her place was being burned to the ground. The flames were too hot and too out of control for this to be an accident.

The firefighters didn't pay the least bit of attention to her as they did their job. She heard laughter and turned her head, seeing one of the younger firemen holding tightly to the powerful blast of water being pushed through his large yellow hose.

"Stop horsing around, Chase," a man shouted.

"Just enjoying my work, boss," Chase called back, his attention never diverting from what he was doing.

She couldn't fault the kid. A lot of children wanted to be firefighters, police officers, or members of the military. They dreamed of saving the world. Not everyone kept those dreams as they grew up, but the elite did, and she knew the ones who'd make it and the ones who wouldn't. Chase would make it. He obviously loved what he did. He also had no idea the owner of the house was standing right there, or he would've toned it down.

She knew it wasn't that he relished seeing something destroyed. He was simply enjoying the thrill of being a part of stopping that destruction—of being the hero called in to save the day.

His chief obviously knew that as well, because he turned and spoke to another of the guys who was putting on heavy equipment. Once they got the blaze under control, if the house was still standing, they'd go inside, see if anything was salvageable.

There'd be nothing left. She could already see that.

Eden *felt* Owen, rather than saw him, when he walked up beside her. She tensed, afraid if he touched her she'd completely fall apart. She couldn't afford that. Too much had happened in too short a time frame, and if she didn't hold tightly to her raw emotions, the floodgates would open, and the flow might be too powerful for her to close the doors again.

It was almost as if Owen could read her thoughts, because he stood close but didn't say a word. She felt the warmth of his body, but he kept a few inches of space between them. It was as if he was telling her it was in her hands, that he was there for her if she needed him, but he'd stay away if she didn't want him. Just knowing this was almost her undoing.

Someone turned and saw them, and she watched as the man's lips turned up. "Owen," he called out, making several other heads turn their way, "why aren't you suited up?"

"I'm off duty," Owen replied. Eden was glad he didn't add it wasn't of his own free will, or that Eden herself had been the one to deliver that news to him. She was afraid they'd push her into the fire instead of try to contain it.

"When has that ever stopped you?" the man called out with a laugh.

"Do we have cause yet?" Owen asked, obviously trying to distract the guy. That's when the other man noticed Eden. She recognized him. He'd only been in town a year, but she'd run into him a few times at the bakery. Sean Adams was his name.

"Sorry, Eden," he said, his grin fading. He looked around at the other men and winced. They hated the destruction fire brought, but they sure loved putting one out. "We didn't know you were here," he offered with a helpless shrug.

"It's okay, Sean. There's nothing you can do now but douse it," she said, hating how choked her voice sounded.

"It's not that we like people losing their houses. The guys just need to let off some steam," Sean told her when Chase laughed again as he shifted his hose, dousing another part of her burning place.

"I understand," Eden told him.

Still, Sean moved away, going over to Chase. The kid's smile instantly faded as he looked over in Eden's direction. She was sure her face was almost eerie in the light of the fire. He bowed his head and went back to work. It made her feel bad that he'd gotten in trouble.

Soon, everyone knew she was there, and their laughter stopped. She wanted to tell them it was okay, that it was just a house. But she couldn't manage to say the words. It might just be a house, but there were things in it that were irreplaceable. She promised herself she could fall apart later. Right now wasn't the time or place.

"Let's go talk to the chief," Owen said. He still didn't touch her, though she found herself leaning closer to him. She didn't quite make their bodies touch, but she was taking silent comfort in his presence. She was sure she'd realize that was a mistake, but for now she didn't care.

Mistakes simply helped a person grow, helped shape them into who they were supposed to become. No one could be perfect, not even those who strove for that. Human error was what made us all human.

The two of them walked to where Chief Eric McCormack leaned against the fire engine. He kept his eyes on his men, but he let them do their jobs. He looked up and nodded at Owen; then his focus was solely on Eden.

"I'm sorry, Eden," he told her. "I know this is impossible." He didn't offer any other words. What else could he say? That it was going to be okay? That she'd be fine after a good night's rest? That she wasn't losing everything she owned? No. He couldn't say any of that because it clearly wasn't true.

"Hi, Chief," she said, her voice quiet, hard to hear over the noise of the fire and engines. She cleared her throat and tried again. "What happened?"

There was a tremendous *boom*, followed by the team of firefighters calling out to make sure everyone was accounted for. She turned, already knowing what she was about to see. The roof of her house had just collapsed, and the walls were folding in. There truly would be nothing left but ashes.

She nearly lost it again.

Even though she'd told herself there was zero hope of recovering anything, she'd still prayed she could at least get those precious things her father had given her. A few tears slipped from her eyes before she could stop them. She faced the fire as she discreetly lifted her hand and wiped them away. She pulled her hand back and saw how black it was. The ash was flying through the air, and her tears were going to be obvious to anyone who cared to look at her.

"We smelled gasoline as soon as we got here," the chief said.

Eden's stomach clenched more tightly. She'd known this fire had been deliberately set, but the chief was confirming it. "Of course, we have to have an arson investigator look at it, but we know what we smelled."

"Yes, you don't do your job as long as you without knowing," she offered. "I don't understand who'd do it."

"Here's a hint," the chief said, holding out a letter. "It was taped to the side of your mailbox. One of the guys grabbed it, and I read it. Keep it in the plastic. We might be able to lift some prints."

Eden was stupefied as she took the plastic-wrapped letter from the chief. Someone had left her a note. What in the heck did that mean?

There was only one sentence typed out in a standard Times New Roman font. There was no signature, nothing to give even the remotest hint of who had left this for her. She couldn't help but recall the notes that had been left for her friend Keera not too long ago. That case was still open.

Had Eden been pulled into this strange universe that seemed to be devouring their entire town? She didn't understand how. She'd never done anything—at least that she could think of—that would make her a threat.

"What does it say?" Owen asked. There was such worry in his voice that she knew beyond a shadow of a doubt he had nothing to do with this. She'd known that all along, but hearing the concern and barely masked fury in his tone sealed that knowledge.

This was Owen—her Owen. No, he wasn't hers anymore, but she knew he could never hurt her this badly. She knew he was too honorable a man for that. She didn't say anything, simply handed him the note. She wasn't sure she could even speak right now.

Owen read the note out loud: "Sticking your nose where it doesn't belong will get you burned."

It made it even worse to hear the words spoken aloud, made it all too real. She might be in danger, though that seemed impossible. *What did it matter?* she decided. They'd already taken everything they could from her. All she had left was her work.

Her eyes narrowed as her tears disappeared. If they thought this would scare her, they'd produced the opposite effect. She was suddenly furious, angrier than she could ever remember feeling.

She was going to find them . . . and they'd pay. They'd all pay. She'd die before she'd quit. They'd taken enough from her, from the town she loved. They'd just made the wrong enemy. She wasn't as weak as she might have seemed. There had to be a ringleader. But whoever was in charge also had minions, and she'd get each and every one of them.

Turning, Eden looked at the shadows cast by the bright blaze, somehow feeling them out there, feeling the monsters who were lurking in the dark.

"I *will* find you!" she screamed.

Neither the chief nor Owen said a word, but their gazes followed hers.

There was no reply. But she somehow knew she'd been challenged. And she also knew they were aware the challenge had been accepted.

Game on.

◆ ◆ ◆

He was close.

Close enough to hear Eden's challenge. He'd been smiling at her devastated look, but at her words, the grin fell away. He'd thought he'd broken her, thought he'd sufficiently scared her, but he quickly realized she wasn't who he'd thought she was.

He now knew scaring her would never be enough. She'd have to die. It didn't matter to him. What was one more casualty in a war?

He tried to smile again, but he was no longer in the mood.

Turning, he walked away from the flames. No one noticed. They were too busy. He was just another concerned community member. He was the last thing on their minds.

But Eden wouldn't always have Owen around to protect her. Even if he was there, it didn't matter. They would both die before this was over.

His smile finally returned.

Yes. Game on.

Chapter Twelve

Eden was shivering. Her anger drained as quickly as it had appeared. This was too much for one person to bear. She knew she was ready to fall to the ground, knew there wasn't a heck of a lot more she could tolerate. She was sort of surprised to find herself still standing.

She almost smiled when she remembered what her father had always said to her: *No matter how bad a day you think you're having, I promise there's someone else in the world who has it so much worse than you do. Don't focus on the negative; appreciate the positive and be grateful you don't know what truly bad is all about.* That was the kind of man her father was. That was the man who'd been taken from this earth too soon. Why him? Why take him when there were so many people out there who didn't appreciate the life they'd been given?

Her shaking grew worse, and that's when she felt the comforting embrace of Owen's arm as he circled her waist. It wasn't an intimate gesture. It was one offered in comfort. He wasn't able to stand idly by any longer when she was obviously going off the deep end.

"You're going to be okay," he assured her.

She wanted to be strong enough to push him away, to tell him she didn't need his comfort. But she'd be lying, not only to him, but to herself. Her father had also told her it was okay to lean on someone stronger once in a while. He'd assured her she'd be that stronger person some days, and someone else would be the next time. It was a circle, where none of us were meant to be alone, none of us were meant to always carry the burden.

"I'll be fine," she finally said, actually feeling that she was going to be. No matter how bad it got, it wouldn't last. No matter what the situation felt like, it couldn't possibly be as bad as she imagined. Why did people want to go to the worst-case scenario right out of the starting gate? Why not think more positively? *Because we're all human, and that means we're all slaves to our fragile emotions.*

She didn't need to stand there watching as the flames took the rest of her house. It was accomplishing nothing to do that. The best way for her to get this mystery solved was to get away . . . to think.

"Can I have a few minutes alone?" Eden asked. She hated asking permission, but she had no idea where she was even going. Obviously she couldn't stay in the house. There wasn't a house there.

"Where do you want to go?" Owen asked.

She looked around. There was a pond down a side trail. It was why she loved this house so much. Not only was the neighborhood wonderful, but she got a piece of nature while still being in town.

"I'm just going to sit on the dock for a few minutes," she said.

Owen looked as if he wanted to refuse. That instantly put an iron rod straight up her back. She hadn't needed anyone's permission in a very long time. She shouldn't have asked. She should have just demanded.

"Let me walk you down," he said.

"Owen . . . ," she began, but he held up a hand.

"I'm not trying to micromanage you, but someone set your house on fire and left you a threatening note. I just want to make sure they aren't hanging around to finish up what they started."

Eden tried to find fault in his logic. But he was correct. She was too worn out to talk, so she simply nodded. As much as she wanted his arm wrapped around her, she wouldn't admit it, so she walked about a foot away from him as they made their way to the dock.

The moon was full, giving them plenty of light, since the farther away they got from the fire, the less light they had. They made it to the dock, and Owen looked around for several moments before he seemed satisfied.

"I'm just a shout away," he told her.

She nodded again. He turned and left her. Eden gratefully sank to her butt and took off her shoes, letting her feet hang over the dock into the cool water. They tingled from the cold, and it was good, letting her know she was still very much alive.

Eden looked down into the blackness of the water rather than looking up at those deceptive stars. She wouldn't be able to see many of them, anyway, since most of the area was covered in smoke. But she didn't even want to see one breaking through the moonlit clouds. She wondered if she'd ever like stars again. At this particular moment, she didn't care.

It was late, but Eden felt the need to speak to someone who wasn't going to get emotional on her, someone who would make her think of anything other than the fact that she was homeless with only the clothes on her body, a broken car, and some cash. How sad her life had become.

She was twenty-seven years old, single, alone, with a job she didn't love, and a life she didn't understand. She wondered if other people had these sorts of thoughts, if they wondered what in the heck the purpose of life truly was. She was sure they did.

A fish came up and nibbled on her big toe, and Eden was shocked when she found herself smiling. She might even be in a halfway decent mood if she had a fishing pole in her hand. Some people found fishing boring. She found it relaxing, especially on a hot summer day with music playing low and a cold beer in her hand.

Sure, the music scared away most of the fish, but every once in a while, a brave one would latch on to her hook. It wasn't about what she caught; it was about the act of doing something so mundane, so leisurely.

Pulling out her phone, she decided to call the arson investigator to fill him in on . . . well, on basically nothing. She didn't really have any information for him, but he'd been the one to choose her to talk to people. Or, more aptly, he'd picked her law firm, and her boss had picked her.

The call was answered just as she was about to hang up. "Hello?"

She realized it was getting late. "Hi, Ron. Sorry to bother you at this hour. I didn't bother looking at the time," she said hurriedly.

"Eden? What's wrong?" He'd seemed distracted when he'd answered, but he was instantly on alert at the sound of her voice. She wondered if there were many emergencies in this line of work.

"Nothing's wrong, exactly," she said. "My house just burned down."

There was a short pause on the other end of the line.

"Are you okay?" he asked, talking to her as if she were a small child.

"I wasn't home when it happened. I got here just in time to see the aftermath," she told him before pausing. "There's something else I need to tell you, though, that I should've already." She pushed out the words quickly so she couldn't take them back. She didn't want to lose this job. It was what she had right now, and it was better than being stuck inside an office at her desk all day long. But she also didn't want this investigation damaged because she hadn't been honest with all the parties involved.

"What is it?" he asked. She couldn't tell by his tone if he was waiting for good or bad news.

"I've had a relationship with one of the people being investigated," she said.

There was another pause, this one a little longer.

"How much of a relationship?" he finally asked.

"We were a couple for about three years, but it ended ten years ago." That was until six months ago, when she'd jumped his bones in his kitchen. She decided she didn't need to add that.

She could tell Ron was doing the math in his head.

"You were teens?" he asked.

"Yes, but you know small towns . . ." She trailed off. Not everyone knew small towns. Maybe Ron had never been to one in his life.

"It's Friday night and there isn't anything we can do right now. But I'm going to have to talk to my bosses and see how they want to proceed with this. Why don't you continue to do your job this weekend, but make sure you're keeping detailed notes," he finally said.

She let out a relieved breath. She might not be on the case come Monday or Tuesday, but at least for now she could still focus on it.

"Thank you. That's exactly what I want to do," she said.

"Tell me what you know," he said.

She spent the next couple of minutes informing him about the injuries on the mountain earlier, and of her conversations with both Owen and his brother. She didn't try to come to any conclusions on what she'd found so far. She wasn't supposed to. That was Ron's job.

"You're doing great. I'll be sorry if you have to be replaced," Ron told her.

"So will I. At first I didn't want to do it, but I've come to sort of enjoy it . . . well, that is, when my house isn't burning down," she said with a humorless laugh.

"I'm truly sorry about that, Eden," he replied. She heard some noise in the background, and it sounded as if she might have interrupted him. Not all people worked twenty-four-seven. Most people had families or friends to hang with. Yes, Eden had friends. But she just didn't want to talk about any of this anymore, so she wasn't planning on seeing any of them.

The background noise at his house increased, and Eden told him goodbye. She got off the phone and sat there at the dock for a few minutes longer. When her feet were completely numb, she pulled them from the water and waited for them to dry enough to put her shoes on.

She was on wobbly feet as she stood and began making her way back up the trail to her diminishing home. She wasn't surprised to find

Owen at the top of the trail. He was far enough away to give her privacy, but close enough to get to her if she let out so much as a peep of distress.

He always had enjoyed being the knight in shining armor. It seemed at least that much about him hadn't changed. She feared she might be planning on making another mistake with him—maybe even tonight.

Why fight it?

Isn't that what she'd thought before? Isn't that what she'd been doing when she'd lost her father? But she truly did have nothing else to lose at this point. Maybe she should simply jump in with both feet one more time.

Chapter Thirteen

"Why don't you come home with me?" Owen asked.

Before she replied, he knew her answer. She shook her head. "No, take me to the motel," she said.

"That's foolish, Eden," he insisted. "I have a huge house. I'll leave you alone if you come with me." He wasn't sure he'd be capable of keeping that promise, but he'd give it one hell of a valiant effort.

"No," she said again. He was growing more frustrated by the second. He didn't want to leave her alone, especially after that note she'd been left.

"How about going to Roxie's, then?" he asked, though it killed him. He didn't want her at his brother's place. He wanted her with him.

"No," she told him. "Take me to the motel."

He was quiet. "What about your dad's place?"

She winced visibly. "You know I can't stay there," she whispered. He felt like an idiot for even bringing it up. Of course she couldn't stay there. He knew he wouldn't be able to stay in his parents' house if something were to happen to them. He really needed to spend more time with them.

"Then come home with me," he tried again.

When she looked up, there was a change in her eyes. There was determination and something else that had him tensing. The look in her eyes said something he didn't want to even hope for.

"Take me to the motel . . . and come inside with me for a little while."

He knew she was trying to distract him. And Owen had to admit it was working. She was beautiful, sexy, and he needed her more than he needed oxygen. So what if he was a fool? He'd take what she was offering, because that was one step closer to his ultimate goal of having her forever.

Without further argument, he placed his hand on her back and led her to his truck, bypassing the firefighters who were still putting out the blaze that had completely consumed her home. There truly wouldn't be anything left. That was something they were going to have to face tomorrow. But he'd be by her side so she wouldn't do it alone.

Eden scooted over to the middle of the seat as they began driving down the road. Owen pressed his foot down on the accelerator, needing to get her into a bed as soon as possible. Many people handled grief in different ways. If it was escape she was looking for, he was glad she trusted him enough to do it with him.

He reached out, his fingers resting on the denim of her jeans, then running up her firm thigh before dropping back down to her knee. His stomach was in knots, and from the way she shifted, he had no doubt she was coming as unhinged as he was.

As Owen rubbed her thigh, her breath quickened, and he felt a shudder pass through her body. He wasn't sure they'd survive the drive to the motel. It was at least closer than his place.

He pulled his hand away, and she grumbled as she leaned into him, her lips trailing along his jaw, tasting the corner of his mouth. He ached so badly it almost felt as if he were being stabbed. His jeans were too tight for the erection he was now sporting, and he shifted, trying to make himself more comfortable.

"What's the matter?" Eden asked. The way she said this shot him straight down memory lane. He remembered driving into the woods with her in this exact same position, the truck just much older. He'd loved how she'd tease him, build up their excitement. They'd nearly driven over a cliff the one time she'd undone his pants, then leaned down and taken his pulsing erection straight down her throat.

After what felt like hours, he pulled into the motel parking lot and cut the engine of his truck. It was long past time he had a taste of her luscious lips. He pulled her onto his lap and pressed his lips to hers. He could swear he saw stars as her tongue danced with his. She pulled back, and now it was his turn to protest.

"Let me get a room," she said, her voice husky, her skin flushed.

"I can do it," he told her.

"No, then they'll think this is a love nest," she said as she climbed off him and slipped from the truck. He was pretty proud to note that she was walking with a definite wobble. He waited impatiently for her to get back, his desire not tempered in the least.

She stepped from the office and waved at him before turning right and going down the long corridor. He practically vaulted from his truck, meeting her at the motel-room door just as she pushed it open.

He didn't give her a chance to catch her breath before he led both of them to the bed, pulling her onto his lap while he began undoing the clasp of her jeans. He had them off in about three seconds flat; then he skimmed the outside of her panties, the silky material saturated with her arousal.

Owen resumed their kissing, pushing her lips apart so he could sink his tongue deep inside the recesses of her mouth. His hands caressed her back, making a moan escape from her sweet lips. She ground her firm butt against him and gasped when she felt the power of his erection pressing against her wet heat.

His hands moved to her center and slowly upward; he was desperate to feel the weight of her luscious breasts in his palms. She arched her back, pleading with him to take care of her. He finally gave her what she wanted, squeezing her tender breasts before rubbing his thumbs across her swollen nipples.

"We have too many clothes on," he muttered, gasping for air as he broke off from the kiss.

"I agree," she told him.

She wasn't going to change her mind. He'd known she wouldn't, though. She needed him as much as he needed her. It had always been that way between them.

Owen pulled off her shirt and took only a second to admire the tiny wisp of a bra that was pushing up her generous breasts. He unhooked it, tossing it aside before taking one of her nipples into his hot mouth, greedily sucking her. He'd always been in love with her dark nipples, especially when they were puckered in pleasure from his touch. When he pulled back and saw his spit gleaming on the beautiful stiff peaks, his erection pulsed in anticipation.

He gave equal attention to her other breast, then stood her in front of him so he could remove her panties and finally take a moment to look at her. She was so spectacular he could barely breathe. Her waist had grown too small in her sorrow. He knew she was forgetting to eat. But even so, her hips flared, beautifully succulent, absolutely made for his grip. And her breasts—oh, her stunning breasts were the perfect handful.

He didn't dare continue looking down her body, afraid he'd explode. Instead, he jumped up and began stripping off his clothes, enjoying her gasp of pleasure as she gazed at his thickness.

"Lie down," he told her.

"No," she said. He stalled at the thought that this had been some sort of revenge for her. He wasn't sure what he'd do if she pushed him out the door. He might actually die.

But she didn't push him from the room. Instead, she climbed onto the bed on her hands and knees, her ass high in the air, her head turning to look at him, a seductive gleam in her eyes. He wanted to lie against her, not take her this way. But tonight wasn't about him; it was about her, and there was nothing he wouldn't do for her.

He moved up against her, his hands reaching out to squeeze her luscious ass, her body trembling beneath his touch. He ran his fingers down the crack of her ass, all the way to her hot core. Pushing his fingers inside her made his erection jump. She was so hot, so tight.

He pulled out and flipped her over, then leaned into her and licked her thighs, loving how her skin tasted and smelled. He didn't think it possible, but he grew even harder, knowing he was on the verge of losing control. He grabbed his erection and squeezed hard, trying to ease some of the pressure. It helped, but only minimally. He kept his lips against her hot skin, licking her up and down before latching onto that bundle of nerves that made her scream when his tongue flicked over it.

His fingers pumped faster inside her, her entire body shaking. Then he swept his tongue over her swollen nerves again and sent her over the edge. Her body sagged as she trembled before him. He loved the flush of her skin, how her chest was heaving, her nipples tight, her thighs wet from her pleasure and his tongue.

"There's never been anyone but you," he said.

Her eyes widened, and he saw a sparkle in her eyes, but she closed them for a few seconds. When they opened, they were once again filled with passion. This moment was something he'd never grow tired of. Now he could take her the way he *needed* to.

"My turn," she told him. She slid from the bed, dropping to her knees in front of him.

She wrapped her fingers around him, then leaned in, her tongue lapping the head of his erection, precome making the tip shine. She licked it up before closing her lips around him, growing more urgent as she took him deeper and deeper into her mouth, moving up and down his shaft, wetting him with her hot tongue.

He grabbed her head, his fingers fisting in her hair as he groaned, praying he didn't let them both down. It had been six months since he'd felt her body on his, and he wasn't sure he was going to make it.

She took him deep, his head entering her tight throat. And Owen gave up. He couldn't hold back. She didn't want him to. With a cry of pleasure, he felt his release rip from him. She hummed against his erection, the sensation giving him even more pleasure. She didn't stop sucking him until she felt his last pulse of pleasure.

Only then did Eden release his still incredibly hard shaft from her mouth, taking a few seconds to lick him from tip to root before sucking his head one more time. He felt his pleasure stirring again. He wasn't surprised—not with this woman, not at this moment.

Owen lifted her up, pushing her onto the bed as he crawled over her. He was no longer in a gentle mood. He felt like an animal, and he had to consume her as much as she was consuming him.

His lips descended, and she eagerly accepted his kiss along with the weight of his body. He didn't hesitate as he aligned their bodies, then plunged deep within her wet heat. She pushed up against him, her breathing becoming labored, her moans mixing with his. He sped up, moving quickly in and out of her wet folds.

Owen reached between them and squeezed her breast as his lips devoured her mouth. He felt her begin to tighten around him, making it harder for him to move. And then she screamed as her body clenched him. He didn't even try to hold on. He let go with her, soaring through an endless expanse of pleasure.

It took a long while for their breathing to return to normal. When Owen was sure he could move, he shifted their bodies, turning so he was on his back, cradling her close to his side. He pulled the covers over them and lay with her head on his chest. He'd missed this. He hadn't felt at home until this very moment.

He was sure she'd fallen asleep when five minutes passed without either of them saying a word. He didn't mind. He could care less where they slept as long as they were together.

"Please be gone when I wake up," she murmured.

Owen stilled the hand that had been rubbing against her back.

"Why?" he asked, trying not to be offended. He couldn't ever remember a time in his life he'd felt used, but he was sort of feeling that way right now.

"I need to know I can be strong. I don't feel that way right now. I feel weak and sad, like the world is weighing on me. I need to know I can make it on my own, that I don't need to have someone there to hold me up."

Her words were tinged with tears, and his caress against her back resumed. "It doesn't make you weak to know when you need someone to lean on," he assured her.

"Please, Owen. I have to do this," she said.

Owen had no doubt he could talk her out of this. But that would show a lack of respect for her. He didn't say anything, and soon she fell asleep. He lay there with her all night, catching a few moments of sleep here and there, but very aware of every movement she made.

When dawn was breaking, she began to stir. And though it killed him to do so, he gently extracted himself from beneath her and quickly dressed. He looked at her one last time before quietly slipping from the rented room.

The only reason he was able to sneak away like a thief in the night was because he had no doubt she'd be with him soon, and not just for a night of hot sex—she'd be with him for all time and eternity.

Chapter Fourteen

Owen stood in his brother Declan's house. He was too restless to sit, so he paced the long den, a stiff drink he hadn't yet touched in his hand. Declan patiently waited for him to get off his chest whatever it was he needed to say. That's one of the great things about brothers—they didn't push.

"Is Eden now a target of this group who was after Keera?" Owen asked.

"I think so," Declan said. Declan never had been one to mince words. Right now Owen was frustrated and grateful for that at the same time.

"You could have lied to me, could have told me she was just fine, that nothing could possibly happen to her," Owen said. He finally stopped and downed the amber liquid in his glass. The burn down his throat was exactly what he'd needed.

"Then you wouldn't be able to protect her," Declan said.

"No one will get to her," Owen said, murder in his eyes.

"I have no doubt about that, but they did manage to get to her home," Declan pointed out. There was a look in his brother's eyes Owen didn't understand. He shook it off and voiced his frustration.

"That's because I wasn't aware anyone was after her. What in the hell is going on in our town? We have drugs, murder, threats, fire. When will it stop?" Owen asked, his voice rising with each new word.

"I'm working on it," Declan assured him.

"Not fast enough," Owen thundered.

Declan didn't take offense. He simply raised his eyebrows as he walked over to his liquor cabinet and poured each of them another drink. He nearly smiled as he looked at his brother.

"I'm going to let you get away with that because I know how much this woman means to you, and I know you're on your last nerve," Declan said as he handed over the drink.

"I'm sorry. That was uncalled for," Owen admitted.

"I'm sure I've said worse," Declan said. "Though I'm so damn perfect I can't imagine when."

The joke was so unexpected, coming from his stiff older brother, that the words stopped Owen once again. He looked at Declan and smiled.

"Man, she has me spinning in circles. I'm so in love with her," Owen said.

This time Declan laughed. "Yeah, that's old news, brother," Declan told him. Then his smile faded. "But you have to be aware that things in life happen that are beyond our control. You might have to accept that."

"What's that supposed to mean?" Owen asked, desperately trying to read the look in Declan's eyes.

"This drug ring has created havoc in our town, and they aren't finished yet. She's definitely on their radar now."

"Are you saying I can't protect her?" Owen asked, irritated beyond words.

Declan was quiet for a moment. "How much do you love her?"

Owen was even more confused than before. "Not that I see what that has to do with my ability to protect her, but I truly am in love with her. The till-death-do-us-part kind of love," he said, as if this were a huge revelation.

Declan laughed again, even more mirth in the sound. It was so odd to hear Declan laugh. His brother carried too much weight on his huge shoulders for a man who wasn't yet forty.

"That means you might make wrong choices where she's concerned," Declan warned. Owen opened his mouth to respond, but Declan stopped him. "Owen, you've always been in love with her, just as she is with you. Now you just have to remind her why she fell in love with you, and why you're trustworthy enough to have her heart again. You have to do this all while trying to keep the bad guys away."

"Wow, okay, Dr. Phil," Owen said. He'd expect this sort of advice from Kian, maybe even from Arden. He never would've expected it from Declan.

"Don't get used to this. I think the town is affecting me mentally. I'm going soft," Declan said, as if that was the worst thing that could happen to a man. In some situations it truly was the worst thing that could happen. "Otherwise, these assholes would already be in jail, and I'd be moving on to the next case."

"I just don't see why these guys have set their sights on Eden. She's barely involved," Owen told him.

"Maybe she's getting too close to something," Declan said.

Owen was shocked by the ferocity in Declan's voice.

"What aren't you telling me?" Owen asked.

Declan turned away, and it looked as if he shook his head. Possibly to clear it. That didn't seem like his brother at all.

"There are some things I can't tell you," Declan said.

"Since when?" Owen pushed.

"That would be one of the things I'm not telling you," Declan said smugly.

"You can be a real asshole sometimes," Owen said, his dark mood increasing as he played word games with his brother.

"That's not the first nor last time I've heard that," Declan assured him.

They were getting nowhere. Owen decided to change the subject . . . slightly. "I'm suspended," he grumbled. He was still beyond irritated over that. "I can't believe there's anyone out there who'd think I'm capable of all this chaos."

"Want me to get it lifted?" Declan asked.

That made Owen laugh. "No. There's not a chance I'm letting anyone say I got out of this because of who I know or what my last name is," Owen told him. "But thanks for having my back."

"Of course you aren't guilty," Declan said, as if that was the most absurd thing he'd ever heard. "But people are just doing their jobs. It's a waste of time, but they gotta do what they gotta do."

"I could care less what the rest of the world thinks," Owen said. "But it'd kill me if Eden truly did believe I could do it."

"She knows you, Owen. She knows you aren't capable of this. She's just doing her job," Declan told him. Then he looked Owen in the eyes. "But you did leave her, so she might not be sure anymore what you're capable of."

"That was a low blow," Owen told him. "And yeah, I did leave her, but you of all people understand why."

"Maybe it's time you told her."

Silence greeted those words as Owen shook his head. "I made a promise," he said, feeling the weight of his loyalty.

"Would he really want you to give up everything?" Declan asked.

"I don't know. I owed him my life," Owen said.

Declan nodded. He understood what it meant to be loyal. He knew you didn't betray someone just to cover your own ass. Owen really didn't know what he should do.

"In time it will work itself out," Declan said.

"You've become quite the counselor," Owen told him.

"Yeah, yeah," Declan muttered. "Tell anyone about this conversation, and I'll hand you over to some experts in torture techniques."

Owen smiled. The sad thing was, he had no doubt his brother did have those contacts. He felt sorry for anyone who dared to cross Declan. It wouldn't go well for them—not well at all.

"What evidence do you have, Dec?" Owen asked.

"Not a hell of a lot," Declan said, his frustration clear. He didn't like being in the dark, didn't like feeling like the bad guys were outsmarting him. If the situation wasn't so serious, Owen wouldn't have minded his brother getting outwitted. It was good to knock his ego down a peg or two.

"It would really help me if you could get this solved," Owen said with a shrug.

"I'll solve it," Declan assured him, a determined glint in his eyes.

"I have no doubt," Owen said. "I've given Eden a full day to herself. I think that's enough time," he finished as he moved toward the door.

"Go get the girl," Declan told him.

"Damn straight."

That's exactly what he planned to do.

Chapter Fifteen

Owen wasn't surprised to find Eden's car parked in the driveway of her ruined home, especially since he'd had it fixed and waiting for her at the motel by the time she could step out her door. Sadly, all that was left of her house besides a pile of ashes was the foundation and a couple of sturdy pillars. The fire truly had destroyed the place, and it hadn't shown a lick of mercy.

It was growing dark as he climbed from his truck, and he took about one second to figure out where she was. He had a feeling she spent a lot of time down at the dock near her place. She was so frustrating sometimes that he wasn't sure if he wanted to spank her fine behind or hold her so tight she couldn't do anything foolish.

Since neither option was acceptable, he locked his truck and pulled out his flashlight as he made his way down the trail. He didn't want to light it yet, didn't want her to know he was there.

He stepped from the trail and could see her sitting at the end of the dock, her feet dangling in the water. He didn't hear a sound from her or around her. That filled him with relief. They had no idea who'd burned down her house, and the one thing he knew for certain was that she absolutely shouldn't be off in the dark by herself.

He walked down to the dock, trying to figure out how to alert her to his presence without startling her too much. She heard him and jumped about a mile off the dock, her body jarring back down as she glared at him.

Good. At least she was smart enough to be afraid. That gave him a bit more peace of mind. Not much, but a little.

"What the hell, Owen?" she yelled. "You scared me nearly to death."

"I'm sorry," he said. "I didn't mean to startle you. But you know I don't want you out here alone right now. I don't think you're taking your safety seriously enough."

"I don't need a lecture from you," she said, but some of the heat in her words had dissipated.

"I don't want to give you one," he told her. "You've been through enough." He made sure to keep his voice calm. "I haven't had the chance to tell you how sorry I am you lost your dad. He truly was one of the good ones, and I know the loss is unbearable for you. I hope you take comfort in knowing he'll be missed in this town. I'll miss him." He grew quieter as he continued to speak. These weren't just empty words. He meant them. He really had liked her father.

She gazed at him for several moments before she opened her mouth, then shut it again. There were tears sparkling in her eyes, but she didn't allow them to fall. He couldn't imagine the strength that was taking.

"I miss him," she finally said, the words coming up through a closed throat. "I'm also angry at him," she admitted, her tone so quiet, he barely heard her. When the words registered, he didn't know what to say.

"I'm here if you want to talk about it," he assured her.

"He left me," she cried. Those tears finally fell as she trembled. He reached for her, but she shook her head. It killed him, but respecting her was more important than his needs.

"He left me, and I wasn't ready to let him go. I didn't even know he was sick. I thought I had forever with him. I thought he'd outlive all of us. He was so healthy, such a man of nature. He was supposed to always be here for me. He promised me he'd be here as long as I needed him. But he left," she sobbed. She was shaking so hard now it nearly killed him not to hold her.

He gingerly moved his hand, resting it on her back. She didn't pull away this time. There was nothing he could say to comfort her. All he could do was let her say what she needed to.

"And he called me right before he died. He called me and I didn't pick up. I was with you, and I thought I could talk to him the next day. I didn't want him to know what I was doing. He never judged me, never made me feel bad about myself, but I still didn't want him to know . . . I couldn't be bothered. And now I'll never get to hug him again. I'll never hear his deep voice again. I'll never feel safe in his big arms. He's my dad, my savior, my hero, and I got so busy I couldn't give him five minutes. Because I thought I'd always have five minutes . . . when I was ready, not when he wanted them. I thought he'd always be waiting right there for me whenever I needed him. And now he's gone, and I'm so broken. I'm sad and mad, and I don't know what to do. I miss him so much."

Her words cut off as she stopped talking, tears tracking down her face. This time when he pulled her close, she didn't fight. She wrapped her arms around him and clung tightly, letting him take some of the burden she'd been carrying for six months. She was forgetting for this moment that she was mad at Owen. There was too much she was dealing with on her own, and he was more than capable and more than happy to help lift that burden. He'd take it all if she'd allow him to.

Several minutes passed with her shaking in his arms. Neither of them spoke. Owen didn't believe in spewing words just to fill an otherwise peaceful silence. Sometimes that meant a situation could be a little uncomfortable, but that didn't matter. The best things in life usually happened when you allowed yourself out of your comfort zone.

"I can't keep leaning on you," Eden finally said.

Owen was relieved to hear a bit of strength returning to her voice.

"Yes, you can—anytime, anywhere," he told her. His hands were now moving up and down her back. He was in heaven doing nothing more than touching her.

Eden looked up at him, and the moonlight was bright enough for him to see the redness of her eyes, the sorrow that still lurked in the shadows of their depths. He wished so much he could take that pain away.

She leaned closer, her chin tilting, a clear invitation.

He took her mouth in a gentle kiss, a reassuring meeting of the mouths. This wasn't about passion; it was about comfort. This was him telling her he wasn't ever going to leave her again. This was him taking a small slice of her burden.

It was so strange to him how much power this one person held over him. If she told him she wanted them to jump off the Golden Gate Bridge, he'd hold her hand while doing it. He'd turn so her body was protected as they hit the water. There really wasn't anything he wouldn't do for her. In time he'd prove that.

He didn't try to deepen the kiss, didn't try to possess her. He simply held her, letting her know she wasn't alone—that she didn't have to be alone again as long as she wanted him at her side.

Far too soon, Eden pulled away, taking a moment to lean against his broad chest, her hand pressed over his heart. He wanted to freeze time and never move, never let this moment slip away. But that wasn't how the real world worked.

"I should go back now," she said as she lifted her head, then scooted away, reaching for her shoes and slipping them on.

Owen rose to his feet, then held out his hand to help her up. She took it after a moment's hesitation. He wanted to tug her against him, but he wasn't willing to press his luck. Instead, he fell into step beside her as they made their way back up the trail to where their vehicles were parked. He held open her door and waited for her to climb in.

"I wish you'd come home with me. I'd leave you alone if that's what you want," he said. He had to at least try.

"Thanks, Owen, but no," she said. There wasn't any anger, just an iron will that he was starting to see appear again in her beautiful eyes.

"Soon," he said.

She looked at him with surprise as he shut her door. He wasn't giving her a chance to deny him his final word. He even smiled as he got into his truck and started it. He drove behind her as she headed to her motel, then honked the horn as he passed by.

At least she was around people. The arsonist wouldn't be so foolish as to light a hotel on fire—or at least he hoped he wouldn't be that foolish. He still made some phone calls and cashed in some favors owed to him to have extra patrols keeping an eye out.

She'd kick his ass if she found out. He smiled, knowing she wouldn't. What she didn't know wouldn't hurt her. And the only way he could even begin to try to solve this mystery was if he knew she was taken care of.

Chapter Sixteen

Eden was exhausted as she fell onto her bed in the cheap motel. She went to sleep almost instantly and had a restless night. The morning came too soon, and she felt as if she hadn't slept at all when she rose from the uncomfortable bed.

She looked around, feeling about as low as she could as she wiped the sleep from her eyes. She wanted to call Owen, have him take away these feelings, even if only for a little while. But she'd told him she needed to be strong, and that's what she intended to do.

The past couldn't be erased, no matter how much she wished it could. No, scratch that, she had to remember that everything about her past had shaped her into who she was now. She didn't want to have regrets, didn't need to have them. Just because things weren't going exactly as she had planned didn't mean every decision she'd ever made had been a mistake.

Still, her heart hurt. She missed her father. She missed the comfort only he could give her, and the way his strong arms would make everything okay. She missed her home, missed the items in that home that had brought her comfort. And she missed Owen. She missed how he made her feel when she was with him.

Talking to Owen about her father the night before, about her sadness and anger at him leaving her so soon, had opened up those wounds a little bit more. Just when she thought she was healing, she'd get pushed back a little bit further. Would this ever end? She wasn't sure.

Owen was sneaking back into her life one moment at a time. Part of her wanted to allow that to happen. The rational side of her knew they'd had their time together, and now it was over. But the emotional side of her had never stopped loving him.

Why had he left her? Had it been that important for him to see the world? Had she truly meant that little to him? Again, the rational side of her came out, and she told herself they'd been teenagers, too young to commit to a lifetime together. But her emotional side told her they'd known all they needed to know about each other, even at such a young age.

The way her mind was bouncing back and forth made her head ache. If she could just focus on her work, she'd be in a much better place—mentally, at least. But come Monday morning, she might not even have that anymore. No, she wouldn't lose her job at the attorney's office, but going back into the small room and sitting at a desk all day seemed a fate worse than death right now. She wanted to stay on this particular case until it was satisfactorily solved, with all the bad guys behind bars.

Her phone rang and she looked at the caller ID. It was Roxie. Eden's finger hovered over the face of her phone. But then she let it go to voice mail. She knew she wasn't going to get away with ignoring her best friend for long. Roxie would come crashing in through her motel door the second she realized the mood Eden was in.

There was a part of Eden that wanted exactly that to happen. The other part of her wanted to be alone to wallow in her misery. Roxie would have a fit about Eden staying in this depressing motel when she lived in a mansion that was plenty big enough to accommodate a guest. But Eden needed to take care of herself—she had to prove to herself she could.

When Eden took a moment to look at herself in the mirror, she was slightly horrified. She'd had a rough few days, and it showed. All of her possessions had burned to the ground. When she'd woken after her night with Owen, she'd found a bag of clothes at the front desk, a note attached to it.

She'd been grateful he'd done that for her. There was nothing that made her feel more gross than to wear dirty panties. She hated taking a handout, but she'd concede in these circumstances. She didn't want to think about all she needed to do, but she also couldn't bury her head in the sand.

She brushed back her hair, then sat down on the bed and picked up her phone. She had to find a place to live, go shopping for more clothes, and restock her toiletries. Those were just a few of the basic tasks she was facing.

An hour later she felt a tad bit better. She had a real estate agent looking for a rental and pulling up listings of houses for sale. One task was accomplished. She had to decide if she wanted to rebuild her house or clear the lot, sell the land, and start over somewhere else. She'd be stuck in a rental for at least six months if she rebuilt. That didn't sound appealing. There was comfort in owning her home, in knowing a landlord couldn't change their mind and give her a thirty-day notice to get out.

Eden knew she had to get out of the small motel room, or she was likely to go crazy. As much as she wanted to avoid any and all company, she got dressed, put on the minimal makeup she kept in her purse, and left the room.

It was a beautiful day, aside from the low-hanging smoke in the air. She'd noticed that her throat had been a little sore for the past week. She was sure the entire town was sucking in too much carbon dioxide, but it wasn't so dangerous that the mayor was advising residents to evacuate yet.

Eden made her way to her favorite café and slipped inside, grateful when she found a table in the back corner. If she kept her head down, maybe no one would notice her. News spread as fast as the wildfire burning on the edges of town. She'd have snoopy people asking her all sorts of questions if she wasn't careful.

Her phone rang again after the waitress, who was new, thank goodness, took her order. It was Roxie again. Eden thought about answering, then silenced the phone after the second ring. She didn't know what to say.

"I knew you were purposely ignoring my calls!"

The irritated voice startled Eden so badly she jumped in her booth, knocking her knee against the bottom of the table. She turned guilty eyes on Roxie, who was standing beside her, her black boot tapping on the cheap linoleum floor.

Guilt consumed her at the sight of her best friend, who looked equally worried and ticked off. She had a right to be mad. Eden would've been upset with Roxie if she was going through hell and didn't call her. Best friends were always there for each other.

"I'm sorry," she said, the words not even enough.

"You know, we're not supposed to suffer alone. We can't allow ourselves to get to such a low place that we don't even take calls from our bestie," Roxie said. Her anger had drained away. She took the seat across from Eden.

The waitress came back, and Roxie ordered some ice tea and a sandwich; then they were alone again.

"I've been trying to make it on my own. It's so easy to lean on other people, and right now that's not the best thing for me," Eden said.

"I disagree. I think at this moment you shouldn't be alone at all. You need support. You've been through hell, and it doesn't appear to be getting any better for you," Roxie said.

"At least it can't get worse," Eden told her, managing to get out a small, humorless laugh.

"You never, *ever* say that," Roxie told her as she closed her fingers and knocked on the table. Eden wasn't even sure the table was made out of real wood, so the gesture was probably futile.

"I'm not worried about anything I say right now," Eden said. "Seriously, if I say something is up, it's bound to be down. I don't think it's possible for me to affect any sort of outcome."

"You've had a rough year," Roxie said, reaching across the table and taking Eden's hand. "Why didn't you call me the second your house caught fire?"

Her friend seemed genuinely hurt that Eden hadn't immediately come to her.

"I told you, I'm trying to do this on my own," she said.

"Where are you staying?"

"I'm at the motel down the road," Eden said, not daring to look at Roxie.

There was a gasp from her friend, and Eden was forced to look up. The horror on Roxie's face was almost comical. The hurt look in her eyes wasn't.

"What's wrong with staying with me?" she asked quietly.

"Oh, Roxie, I didn't want to be a burden on you, on anyone," Eden said.

Now Roxie's eyes narrowed to slits, and Eden knew she was about to get a lecture. She sat back and waited. She deserved this.

"It's absolutely unreal that you'd say that to me. I know I left this town behind, just like Owen did." She paused and Eden swallowed. Two of the most important people in her life had left her behind. Maybe that was why she had so many issues about not leaning on anyone but herself.

"You had to get away. I understood," Eden told her.

"No, I was running away, and I left everyone behind, including you. I was selfish and didn't think about how it would affect you. Now I realize that, and I'll continue to make it up to you. You're coming home with me. I won't take no for an answer."

Roxie leaned back and folded her arms, her expression stubborn. Eden had no doubt if she tried to refuse, Roxie would call in some favors and have Eden dragged to her house, even if they had to handcuff her.

"I already paid for the motel," Eden said.

Roxie rolled her eyes. "I don't care. Cancel it. I'm not leaving your side until we get to my place."

There was nothing else Eden could do. And she had to admit she was truly grateful for Roxie insisting she come home with her. She didn't actually want to be alone. She was simply being stubborn.

"Thank you, Roxie," she finally said, hating how close she was to tears.

"There's no need to thank me. You're more than my best friend. You're family," Roxie assured her.

Eden wasn't able to stop a lone tear from falling down her cheek. That made Roxie tear up, and one of her own fell. The two women looked at each other, then laughed at how silly they must look. But the laughter was exactly what Eden had needed.

"Really, thank you for not letting me be foolish," Eden said after a while.

"I expect you to do the same for me when I'm being an idiot," Roxie said.

"That's a deal," Eden assured her.

They rose from the table, and Roxie gave her a big hug. Eden wasn't alone, no matter how much she might think she was—she was never alone. If she closed herself off, it was by choice. There were people out there who loved her, people who'd be sad if something happened to her. That was so much more than some had.

Roxie stayed true to her word; she didn't let Eden out of her sight as they went back to the motel and Eden grabbed the few items she had and checked out. Then Eden's best friend followed behind her in her beautiful silver Lexus as they made their way through town, up the hill to Roxie's place.

The day was going a heck of a lot better than it had begun. Maybe this was a start to the newest chapter in her life. Maybe things were about to take a turn for the better. Maybe her smiles would become real again.

"Thanks, Dad," she whispered. "I'm sure you were talking to Roxie in her sleep. I guess I didn't want to be alone, after all."

She felt warmth surround her heart, and tears blinded her for a moment. She had to quickly wipe them away so she didn't crash her car. She was sure her father was right beside her at that moment, and he was telling her he loved her, that she would never be alone again.

More tears fell.

◆ ◆ ◆

Rage filled him when he saw Eden leave the motel, followed by Roxie Forbes.

He'd had plans for her that night. No, he wasn't a fool. He'd seen the patrols, seen how closely Owen had her guarded. But it wasn't close enough. He would have gotten to her that night.

She would've died.

But not before he had a little fun. He wanted to make Owen Forbes suffer. He wanted to make all the people who'd interfered suffer. And there was no better way to do that than to mess with someone they thought they were protecting.

He'd have to rethink his strategy now, because there was no way he'd get to her if she was staying at Kian's place. He was good, and that meant he wasn't foolish.

He forced his rage down. He'd be patient. His time would come . . .

Chapter Seventeen

Eden sat on Roxie's plush leather sofa and curled her feet beneath her. Her friend handed her a cup of coffee, and she took a sip, then nearly spit it out, her throat on fire.

"What in the world is in this?" she asked as she coughed several times.

"It's my special mix, and it will help you sleep like a baby tonight," Roxie told her as she took a sip of her own coffee before sighing.

"Or it will burn through the inside of my throat. Seriously, what's in it?" Eden took a much more cautious sip; it didn't taste too bad when taken in small doses.

"It's probably better for you not to know," Roxie said with a laugh. "Enough about coffee. I need to know why you've shut me out. Are you still upset with me because I left?" There were tears in her friend's eyes that instantly had Eden feeling terrible.

"No," she assured her friend. "I do have severe abandonment issues. I'm not going to even try to deny that. But I swear that's not why I haven't called. I know you were dealing with your own problems when you left town. You had terrible parents and a sister you didn't get along with. Then with you and Kian being a hot mess, you had to go." She stopped as she took another drink. "I did miss you horribly, though."

"I missed you, too. I was so lost. I didn't know what else to do. I don't want to see you hit the same rock bottom that I hit. It was a horrible place to be in, and I have so many regrets about that time. If I'd stayed . . ." She stopped as she gulped. "I lost so much time with Kian because I was lost and afraid. I would give anything to have that time back."

"But would you be who you are if you'd have stayed?" Eden asked.

Roxie was quiet for several moments. "I don't know," she answered honestly. "I might have needed to get away to figure that out. And it did all work out beautifully. We have our daughter. I'm sad that my sister's gone, and I regret I didn't try to understand her, that I didn't help her . . ." She paused again, this time taking so long Eden wasn't sure if she should say something. "I've learned, though, to not have regrets. There's nothing that can be done about the past. All I can do is change how I want to be for the future. I love my husband, my children, and my friends." She looked pointedly at Eden. "There's nothing I won't do for any of you."

"I'm trying to be stronger. I've leaned on people for too long, and what's happened is I don't know how to rely on myself. And the harsh reality of the world is that sometimes all we have is ourselves. People disappear, and our lives change forever. Fate is a cruel bitch that doesn't take prisoners," Eden said.

"Sometimes that's true. But now I like to think that it all happens for a reason," Roxie told her.

"You think there's a reason my dad died?" Eden questioned, hearing the anger in her voice.

"No. I think death is awful, and something we can't explain. I tried to understand it when I lost my sister. I tried to blame myself and everyone around me. But in the end, I discovered there were no answers. Your dad was an incredible man, and he shouldn't have been taken from you. You're going to have to grieve, and there's no way I'll sit here and tell you it's all going to be okay because it's not. It's going to hurt like hell. The only thing that can make it better is for you to realize you aren't alone, that you have people who love you and who you can grieve with," Roxie assured her.

"I'm just so mad. Is it okay for me to be mad for a while?" Eden asked.

Roxie smiled at her. "You can be sad and angry, hurt and distrustful. You can go through every emotion there is, and I'll still be here for you. I'll go through it with you," Roxie assured her.

Eden was silent as she sipped on her coffee, feeling warmth deep in her belly. The more she drank, the more she enjoyed it. It was apparently what she'd needed.

Roxie didn't try to fill the silence with empty words. She was letting Eden know she truly was there for her for anything she needed. Knowing that gave her more strength than just about anything else had in a very long time.

"Can we not talk about any of it, or think about any of it, for a few hours?" Eden asked.

Roxie smiled again. "We can definitely do that. Let me make us another cup of coffee . . . maybe a little less strong. We can chat about anything at all that you want, or we can snuggle up and watch a good movie. It's up to you."

So that's what they did. And for the first time since she'd lost her father, Eden felt a small measure of peace. She hoped it would last, but she was sure her worries weren't quite over.

At least she knew she wouldn't have to go through it alone. She shouldn't have been trying to for so long. She was finally realizing her father was right, that it didn't make her weak to lean on her friends.

"I need to go to his house. I need to clean it out. I haven't been able to do that yet," Eden said after they finished a movie.

"I'd love to do that with you," Roxie told her. "I know it won't be easy."

"I lost everything in the fire. So maybe it's a blessing I haven't had the strength to do it yet. At least I'll still have my father's things—a small piece of him," Eden said.

"Oh, Eden, you will always have your dad because he's in your heart," Roxie assured her. "Just like my sister's in mine."

"It doesn't feel like enough," Eden told her.

"I don't think it ever will feel like enough."

Maybe nothing would be fulfilling ever again. But at least Eden was no longer alone. She had Roxie in her life . . . and she had Owen. She wasn't sure what she was going to do about him, but it didn't seem as if he was going away.

Only time would tell what came next. She hoped she was ready for whatever it was.

Chapter Eighteen

Eden didn't get to sleep until almost two in the morning, so when her alarm went off at six, she groaned, reaching out and hitting the "Snooze" button. Normally she'd fall back asleep instantly, but with all that had been happening, it appeared that wasn't going to happen on this day. It was Monday, and that meant it could be her last day working on the case.

She lay there awake, her mind reeling. She wasn't even sure what she needed to get done for the day. She knew she still had to conduct interviews. She had to assume all the men on her list were guilty. Yeah, she knew innocent until proven guilty, but lives were being lost, homes were being destroyed, and until the person was caught, more damage would occur.

Today she was meeting with Sherman Armstrong, who was a close friend of the Forbes family. She knew he wouldn't willingly give up anything that might indicate guilt, but once you got someone talking, they were bound to give up information they had no idea they were revealing.

Giving up on the idea of an eight-minute snooze, Eden rose from the incredibly comfortable bed in one of the many guest rooms in Roxie's home and hurried through a shower. Her friend had left her more clothes and a full arsenal of cosmetics. She'd never have thought she'd be so grateful for a fresh container of deodorant. It was funny how you always had certain items on hand, things you just grabbed every time you went to the store. They added up through the years. Then a fire had taken it all away in minutes.

That thought made her want to catch the arsonist that much more. Arsonists had no boundaries when it came to people's lives. How selfish could a person be? She'd never know the answer to that, because such cruelty wasn't in her genetic makeup.

Roxie wasn't yet awake when Eden came downstairs. She scarfed down a donut while she made a quick cup of coffee, grateful when she found a mug she could take with her. She quickly hurried out the door and headed to the address Sherman had given her.

When she pulled up to a small airstrip, she felt a bit of anxiety. Why were they meeting at a private airport? She'd seen Sherman around but hadn't ever talked one-on-one with the man. She realized she didn't know a heck of a lot about him.

When a white-haired gentleman came out of the large hangar wearing a sweater-vest and holding a cane, she let out her breath. There was no way this man was dangerous.

"Hello there, young lady," he said. He moved pretty dang spryly for a man with a cane. She wondered if he used it for visual effect instead of necessity.

"Hi, Mr. Armstrong," she said, holding out her hand.

He gripped her fingers and squeezed as he waved his other hand in the air. "There's no need to be so formal. We're all friends here. Please call me Sherman," he told her.

"Thanks so much for taking the time to speak with me today, Mr.—" She cut herself off. "Sherman," she finished.

"I always take time to talk to a pretty lady," he said with a wink. She couldn't help but smile. He reminded her a lot of her father—in all the good ways.

"You probably know I've been asked to look into this wildfire," she said, not wanting to be deceptive. "I've heard you know just about everyone in this town, and I was hoping we could talk some things out. The sooner we figure out who's causing this damage, the sooner we can put an end to it."

"You might be getting more than you want," Sherman replied with a chuckle. "I do love to talk. Follow me."

She was left with no choice but to tag along as he moved inside the hangar, where a pretty blue plane was sitting, the windows sparkling in the morning sunlight. He moved over to the plane and began walking around and checking different areas of it.

There was nowhere to sit, so it seemed she was just going to trail after him. She was sort of unsure where to begin. She didn't want to dive right in and ask about Owen and make him instantly suspicious of her motives.

"Have you been up in a small plane before?" Sherman asked, making her stop in her tracks.

"No. I've never wanted to," she told him as she eyed the plane before her with suspicion.

"Nonsense. Everyone needs to go up at least once in their lifetime. But I'll warn you that most people get the bug once they do it," he said as he moved over to the passenger side of the plane and opened the door, holding out his hand.

"You want me to get in?" she asked, taking a step back.

"Sure do. We're going to go for a little flight while we visit," he said. He was still smiling at her, but she had no doubt he wasn't compromising. If she didn't fly with him, he wasn't talking with her.

"Can't we just talk here on the ground where it's safe? Then you can go for a flight," she suggested.

"I don't like to fly alone," he told her. He continued to hold out his hand.

Eden could tell him to have a nice day and then quickly turn around and leave, or she could face her fears and possibly get closer to solving this arson case. She chose the latter. With reluctance she moved over to the plane, grabbing hold of the bar and pulling herself inside. It was so small. She felt a tremor shake her body.

Sherman closed the door, then moved over to some device that began pulling the plane from the hangar. Eden's stomach was tense as the plane was tugged outside. She couldn't believe she was about to do this.

Once they were clear of the hangar, Sherman stepped inside the plane and sat down. He showed her how to buckle up, then grinned as he handed her a set of headphones to wear. He clicked a button; then she heard his voice through the noise-canceling earpieces.

"I know you're a little nervous, but I promise this will be a blast," he assured her.

"I doubt that," she muttered, and he laughed. She hadn't expected him to hear her.

Eden clutched the seat on either side of her legs as Sherman started the plane and began to taxi out to the runway. Voices came over the radio, telling him which direction to go, what the wind speeds were, where visibility was worse than other places. She also heard other pilots talking about water drops and commenting on how the fire was getting more out of control.

For once Eden wasn't thinking about the fire. Even though that's why she was in this predicament, she was more worried about plunging to her death in this contraption Sherman expected her to feel safe in.

They immediately began picking up speed as Sherman played with the controls; then they were lifting off. Eden was fascinated as the ground grew farther and farther away. She couldn't help but look out at the houses and vehicles. They grew smaller, and the sensation of floating was almost euphoric. She'd flown before—of course she had—but never in a plane like this, never with this view.

She didn't want to admit it, but Sherman was right. She could see this becoming an addiction for her. Without her being aware of it, her fingers unclenched, and her lips turned up in a smile that was so big it hurt her cheeks.

"Wow," she breathed as he took a pass over Green Lake Park. It was all so breathtaking. Then he circled, and she gasped as she saw a sky view of the fire. It was even more devastating than she'd realized. Her smile fell away.

"This fire's getting worse," Sherman said, his voice subdued as he circled the outer edges of the wildfire. "It breaks my heart. Not just for the loss of all this beautiful greenery, but for the men and women down there fighting it. I know these kids, have known them their entire lives. I even know the hotshots, as they've come in before. Most of them are so young, but it takes special people to go out there and risk their lives for others."

"Is there anyone you don't know around here?" Eden asked. This was as good an opening as any to get him talking.

"Not really. I like to know the people where I live. I think if we all got to know our neighbors a lot better, there'd be a whole lot less anger and destruction in this world," he told her.

"I agree with that," she said. "Maybe it's time I stopped keeping to myself so much."

"I won't argue with you there," he told her. "You can't keep yourself cooped up. It gets too darn depressing."

"Do you have any family fighting the blaze?" she asked.

"Yeah, my nephews are helping. Ace is my youngest, and he's a pilot. They're all pilots, but Ace is definitely the hotshot of the crew. He and his brother Maverick have been dropping water for the past two weeks. It gets dangerous out there when you're dealing with hot pockets of air. But those boys don't mind flying into danger. I'm a bit too old for it. I tend to stay on the outskirts of things now."

"I have a feeling you're more of a hotshot than you want to admit," she said, smiling again. It was hard not to when she was with this man.

"I might have been a long time ago," Sherman said with a chuckle. "I leave all that madness to the kids now. My boys are up in the air. Of course Owen's on the ground right next to the flames, and I think of him like a nephew. I worry every day he's out there."

She hadn't expected to get to Owen so quickly. She was a bit disappointed. She found she didn't want to interrogate Sherman about Owen. She knew it was a waste of time, but with her suspicions of Declan growing, maybe Sherman would be able to answer something without realizing he was answering it. She could possibly get information about Owen and Declan and others on her list.

"Has Owen told you what it's like down there fighting it?" she asked.

"Yeah, we've talked. Not much, though. He pretty much fights the fire, sleeps minimal hours, possibly grabs a bite to eat, then rushes right back out there. He won't stop until this thing is out. He won't let it take his hometown."

"Does he have any suspicions on who started the fire?" she asked. Then thought she'd better add more. "Does anyone have any suspicions? Do you?"

Sherman kept his eyes forward, continuing to fly. He circled the large perimeter of the fire, making sure to stay out of the way of the other aircraft dumping water; then he turned to start heading in another direction.

"Hey, Uncle Sherman, are you finally joining us?" a voice asked over the radio.

"Not a chance, Maverick. I'm taking a pretty lady out for a flight," Sherman responded, turning toward her and winking.

"Way to go, Uncle," Maverick replied. "Want to send a selfie?"

Eden found herself blushing, though she didn't know why.

"It's not like that, boy. Get your mind out of the gutter," Sherman scolded.

Laughter came through loud and clear over the radio before another voice joined in. "I don't know if I believe you, old man," it said.

"That's because you're as bad as your brother Nick," Sherman replied. These must be the nephews he'd been talking about.

"We wouldn't mind if you had a special someone in your life," Maverick told him.

"Copy that. Maybe it's time we meddle in your love life like you've meddled in ours," Nick said. There was a lot of chuckling through the headphones.

"Don't be crude, boys," Sherman said. Eden was fascinated to see a blush come over Sherman's cheeks. She wanted to say something but didn't know how to respond. "And I think I deserve some thanks, considering the lovely women you've married."

There was only a slight pause. "You sure do," Maverick said. "I've never been happier."

"Ditto," Nick said.

"Well, that's better," Sherman said, a grin taking at least ten years off his face.

"Okay, we'll leave you be, then, and get back to beating this bitch," Maverick said with another laugh. He sounded as if he was in his element and having the time of his life.

"Sorry about that. The boys lost their dad when they were barely out of their teens. I've tried teaching them manners, and their sweet mama has, too, but it wasn't until recently when they finally settled down that some manners began sinking in. Of course, when they're away from their wives playing with their airplanes, they once again forget," Sherman said. But there was such fondness in his voice that she had no doubt he loved those boys very much.

"It must be nice to have a large family," she told him.

"I thank God every morning I wake for another day with them," Sherman said. She could picture him climbing from bed and dropping to his knees to do just that. She couldn't help but like this man. She wished she had him for an uncle.

"Enjoy every moment," Eden told him. She didn't want to feel jealous, but she was, the slightest bit. And her heart hurt as the ache of missing her father tried to consume her once more.

"I'm sorry about your dad. I can't imagine how much it hurts," Sherman said. She knew in a small town there were no secrets, but she didn't want to grieve right now. She wanted to work and to enjoy this time with a kind man.

"Thank you. I'm trying to move on. It hasn't been easy."

"Well, you have good people in your life. Don't be afraid to lean on them. There are some things we can't do alone," Sherman said.

She was too choked up to respond, so she turned and looked at the ground below them. Thankfully, Sherman didn't push her, allowed her to pull herself together. She appreciated him that much more for it.

They flew around for a while longer, and Eden attempted to get information out of him that she didn't already know.

"How long have you known the Forbeses?" she asked, hoping to keep her voice casual.

"I've been friends with their daddy since before the kids were born. They're a good family," he answered with ease.

"I've known them a long time . . . ," she said. "Especially Owen. Do you know him well?" She hated the slight pitch to her voice. She took a calming breath.

"Owen's a good man. He's always been a hero, just like my nephews. He doesn't need credit for the lives he saves, and that makes him an even better man," Sherman told her.

"I've heard some firefighters like to start blazes so they can then play the hero," she said, trying to sound as if she was doing nothing more than making conversation.

Sherman paused for a moment, and she wondered if she was busted. Then he spoke.

"It's truly sad when that happens, but we're in a real good place here. I know none of our men or women would do anything of the sort." His voice was just as casual as hers.

She sighed. "Have you noticed any odd behavior from any of the men or women fighting the blaze?" she asked, trying a new tactic.

Sherman thought about her question for a few moments before he shook his head. "It's not one of our guys. I'd bet my life on it," he told her.

That turned her suspicions back to Declan. If no one thought any of the firefighters capable of starting the fire, then it had to be someone else.

"What do you know about Declan?" she asked.

This time Sherman took his eyes off the sky and looked at her with a bit of confusion. He waited for her to elaborate. She knew she was busted now. The man had no doubt about the fact that she was interrogating him.

"He's been working on this drug case a long time. Has he shared much about it?" she continued.

"Do you think Declan is capable of having anything to do with this?" he asked. It didn't feel like a scolding, but his words made her look out again at the large plumes of dark smoke hanging over their town.

"I'm just asking questions," she told him. "I can't come up with any conclusions until people share with me what they know."

Sherman gave her a look that she thought was respect. She certainly didn't want to offend him, and it appeared as if she hadn't.

"Declan has always kept to himself, from the time he was a little boy. He's fiercely loyal and a good man. I would bet my life on the innocence of any of the Forbes men," Sherman told her.

"You know that in a lot of cases where a serial killer has been caught, the family and friends have all expressed shock, saying they never would've suspected the person of such horrific acts," she pointed out.

"I've read the same facts," Sherman told her. "But trust me, I know people, and I would lay my life on the line for family and those I love just as much as family. Declan and Owen *are* family."

Was she completely wrong in her assumptions? Or was Sherman blinded by love?

She asked a few more questions, but she knew she wasn't going to find answers with Sherman. Either he'd protect the ones he loved to his dying breath, or he truly knew nothing. After more than an hour of flying, she found herself disappointed as they began making their descent back to the runway they'd taken off from. She felt her stomach jump a bit as they touched down, but she still wore a smile. Sherman taxied to the hangar, then turned off the plane, shifting in his seat to look at her.

"Did I put the bug in you?" he asked.

She hated to admit the truth. "You sort of did," she said, not wanting to lie.

"And do you feel any better about Owen's innocence now?" he asked. "Or Declan's?"

She was shocked by the knowing look in his eyes. She felt a little guilty. She hadn't fooled this man. Her cheeks heated the slightest bit, but she didn't do him the discourtesy of looking away.

"I haven't found anything to prove guilt or innocence," she said.

"You'll get it worked out," Sherman assured her. "I promise."

"I hope so. I don't think I'll be on this case much longer, and it's become personal since someone burned down my home," she told him.

He shook his head. "It takes a real heartless person to destroy someone's home. That absolutely hurts my soul." He reached out and grasped her hand. "You just let me know if there's anything I can do for you."

She knew those were just words people said to each other, words that didn't really mean anything. But as she looked at Sherman, she realized they weren't empty words to him. He meant them. She reached across the space between them and gave him a hug, the urge too overwhelming to ignore. He hugged her back.

"Thank you for today. It was just what I needed," she said.

"Anytime, young lady," he said. She knew he meant that as well.

She was sad to go a half hour later. She insisted on helping him get the plane back in the hangar and washing the windows with him. He'd given her a beautiful gift today, and if that was the only way to thank him, then she was more than happy to do it.

If she had to make her case right now, she'd be left with little choice but to admit her total incompetence. Maybe she was too close to this case. It was probably a good idea for them to bring in a new person to take over.

The thought of that took away some of the joy she'd found while high in the sky. *One step at a time,* she told herself. She had to take things one step at a time. She exited the hangar and looked up, not at all surprised when she saw Owen leaning against his truck, a smile on his lips.

Chapter Nineteen

Owen was usually grateful to live in a small town where everyone shared information. Sometimes he wasn't as grateful, like when there were family matters he didn't want talked about, but right now he was glad because that's how he knew Eden was currently taking a flight with Sherman Armstrong.

Owen smiled as he thought about what she'd be hearing right now. Since Owen had nothing to hide, he wasn't worried about what she'd learn about him. He did, however, enjoy the fact that her ear was definitely getting talked off.

Eden had always been a private person. She wasn't one of those people who threw their arms wide and invited the world in. There was a dignity and class about her that had originally made him fall in love with her. If it hadn't been for his obligation to his best friend, he didn't think he would have had the will to leave town, even if he had wanted to find himself.

Sure, he'd felt the need to see the world, but he'd always pictured doing it with her by his side. The two of them had been so young, though—too young to make permanent decisions. Maybe if they'd stayed together then, though it seemed pretty damn appealing right now, it would have ruined them. They wouldn't have found who they were without one another. Sometimes you had to be set free to know there never had been chains holding you down in the first place.

He'd had another restless night of tossing and turning. Not only was he stressed not to be on that mountain putting out the worst fire to hit his hometown in too many years to count, but he was also worried about Eden. He'd felt a hell of a lot better knowing she was out of that crappy motel and staying with his brother. If she'd been at the motel one more night, he was planning on buying the damn thing and installing a twenty-four-seven security staff as his first executive decision.

He was grateful now he wasn't the owner of the dive. Though maybe he should buy it anyway and fix it up—bring back some class to it. That was definitely food for thought.

For now, he was leaning against his truck as he waited for Sherman to fly back to the airport. He and Eden needed to spend more time together. For one thing, he couldn't very well prove his innocence to her if they were never together. For another, it was simple. He missed her.

Owen stood there looking up at the sky, and he was relieved to finally see Sherman's plane off in the distance. They were probably ten minutes out. Owen never had gotten the flying bug, but he'd gone up with friends every once in a while, and taking a private jet to some resort was a great way to travel. He'd just never felt the need to learn to pilot one of the planes.

Sherman always told him it was never too late to learn. That old man thought it was a sin for anyone not to know how to pilot. He'd tell them they'd all sink into the sea if a big one ever hit unless they could grab some wings and soar. Owen figured he'd take his chances with a tidal wave. Hell, he could captain a boat like no one else. He could ride the waves.

His peace and quiet were disturbed when he heard a car approaching. This was a private landing strip, so there weren't too many people who'd be headed this way. He turned, then smiled.

A tall man emerged from a Porsche 911. He walked over, confidence in his gait as he approached Owen with a friendly smile. Chaz Rock was Owen's age. They'd gone to school together and had gotten into more trouble than Owen cared to admit. They didn't hang out nearly as much anymore since Owen had left town and returned. Chaz was always on the go with his real estate empire. But old friends had a way of coming back together.

"I thought you'd rather be caught dead than sitting at an airport watching planes come and go," Chaz said.

"Not when a pretty girl is about to touch down," Owen told him.

They both laughed. "Yeah, the things we put ourselves through to be noticed by women," Chaz grumbled.

"I've been chasing this girl my entire life," Owen admitted.

"Must be Eden," Chaz said with a wink. "It's my understanding you had her caught in your net when you released her," he pointed out.

"That was the stupidest thing I've ever done," Owen acknowledged. It wasn't too often he confessed to his shortcomings.

Chaz nodded in agreement. "Are the rumors true?" he asked.

"Probably?" Owen said with a grimace. "Which ones are you referring to?"

Chaz laughed. "Have you been banned from fighting the fire?"

"Yep," Owen said. "They think I might have started it."

Chaz looked at him incredulously. "That's insane. This is your town."

"I can't seem to convince the powers that be that I love it here, even if I did leave for a while."

"How you holding up?" Chaz asked. He leaned on Owen's truck as the two of them watched Sherman's plane draw closer.

"I'm good. I'm trying to get this matter cleared so I can get back to work. We have a real arsonist who needs to be caught before this situation gets any worse."

"Well, rumors spread faster than butter on a hot sidewalk in this town, but at least you can take comfort in knowing not a single person here thinks the rumors are true," Chaz assured him.

"I'm sure there are some who might believe it," Owen said. "But that goes with the territory. There are people who won't like me because of my last name, and there are others who'll do a jig for a juicy piece of gossip. But I'm confident that the people I care about know it's not me. That's good enough."

"Sometimes we can't outrun our pasts, though," Chaz pointed out. "Those rumors might continue to spread."

Owen was silent for a moment. "Then I'll just have to be me and let fate decide what happens."

Chaz shrugged as if it didn't matter either way. "I'm taking my plane up," he said. "Want to get your mind off things for a while and go for a ride?"

"Maybe another time," Owen said as Sherman's plane touched down. He let out a breath of relief that Eden was back on solid ground. He knew Sherman was an ace pilot, but Owen wanted to keep Eden safe, even if that meant he was somewhat illogical about what he deemed safe or not.

"Sounds good," Chaz told him with a grin before giving Owen a wave and heading to his private hangar. Owen turned back to see Sherman's plane taxiing toward him.

Owen didn't think Sherman or Eden saw him when they pulled into the hangar. He was parked off to the side. He wouldn't interrupt. He'd let them finish up and wait for Eden to come out. He was parked near her car, so there was no way she'd miss him.

He stood there long enough to watch Chaz pull his plane from the hangar and taxi to the runway, flying down it and lifting off into the air. Owen waved, not sure if his friend saw the gesture.

Finally, Eden came out of the hangar. Alone. She was grinning until she looked up and saw him. Then her smile wavered, and she seemed to take a fortifying breath. That hurt his gut a little. It wasn't a good sign if she had to build up her courage to come around him. Owen wasn't sure what he was going to do to change her opinion of him, to show her he wasn't the same selfish teenage boy she'd once known.

"I guess an entire day is more than enough time to be apart?" Eden asked as she approached. She smiled, giving him a bit of hope. Maybe she wasn't entirely disappointed to see him. Maybe they did have a chance.

"It was way too long," Owen told her. "Want to go for a ride and chat?"

"About anything I want?" she asked.

"Sure," he said, not at all worried about anything she would ask him. If he could help her solve this case, his town would be safer. Plus, when they didn't have this hanging over their heads, they could focus on just the two of them.

She smiled. It was a smile of victory, as if she knew something he didn't. He looked toward the hangar, but Sherman hadn't yet emerged. He went through his mind trying to think if there was anything in his past that Sherman knew about that he could have shared with her.

He honestly didn't think so. Had she spoken to Declan again? He didn't think that, either. Declan wouldn't tell Owen's secrets. They weren't his to tell. His brother was too honorable to share them on purpose and too smart to slip.

Owen opened his truck door for Eden, glad when she hopped inside. They could pick up her car later. Right now he didn't feel like following her. He wanted her by his side. He felt danger was growing closer, and that scared him far more than her finding out secrets he didn't want her to know.

He'd die for this woman. Maybe it was time to fess up to the sins of his past. He knew they weren't going to be able to move forward until he did exactly that.

Chapter Twenty

Eden was nervous as she waited for Owen to climb inside his cab. She had nothing on him, but she'd learned long ago that if you acted as if you knew something, then sometimes people would panic and try to get their side of the story straight, giving up valuable information.

She was playing a cat-and-mouse game with somebody, and whether Owen realized it or not, there might be knowledge buried inside him that he didn't understand was valuable. That often happened with people who were close to a crime. Their town was in danger, and someone out there had the answers that would stop the blaze.

"Is there anything you want to share with me?" Eden asked in a knowing voice, as if she already had the information and simply wanted him to confirm it. He started the truck but just sat there, leaving the engine idling.

"That trick doesn't work on me," he told her with a shrewd grin that had her teeth grinding together. Of course it wouldn't work on him.

"I guess we have nothing to talk about then," she said. She reached for her seat belt to undo it when he stopped her.

"Give me a minute," he said. There was resignation in his voice that stopped her from leaving the truck. It appeared as if he was going to talk. Not because she'd fooled him, but maybe because he didn't like that she didn't trust him. That made her heart do a funny little twitch.

"I didn't want to leave you ten years ago," he began. There was such resignation in his voice that it was hard for her not to believe him.

"This fire and who started it doesn't have anything to do with you leaving me ten years ago," she pointed out.

"It might," he said with another sigh, and her pulse pounded that much harder.

"About six months before I left town, I got into some trouble," he began.

Eden searched her mind in confusion. She didn't remember him getting into any trouble. Then again, he was a Forbes, and if he'd done something wrong, his family certainly had enough money to pay people off so nothing would stick, and no one would know. But that didn't sound like his family. They weren't the type of people to cover things up. It was one of the many things she respected about them.

"I kept it to myself because my dad and siblings would have kicked my ass if they knew," he told her. "I was hanging out with this guy named Mario. He was an okay guy, or so I thought. He was dangerous, and I was trying to figure out exactly who I was outside of my family. I liked that he did crap that wasn't always aboveboard. I liked that my adrenaline pumped with him."

"Are you talking about Mario Vasquez?" she asked, horrified. He was a bad, bad man.

"Yeah, one and the same. We didn't have a very long relationship, and I kept it from you and my family," he told her.

"I can understand why," she said, disappointed he'd been hanging out with a thief and drug addict. "Did you get into drugs?" The thought made her stomach turn.

"Not a chance," he said with such disgust that she knew he was telling her the truth. "I simply liked the adventure of it all." He sighed as he paused. "Do you remember my best friend, Bill?"

It took a moment for her brain to catch up to what he was saying. "Yeah, you guys were tight."

"Yeah, we were. Then he got mixed up in the same crowd, but unlike me, he got into drugs."

"I don't understand what you're trying to tell me," she said. None of this was making sense.

"I was hanging out with Mario because of the thrill of it. I liked being around people who were what I considered dangerous. I felt as if my life was in a rut . . ." He stopped when he saw her expression.

"Was it that bad being with me?" she asked, hating the vulnerability in her voice.

He reached for her, but she scooted away. She couldn't let him touch her right then.

"It wasn't about you and me. It wasn't about anyone but me. I was revered in this town, not because of who I was but because of my family name. I felt as if that was holding me down, and I went through a rebellious stage. I didn't want to do anything too bad, but I wanted to feel something different, I guess," he tried to explain.

"Something you couldn't feel with me," she said. He was hurting her, though she knew he wasn't trying to.

"I wanted to feel like anyone except myself," he said.

"And so you thought hanging with the bad crowd would help you accomplish that," she inserted.

"Yeah, I did. But I was a fool to think that way. It quickly got out of hand. My best friend was getting more and more involved with these people. I was trying to figure out a way to get him out when one night I stumbled onto something I wasn't supposed to see." A shudder passed through him.

"What was it?" she asked.

"A drug deal gone wrong . . . two dead bodies."

She gasped, her heart in her throat. "Oh my gosh . . ." She was too shocked to know what to say.

"They were going to kill me. There was nothing I could do to stop it. I felt so bad for you, for my mom, for my brothers. Because I had no doubt they'd dispose of my body, and all of you would have searched and searched to no avail. That's probably the most scared I've been in my entire life," he admitted.

"Oh, Owen, why didn't you come to me? Why didn't you go to your family?" she asked, desperately wanting to reach out to him.

"I didn't leave because of that," he told her. "Bill saved my life. He stepped up and agreed to work for them if they let me go. He swore neither of us would tell anybody." Owen was almost shaking as he told her this.

"What happened?" she asked.

"They obviously let me go, and that was the end of my association with them. I'd see them once in a while, but they wouldn't speak to me. I was okay with that, except I had this monster guilt hanging over my head about what Bill was going through. He changed so fast. He became harder, got more and more into drugs, and it was killing him." He stopped as he wiped a hand down his face, clearly shaken up by this conversation.

"Why didn't you tell me?" she asked again. "I wouldn't have liked any of it, but I would've been by your side." She was on the verge of tears now.

"I couldn't tell you because they told me they'd kill anyone I told. They said they had ways of knowing everything. I was young and stupid. I knew what they were capable of, and I knew they weren't bluffing. They have so much power in this town, power you can't imagine. They work in the shadows."

"That doesn't explain why you left," she told him.

"At the time I blamed myself for Bill's situation. I thought it was my fault he was so mixed up in drugs. I thought he'd sacrificed his life for mine," Owen said.

"And did you learn differently?" she asked.

"Yeah, but not for a while after we got out of town. Bill had already been into drugs and had been selling them on a smaller scale before that night. But as his addiction grew, he needed to make more money, so he was getting far too involved with that crowd."

"I still don't know why you left," she said, needing him to come to the conclusion.

"I needed to get him out of here. I was planning on getting him set up somewhere and then coming back. I didn't plan on leaving forever. But then we got to New York. Bill cleaned up . . . for a while. I found I liked being there, liked the fact that no one knew who I was," he admitted.

"Liked being without me?" she said, hating how pathetic she sounded with those words.

"No. I never liked being without you, but I needed to save Bill . . ." He paused for a long moment. She said nothing. "And I think I needed to save myself, too. I didn't know who I was without being a Forbes. I didn't know what I was capable of on my own."

"You had to leave to figure that out," she said. It wasn't a question.

"I did it wrong. I found an opportunity to get Bill away without them trying to stop us, and I didn't think. I promised him I'd never tell anyone what he was doing. He wouldn't leave unless I promised that. I also knew if I told you or my family, you'd try to stop us, so I ran. I screwed up." He stopped talking and Eden realized tears were running down her cheeks. He wasn't looking at her, and she was glad.

"Was it worth it?" she asked. She hated how vulnerable she felt.

"Bill was all sorts of messed up when we left. It took months for me to convince him I'd done the right thing. Then he told me if I left him there, he'd find another family, and what he meant by family was the bad kind. I still thought at the time that he'd saved my life, and that's why he'd become the man he'd become. It was my turn to sacrifice for him."

"That doesn't explain why it took you so long to come back," she said.

"After a while I was ashamed. I knew what I'd done to you and my family. It didn't take my brothers long to track me down, and they were furious, but they respected my decision, told me the life I wanted to live was my choice, but that I'd better not disappear on them again. I told them I wouldn't. I didn't come back because I feared I'd stay, and I wasn't ready to abandon Bill."

She was quiet. She didn't know what to say about that. He'd left her, and while he might feel some remorse about the way he'd done it, he obviously still felt it had been the right thing for him to do.

"Why are you here now?" she asked. She was thankfully beginning to feel a little numb.

"Bill died of an OD a couple of years ago, and the longer I was away, the more I knew this was where I belonged. I missed my family," he said before turning, waiting until she looked at him. "I missed you."

Eden was silent as she took in all that Owen had just told her. It was a lot to handle. He hadn't left because he hadn't loved her; he'd done it because he loved his best friend. He'd sacrificed himself for another, which was nothing new for him. But he'd stayed away because he'd been searching for himself.

"Why did you still keep his secret?"

"It's hard for me to break a promise. I told him I'd never tell . . ." He stopped and took a breath. "But I promised you I'd never leave, so it looks like I can't keep my word."

He'd chosen to leave her. Just because he now wanted her back didn't mean she should change her own plans. It didn't matter if she still loved him. Love had seemed to cause her nothing but grief her entire life.

"Your homecoming hasn't been fully embraced," she finally said.

He shrugged. "I ticked a lot of people off with how I left."

"So then you can understand why you'd be a suspect with the arson investigators," she told him.

He sighed. "No, I don't understand that. I might have run away from home, but I didn't do it because I had animosity toward this town or the people in it. My family lives here, and the people I care the most about in this world live here. I'd never do anything to hurt this place." Sincerity rang in his tone.

Her shoulders slumped. She was angry with him, but she knew she was wasting time with investigating him, even if his name was on the list. She was perfectly within her rights to check off his name and tell the investigators to search elsewhere. She should've done it after her first conversation with him.

Of course, her life had never been that cut-and-dried, and the fates certainly wouldn't give her such an easy out. They hated her, much preferring to toy with her than to help set her free.

"I didn't do this, Eden. I need you to believe me," he said quietly. She gazed at him for a long moment before speaking.

"I never thought you were guilty," she finally admitted.

His lips were pressed together as he gazed at her. "I need you to know with every fiber of your being that I'm not capable of this," he told her.

"I've known all along you couldn't do this, Owen. I've just been so hurt, so bitter about how things ended with us, that I took a bit of pleasure in trying to make you squirm. And then I've carried so much guilt from our night six months ago, about losing my dad, wondering if I could've saved him. Maybe in the beginning there was a part of me that wanted you to be the bad guy so I could alleviate some of my guilt," she said, not trying to stop the tears.

"I'm sorry you've been hurt so much. I'm sorry I've been such a huge part of that pain," he said. His eyes burned as he looked at her. His voice was quiet as he continued, but his words were unmistakable. "I do love you," he finished.

She shook her head. "Please don't, Owen. I can't handle that right now," she begged.

"I understand," he told her. He reached out and she allowed him to take her hand.

"Let's do this together, Eden. Let's find out who's causing this destruction to our town." There was such urgency in his voice, she knew he needed answers as much as she did.

She was tired of being alone, tired of putting herself through it. She had no doubt it was by choice. There were many people she could ask to be by her side who wouldn't hesitate, but the only one she seemed to want to be there was Owen. She was tired of fighting that.

"What if it's someone you're close to?" she asked.

He looked confused. "Do you have names?"

"Maybe, but none I'm willing to share right now," she told him.

He paused. "I'm assuming it's someone I know. But it wouldn't be anyone I'm close to."

"You can't know that for sure," she said.

"Yes, I can," he told her with just as much determination.

"I might be taken off the case at any minute," she told him.

"Why?" he asked as if that was absurd. It made her feel slightly better.

"Because you and I have history, and now I'm eliminating you as a suspect. This might be the final nail in my coffin."

"Then let's do what we can for as long as we can," he suggested.

She gave him a half-hearted smile. "We can try to be a team on this, but it might not work," she finally said.

He smiled. And though Eden knew they were far from being okay, she somehow felt more peace than she had in a very long time.

"We're working together, that's all," she said, squeezing his fingers once before releasing them. "We'll attempt to be friends."

His lips turned up even more as he gazed at her.

"I'll accept that for now," he told her.

She wanted to argue, but she didn't get the chance. Because they were interrupted when his phone rang.

Chapter Twenty-One

Owen's entire body tensed as he took the call and listened. The color washed from his cheeks. Eden sat waiting, knowing that whatever was being said was bad news.

"Who?" Owen finally said, his voice low.

Something horrible had happened to shake up Owen this badly. It was someone on his crew, someone who'd been hurt. She had no doubt about it.

"You smelled gas? You're positive?" he said. His voice had grown quieter. "I'm on my way." He hung up the phone and threw the truck into gear.

"Owen?" she said. She had a feeling he'd forgotten she was even there.

His body was tense, his jaw ticking as he ground his teeth together. He was barely containing the fury and anguish he was feeling. This was bad. It was really bad.

"The winds have been unpredictable with this fire, and she took a shift for the worse. The men were lighting a line, trying to save a development the fire was moving straight toward. There was an explosion," he said, choking on his last words.

"Did I hear you say something about gasoline?" she asked.

His jaw clenched as his eye ticked. He was barely holding it together. She had to hold on tight as he took a corner far too fast, and the truck skidded. Only when she was slammed into the door did he let off some of the pressure on the accelerator.

"I'm sorry," he said.

"Don't apologize. Just tell me," she insisted.

"Someone did this. Someone poured gas on the ground, knowing exactly what we'd do next," he said, barely containing his rage. "It was Ben this time. He was in the middle of grass saturated with gas, and a spark came down from the wildfire, instantly lighting him on fire. He didn't have a chance, but they took him to the hospital, anyway."

He sounded close to tears. She knew part of his frustration was from the fact that he wasn't out there, he wasn't helping.

"There's nothing you could've done to stop this," she told him. She didn't dare reach out to him. He was wound so tight he was likely to drive them off the side of the road if she startled him.

"It might've been me and not him," Owen said, slamming his hand against the steering wheel.

Eden shuddered at the thought. "That doesn't help us, Owen. We need to get this case solved so this stops," she tried to reason.

"Whoever is doing this is constantly one step ahead of us," he said, his voice rising.

"We'll find him. I promise you," she insisted.

"It might not be a him," he pointed out.

"I know, but most arsonists are males," she said.

"I don't give a damn about statistics. I just want this case solved. I want this bastard caught." They pulled into the hospital ER, and Owen parked crookedly, opening his door almost before the truck had settled to a stop.

She was right behind him as they ran inside.

The screams were the first thing that greeted them. The smell of charred flesh was the second, making Eden try her best not to throw up on the pristine floors.

Activity hummed around them as doctors fought to save the life of this rookie firefighter who should've been perfectly safe where he was, would've been safe had he not been in a field saturated with gasoline. Who could do that? Who could watch a person die the most agonizing death possible?

Owen went over and spoke to his chief, both their heads bowed. A petite brunette stood in one corner weeping, with one of the firefighters holding her up as he whispered comforting words to her. Other than that, there was silence in this large space. The people in the room knew the firefighter wasn't going to make it. And if he did, he'd wish he hadn't. The pain would be so intense he wouldn't be able to come out of a coma for a long time. He wouldn't be able to bear it.

Eden felt like an intruder in this intimate moment. She'd been the one to deliver the news that had suspended Owen, leaving them with one less person. She was the one looking for a traitor among them. And the traitor might not even be a firefighter. She was beginning to doubt it could be. No firefighter could set a trap like this, stand by as one of their brothers burned alive.

The screaming finally stopped, and Eden realized tears were falling down her cheeks. The man had either passed out, or they'd drugged him. She refused to think it was because he'd succumbed to his wounds. He had to fight. Obviously there were a lot of people in this room praying for him.

Owen finally walked over to her, and she didn't turn from him when he pulled her into his arms. She knew it was him needing comfort more than her, and it was the least she could do.

"He's been burned on over eighty percent of his body," Owen said in a hushed whisper.

"Oh, Owen, I'm so sorry," she said, her hands gently rubbing up and down his back. He squeezed her hard. She tried to lend him what little strength she had.

"We have to find this person. He needs to be punished," Owen told her.

"I promise you we will. We won't rest until whoever is doing this is behind bars," she said, fury rising in her voice.

They stood that way for a long while. Owen was thinking of the people who'd been injured in this fire, and Eden was lost as to what to do next. The strange thing was, though, that she felt safe where she was, felt like she could figure it out. She'd always felt that way when she was in Owen's arms. She most likely always would.

"I'm sorry, Owen," she told him, hating that she didn't have more to offer.

"Me too," he said.

She wondered if they were apologizing for more than just the current situation. Maybe when this was over, the two of them could figure that out.

"We can't stay here. We aren't going to know anything for a while."

"What do you want to do?" she asked.

He shook his head, and she saw determination enter his eyes. He'd leaned on her for only a brief moment, and now he was drawing back, gathering his strength. His need to be the savior, to be the one to sacrifice, was so ingrained in him that he needed to take care of her instead of letting her take care of him.

She hated that she wanted him to do just that.

The chief approached them. "They want us to clear out of the ER. There's too many of us in here. Why don't you get out of here? I promise to let you know as soon as I hear anything," Eric said.

"I feel like a traitor for leaving," Owen told him.

"Go get some food. You need to keep your strength up. We're going to need you," Eric told him. Owen didn't say anything, and Eden felt her stomach turn at the thought of food.

"I don't think I can eat," she said. Especially after smelling charred flesh. She trembled as a new wave of nausea hit her.

Eric looked as if he completely empathized with her, but she knew Owen had to get out of there, that he wouldn't go unless he thought it was for her.

"I won't eat if you don't, and I'm hoping to get back on that mountain soon, so I need the energy," he said. He was obviously trying to guilt her into taking care of herself. It worked. It seemed they wanted to take care of each other.

"Okay, let's go," Eden told him. She let him take her hand as they left the hospital. She was almost grateful for the breath of smoke-filled air she took once outside the tragic ER. It might be irritating her throat, but it was a hell of a lot better than the taste that had been in the hospital air.

This would be her last fire investigation. She knew that for damn sure. It was too emotional, and she'd had her quota filled of what she could handle. She knew when to give herself a much-needed break.

Owen held the truck door for her, and they drove away much more slowly and quietly than how they'd arrived. Both of them were lost in their thoughts. She couldn't help but think of the woman who'd been crying in the ER.

That had to be the young firefighter's wife. She was most likely going to lose her husband. Eden couldn't imagine how she was feeling. She cast a sideways glance at Owen.

Eden knew beyond a shadow of a doubt she wouldn't be able to handle another loss in her life. What would she have done had it been Owen on that table? A shudder passed through her.

She'd been willing to let him go when she'd realized he wasn't coming back to her. It had nearly killed her, but she'd had no other choice. Could she possibly let him back into her life only to lose him again?

Closing her eyes, she knew that wasn't something she could handle. A person could only go through so much before they couldn't take any more pain. She'd hit her quota a long time ago.

As much as she loved this man, the distance between them gave her a sense of protection around her fragile emotions. If she let him all the way back in, she was afraid the glass walls barely surrounding her would shatter into a million pieces. She'd never be the same again.

It was time to make some solid decisions in her life. She just wasn't sure what those decisions had to be.

Chapter Twenty-Two

Owen was somber as he drove Eden to a small diner in town. Food was the last thing he wanted after what he'd witnessed in the hospital, but he needed to make sure Eden was being taken care of. They were both running on empty at this point.

Owen parked the truck and was glad when Eden waited for him to come around and open her door. He wasn't sure if she was allowing him to be a gentleman, or if she was just so tired she didn't have the energy to reach out and push the handle to release the door. Either way, it was something he'd always done for her, something his mother had taught him was essential if he wanted to earn a woman's respect, so he was glad to do it. The small act helped him keep his feet planted on the ground.

They walked into the café, the place scarcely populated with the lunch rush gone and the dinner rush not yet there. He was glad. He didn't want to run into people who knew him, and that was difficult to accomplish in a small town. The waitress wasn't around, so Owen led Eden to a corner table with a large window offering them a view of the mountains.

"So much has changed since I left and came back," Owen said. He instantly wondered if he shouldn't speak about his departure. But what good did it do either of them to pretend it hadn't happened? Maybe it was better to face it, talk it out, and see if the two of them still had a future. Their talk earlier hadn't gone nearly as badly as he'd thought it would. He knew she was still processing what he'd told her, but at least things were getting laid bare. At least these shadows that had been hanging over them for too long were finally receiving a little light.

"Not a lot has really changed," she told him. "Maybe the decor has improved, and maybe some new businesses have arrived, but at the end of the day, it's still Edmonds. It's still a beautiful place to raise a family."

There was a small hitch in her voice, and he wondered if she was thinking about their past dreams of raising their own children in this town. They'd both been so young and naive back then. They hadn't made any other plans than to be together and have a family.

Right now that dream sounded just about perfect.

Angela Lincoln approached their table, a big smile on her lips. "Owen, it's great to see you," she said before turning to Eden with a pointed stare. "You've been avoiding me," she said.

Angela worked for Arden part-time, and apparently was also working at the café. Owen knew his brother had offered her raises, but she was a woman determined to prove herself, especially as a single mother, and she'd told Arden she'd only accept raises in appropriate amounts— that her son was now in school, and she could work two jobs. What amused all the brothers was how much her stubbornness seemed to bother their oldest brother, Declan. Owen was waiting for the fireworks to start up between the two of them. He had a feeling he wasn't going to be waiting long.

"I'm sorry," Eden told her. "I've been sort of reclusive lately."

"Sort of?" Angela said with a raised eyebrow.

"Okay, I've been *very* reclusive . . . ," she admitted with a long pause. "But I'm out now," she added with a smile, hopeful that all would be forgiven.

"I miss you," Angela said. Owen noticed the stress around Angela's eyes. Maybe he'd have to talk to his brother and find out if everything was okay with her. Angela was a good woman, and she worked for one of his family members, so that meant they had to keep an eye out for her, especially since there was something that had made her run away from wherever she'd lived before.

"I'm truly sorry," Eden said. It sounded like she meant it. "I've been dealing with a lot, and I thought retreat would be best."

Angela shook her head. "Trust me, I get that," she said, a knowing look in her eyes. "But don't underestimate your friends."

Owen wondered if she realized she should be taking the same advice. He decided now wasn't the time to tell her that.

The bell on the door clanged, and a group of men walked in, their laughter preceding them.

"I better get your order and rush it in. These guys come in every Friday, and they order big," Angela warned.

"I'll have fish and chips," Owen said.

"How about a bowl of clam chowder?" Eden asked.

"Perfect," Angela said before walking away and slipping their order to the chef before she greeted the new group.

Eden was quiet as she watched Angela interact with the men. Owen enjoyed doing nothing more than sitting with Eden while he tried to figure out exactly what it was that went through her mind.

"You sort of got in trouble," he pointed out after a few moments.

She turned her attention back to him with a slight turning of her lips. "Yeah, I guess I did," she said.

"So I'm not the only person you're holding at bay."

"I guess not," she told him with a shrug. She wasn't offering anything more.

"Angela is pretty stubborn. I don't know why she's working two jobs when my brother has offered her a raise," Owen grumbled.

He must've said the wrong thing, because Eden's shoulders stiffened as her eyes narrowed. She took a drink of water before replying. He thought it might be best to just wait to hear what she was going to say.

"Not all women are damsels in need of rescuing. Maybe some of us want to save ourselves," she finally said.

"And maybe sometimes it takes a stronger person to admit they can't do it alone," he quickly replied.

They sat there in a standoff for a few moments, neither willing to back down. What was wrong with wanting to help someone you cared about? He didn't get it. Before he could open his mouth and put his other foot in it, the door clanged again, and Owen automatically turned to see who'd come in. It was Eric.

He spotted them and quickly weaved through the tables as he approached. The man looked as if he'd aged ten years in the past two weeks. Not only had he lost men, but his town was on the verge of being overtaken by fire. He wasn't a man who'd go down without one hell of a fight. He was that captain that wouldn't abandon ship.

"I'm glad I found you," Eric said as he pulled out a chair and sat.

"Have you eaten?" Owen asked.

He waved his hand as if he couldn't be bothered with such a task as shoving food in his mouth. When it came to his men, Eric always made sure they were taken care of, but when it came to himself, he obviously wasn't as concerned. Maybe the guys needed to have an intervention with the man before he ran himself too ragged. It was close as it was.

"I have news," Eric said before they could try to talk him into eating.

Owen tensed. "What news?"

Angela appeared right then, setting down their orders. She also placed a sandwich and fries in front of Eric, and he looked at her in confusion.

"I saw you come in, and I stole this from one of the guys. I know club sandwiches are your favorite, and that group can wait. You look as if you could be blown over by a stiff wind," she said, her voice firm.

Eric looked down at the food and cleared his throat before looking back at Angela with a soft smile that shocked Owen. The chief never smiled.

"I don't know how our town got so lucky as to earn you and your sweet boy, but I'm glad we have you," Eric said as he picked up a fry and took a bite. It appeared it had to be a pretty woman offering the food before the chief would eat. That was a mental note Owen stored for later.

"I just know a person in need when I see one," Angela said with a smile. "Now, I'll leave you guys alone to eat." She disappeared before they could talk her into joining them.

Owen turned back to the chief. "What did you want to share?" he asked.

The chief held his sandwich without much interest, taking a bite and looking as if he wasn't even tasting it. He washed it down with some water before responding.

"We had some tests run where that explosion took place," Eric said, his face seeming to go even more ashen. "There was a special fertilizer used." He shook his head, seeming to age a few more years right before their eyes.

"That's good. It'll help us narrow our list of suspects," Eden broke in.

Owen was studying the chief, dread filling him. He'd known Eric his entire life and knew he wasn't a man to hesitate over anything. The chief was reluctant to share this news with Eden, which meant only one thing . . .

"Say it, Eric," Owen said, giving him permission. Eden looked confused.

"What's going on?" she asked as she set down her spoon. It appeared as if they'd all lost their appetites.

"The Forbeses use a special blend for their fields . . ." The chief's voice trailed off. Owen watched Eden's face. It didn't take her long to figure out what wasn't being said.

"And the tests show that's what was used to essentially make a bomb with gasoline and fertilizer," Eden concluded. When fertilizer was mixed with gas, it was literally explosive.

"Yep," the chief said. He looked downcast. "I know this doesn't look good for Owen, who's on your suspect list, but you need to know those are my men out there getting hurt, and I'd trust this man with my life and the lives of all the firefighters in this department. Someone's trying to set him up," Eric said, his fist hitting the table.

Eden turned and looked at Owen in a way that didn't tell him what she was thinking. All he knew for sure was that someone out there didn't like him. Not only that, but someone was trying to make sure he spent the rest of his life behind bars.

He might not only lose the girl. He might lose his freedom as well.

Chapter Twenty-Three

Eden lost any hint of an appetite as Chief Eric's words sank in. There was now evidence pointing at the Forbes family. She had no doubt that Owen was innocent.

But the person doing this was coming after Owen. Her time on the case was running out. What if another investigator came in and didn't look closely enough, and Owen got convicted of a crime he didn't commit? She was frustrated.

"I'm done eating," she said as she pushed her plate aside. She had a feeling she'd never have an appetite again.

"Maybe we should take a break from all of this," Owen suggested. She noticed he seemed to be leery of her.

"I don't think you did it," she told him. She needed to give him that—put his mind at ease.

"Thank you," he said, the words rushing out.

"Atta girl," Chief Eric told her. He stood, his food gone. He'd been far hungrier than he'd either known or been willing to admit. He tossed a twenty on the table, said goodbye, and walked out just as quickly as he'd come in. He had a fire to fight.

"It was petty and foolish of me to think anything else," she told him.

"We've called a truce," he reminded her. "I need some things from home, and you're stuck in my truck, so let's take another ride. Hopefully this one won't be as stressful."

Eden was afraid of going to his house with him, afraid of herself, afraid she'd take one look at his kitchen and either fall apart or attack him. Neither option was acceptable. Of course, she could always just avoid the damn kitchen.

"Why don't you drop me off back at my car instead," she offered. He was shaking his head before she got a chance to finish the sentence.

"There's someone out there who burned down your house and who obviously has a vendetta against me. I'd feel better having you close," he said. She opened her mouth to argue as he held up a hand. "Remember, we all need someone at certain times in our lives. Even if you can't admit you need me right now, maybe you can admit I need you."

His words were a direct hit. She loved that he was always the hero, loved that he was more than willing to rescue anyone who needed it. But he was giving her the chance to save him, even if it was only for the briefest of moments. She couldn't possibly resist that. Not when he never asked to be saved by anyone.

"I'll ride along with you, but only because I don't ever remember you asking for help before," she finally said. She took out her wallet and added two more twenties to the one the chief had thrown down. She glared at Owen, daring him to say a word. She loved how uncomfortable he looked with her buying him a meal. It improved her mood greatly.

He stood there as if not knowing what to do. She wondered if a woman had ever paid for him. She highly doubted it. But his discomfort at the situation made her feel a whole lot better.

She stood and waited, making sure he wasn't going to try to grab the money and slip it into her purse while throwing out his own. After another silent moment, he turned and practically stomped from the café, looking like a toddler who hadn't gotten his way.

She smiled—a real smile—a smile she had only ever used when she'd been with Owen.

There was more silence as Owen held open her truck door and waited for her to climb inside. She took her time, needing to feel empowered. She knew he'd be looking at her ass as she leaned over, brushing dust from his seat before she sat.

There was already too much fire in this area, and she was certainly playing with it, but she didn't care. It was getting her mind off her worries, off her stress, off everything.

They listened to music on the way out to his place, and Eden found herself comfortable. She didn't mind silence with Owen. Maybe it gave her too much time to create scenarios within her own mind, but there had been a time she'd enjoyed doing even that.

Eden absolutely didn't want to go to that place that led to her dreaming of a happily ever after with this man. She'd been there, done that. It was time to move on, but maybe the two of them could be friends. That's the way they'd started out, and maybe that's the way they were meant to end.

They arrived at his house, and as she looked at the massive walls, she felt her nerves return. It would be just the two of them in there. Of course he took them around back, leaving them no choice but to enter through the back door that led straight to the kitchen.

She hesitated as she followed him from the truck. He opened the door and they stepped inside. She took one look at the island and images of the two of them wrapped around each other, their bodies slick with sweat, their hearts beating erratically, their cries mingling in the air, played in vivid color through her mind. She was instantly aroused.

She looked at Owen and wondered why in the world she was trying to fight this. It was useless. The connection between them was too great to deny. And she wanted to forget all the pain she'd been through—she wanted to forget everything but him and what he could make her feel.

She knew her thoughts were showing in her eyes because his entire body tensed as if he was accepting an unspoken offer she'd posed. Maybe it was the trauma of their lives right now. She didn't care.

She just wanted him.

Friends with benefits? That term existed for a reason. Maybe it wasn't such a bad thing. She would justify this situation in any way she could at the moment, because she desperately wanted to feel anything other than sadness or confusion.

And only Owen could bring her the pleasure she so desperately needed.

Chapter Twenty-Four

Owen was most certainly giving himself credit for not running straight to Eden, lifting her onto that smooth granite counter, and ripping away her clothes. With the way she was looking first at the counter and then at him, he figured he deserved a medal for his restraint.

"Owen . . ." He could tell she was giving in to some internal battle she'd been fighting. She wanted him just as desperately as he always wanted her.

"Just say the word, and I can put us both out of our misery," he promised. He was practically ripping off the back of a chair to keep himself from advancing on her.

Yes, he enjoyed her company, and yes, there was so much more to this woman than just a simple roll in the hay. But he'd had so little of her for so long. If they could sate their mutual needs, then maybe he could think with his heart and brain a hell of a lot more than with other body parts. Right now, though, he couldn't look at her without wanting her, and he couldn't even think about anything but her. That was saying a whole lot, considering they were being surrounded by fire and people intent on destroying them.

"Coming here is difficult," she said. He found he desperately wanted her to admit she desired him as much as he did her. He needed for her to want to stay, not for him to just give her pleasure and then disappear like he'd never been there.

"I can't keep playing games, Eden. We don't have to figure out our entire futures, but let's stop pretending we don't feel something—that we don't still need each other. Why fight the inevitable?" he asked.

"I feel guilty," she told him.

"For what?"

"I feel guilty for wanting you when you hurt me. I'm afraid you will again," she told him. That hit hard. "And I feel I'm betraying my dad because he needed me, and I chose you instead."

All the fight drained from Owen as her heartbroken words seared his soul. He'd give anything to take her pain from her. He couldn't do that, but he could tell her with surety what her father would want.

"He'd never ask you to blame yourself for his loss," Owen assured her. "And I know I hurt you, but I promise I won't again." She tried to speak, but he held up his hand. "I know you don't want to hear promises from me. I know you can't trust me yet. But we can't seem to keep away from each other, so why don't we agree to forget about the past until this situation is over?"

"I'm not sure I can," she told him.

"Let's put it on pause for one night, then. I need you, Eden," he said, giving her every ounce of vulnerability in him. He was broken, and only with this woman was he willing to show how much.

She opened her mouth to speak when there was a noise outside, something that made him nervous. The hair on his arms stood up, and Owen knew something was wrong—something was seriously wrong.

"Get down, Eden," he said, his voice urgent.

She looked at him as if he'd just asked her to strip naked.

The sound of glass breaking and his wall exploding unfroze him as he jumped at Eden. She barely had time to register the danger before he was tackling her, their bodies flying through the kitchen.

He turned them, but not enough, both of them hitting the hard tile floor on their sides, their breaths exploding from them. Owen was staring at her face as her head slammed into the floor, her eyes instantly rolling back in her head.

Someone had fired a shot into his house.

He held her tight as he heard three more shots shattering his windows and destroying his walls. He didn't give a damn about his house. All he cared about was that he might have done more damage to Eden than the shooter had been attempting.

She'd hit the floor too hard, and he nearly had a heart attack when he saw a trickle of blood dripping down her face. He wasn't sure if it was from flying debris from the bullets or if he'd knocked her head that hard on the floor. Either way, he'd never forgive himself if she was injured.

"Eden!" he shouted as he shook her shoulders. The shooting seemed to have stopped, but whoever it was could be circling his house. He shook her again. A groan escaped her as her body began shaking. He wrapped her more tightly against him as he scooted them back, using the protection of the island that kept them out of view of the windows.

"Eden, are you okay?" *Please be okay.* It had happened too quickly. He hadn't had time to think, to protect her from the impact of the ground. He rubbed his hands up and down her back, grateful when he didn't feel anything sticky. "I need to know if you've been shot. I need to look at you," he told her as he tried to pull back. She clung more tightly to him.

"Don't let go," she told him, and he was helpless to do anything other than obey her. He kept her cradled against his chest, one arm wrapped snugly around her while the other reached for his cell in his pocket. She didn't say a word as he called in the attack. They'd soon be surrounded by people.

"I don't understand what's happening," she said, the trembling in her body beginning to ease.

"Someone has it in for me, or us, or this entire town, or maybe all of the above," Owen said. He was furious with himself that he'd once again allowed danger to get so close to her.

There was silence for the next few moments. All was quiet outside. The shooter had to have known he'd call for help, and they had to know his brother Declan would catch them in seconds if they were still near.

"I think they're gone," he told her. She pulled back the slightest bit so she could look at him. He was surprised to find such courage in her eyes.

"I'm sorry I fell apart," she said.

He looked at her incredulously. "What are you talking about?" he asked.

"I froze," she admitted.

"Eden, anyone would freeze. I froze," he said.

"Not for long enough to make a difference," she told him. "If I would've been in charge of us getting to safety, we'd both be toast right now." She reached up and rested her slim fingers against his cheek. Owen felt as if he'd died and gone to heaven. There was such trust and love in her eyes. He prayed he wasn't just seeing what he wanted—desperately needed—to see.

"We don't know what we're capable of until we're faced with our deepest fears. You can easily say that's what you'd do and that's what would happen, but I know you, Eden, and I know you're stronger than you think you are." Her eyes brightened at his words as she leaned forward, pressing her forehead against his.

Damn, he loved her, loved her so much that it was almost too powerful for him to contain. He wouldn't live without her. Too much time had already gone by with them apart.

"You've run your hands over every inch of my body," she said with a chuckle as he rubbed his palm down her calf. He looked up.

"I was . . . just caressing you," he said slowly.

She laughed, shocking him even more. "Yeah, that's not the touch of a lover. That's an exam from a doctor," she countered.

"I need to make sure you're okay," he said as he brought his hand back up and rested it on her lower back.

"How about you?" she asked.

"What about me?"

"Maybe I need to rub you all over to make sure there aren't injuries," she said, her hand slipping from his cheek and running across his shoulder and down his arm.

Owen flipped so quickly onto his back, it brought out another giggle in her.

"Examine away. There's definitely a shooting pain right near my zipper," he told her, all thoughts of the attack wiped from his mind just that quickly.

Eden laughed, really laughed, this time as she moved her hand past his palm, then up the underside of his arm and down his rib cage. Owen found himself holding his breath as she neared that bulge he'd just mentioned. But her fingertips danced just on the other side of his ache, smoothing down the top of his thigh, making his body jump.

Owen was about to grab her hand and place it exactly where he wanted it, but then he heard the crunch of gravel as a car whipped up his driveway. There was a screech of tires, and within three seconds his door was demolished as it was kicked in.

Eden's face washed of color as she gripped him tightly, all thoughts of foreplay gone. He was going to kill someone—a certain someone.

"Owen," Eden said in a hoarse whisper. He held up his hand, stopping her.

"My brother's here," he grumbled. "Perfect timing, as always." It was only seconds before Declan was with them.

"Are you both okay?" Declan asked.

"A little bruised," Owen answered when Eden didn't say anything. "We're good here. You can take off," Owen said. "But thanks for coming so quickly."

Declan didn't take the hint. "Get off your ass. Let's take a look outside," Declan told him.

Owen let out a frustrated sigh. Eden was going to pull back the second he let her go. Declan didn't move. Owen gave up as he reluctantly pulled himself from Eden's arms.

"I'll be back," he said, his voice low and husky. He was shocked speechless when she gave him a tentative smile, then . . . winked at him.

"I'll be waiting."

Declan hauled him to his feet and practically dragged him away. Owen smiled as he realized Eden wasn't going anywhere. Their night was just beginning.

Chapter Twenty-Five

Declan might have been the first to arrive, but by the time Owen and Declan stepped outside, Owen could hear another car racing down his driveway. It squealed to a halt, and the driver and passenger doors flew open as Kian and Arden jumped from the vehicle, their eyes looking wild.

"What in the hell is happening around here?" Arden yelled.

He looked Owen over from head to foot before seeming satisfied that his brother hadn't been harmed.

"Seriously?" Kian said, moving closer as he really gave Owen the once-over. He wasn't as willing to take a quick look. Owen wasn't letting his brother examine him, though.

"I'm fine," he told them.

His phone rang and he wanted to ignore it, but he knew better. He didn't even need to look at the caller ID to know who was calling.

"Hey, sis," he said.

"You were shot at!" Dakota cried. He held the phone away from his ear. She'd found out fast, dang it.

"News travels quickly when you don't want it to," he said with what he hoped was a nonchalant chuckle.

"This isn't funny, Owen. What in the hell is happening in my hometown?" she demanded. "Ace and I are on the way there now."

"I thought Ace was already here fighting the fire," Owen told her.

"He's been doing the afternoon drops, so thankfully he was home. I don't think I could drive right now, I'm so dang upset." His sister wasn't an overly dramatic person, so he felt utterly subdued as he heard the tears in her voice.

"I promise you I'm okay. I don't know what happened, but our brothers are here, and we're going to figure it out," he assured her.

"I'm scared, Owen. It's obvious someone is targeting you directly," she said.

"And Eden," he told her. "But I'm being careful. I promise you. I'm keeping her safe."

"You better keep both of you safe. I love you, and if something happened to you, I'd . . ." Dakota's words broke off as a sob ripped out of her.

"I love you too, sis," he assured her. "Nothing will happen to any of us. But these bastards are going to be caught, and they will pay."

"I'll feel better when I get there," she said. "I need to see with my own eyes that you're okay."

"I know," he told her.

"Stay put. I'll be there in forty minutes," she told him. It took another couple of minutes, but Owen finally managed to get his sister to hang up. Then he turned and looked at Kian, Arden, and Declan, who all appeared just as worried as Dakota had sounded.

"Why are they targeting you?" Kian asked.

"I don't know. Maybe because Eden's investigating this thing?" Owen suggested.

They moved away from the house and stayed together as they searched his property. There wasn't a sign of anyone around. They enlarged their perimeter, looking for even the smallest of clues.

"I think this has to do with a hell of a lot more than Eden," Arden said.

"Yeah, because they were deliberately trying to set you up. But with this shooting, it seems they're growing impatient and not even trying to hide the fact they want you gone. That scares the shit out of me," Kian said.

"It should scare you. Desperate criminals are unpredictable," Declan said. He was gazing into the distance, and Owen was sure his brother had found something.

They followed Declan, and sure enough, they found the casings of rifle bullets.

"They have long-range rifles. These aren't amateurs," Declan said as he pulled out a plastic bag and carefully stowed the casings as he looked at them through the plastic.

"They're bound to mess up soon, and then we'll have them," Owen said.

"I know they will, but I don't want it to be too late at that point," Declan said, obviously frustrated he hadn't already solved this case.

"It's already too late," Owen told him. "Lives have been taken."

"I know that, brother," Declan told him. "But right now your life matters the most to me."

"We're family. We take care of each other," Arden said.

"I've seen too much death from this already. I can't handle seeing you in my ER again," Kian said.

"Then let's stop these assholes," Owen insisted.

"You think there's more than one?" Kian asked.

"Yeah, I think there's a bunch of them," Owen said.

"If we get the ringleader, we get them all," Declan said.

"Then that's what we'll do," Arden said.

"I'll find this guy. Enough of my men have been hurt already. I can't sit back and let it keep happening," Owen insisted.

"You know it doesn't always have to be you saving the world," Arden told him. "You have family here who'd do anything for you. Let us help you. Let someone else be the hero this time. You should grab Eden and get the hell out of town."

"I'm not sure I know how to sit back and take help," Owen admitted. "But I sure as hell know I won't run." His brothers nodded. They knew that was an empty suggestion. None of them were capable of running from a fight.

Kian smiled as he looked toward the front of Owen's house. They'd searched the entire perimeter and were back where they started.

"Well, we'll start by fixing that door. It looks pretty bad," Kian said.

"That wasn't the bad guys. That was our brother dearest," Owen said as he sent a lopsided grin Declan's way.

"I didn't know if they'd breached your house, and I wasn't going to sit there and knock on the door," Declan said, shifting on his feet.

"Yeah, I'd have done the same if it were you who'd been shot at," Owen admitted.

Declan laughed. "You couldn't have broken down my door like that," he said, arrogance shining in his eyes. "My house is a damn fortress."

"Oh, we'd have gotten in," Arden said with a laugh.

"Not as easy as I got in here," Declan said.

"I haven't ever needed a fortress before. I hate that our town has become this crazy," Owen said.

"We're going to fix it," Kian said. "We'll do it together."

Owen didn't know how to accept the offer of help very easily. But he did know he loved his brothers more than he loved himself. His family meant the world to him. He included Eden in that tally of family members.

They'd get to the bottom of this, and maybe at the end of the day he'd be able to accept help. He wasn't sure. He knew for damn sure he could accept some help fixing the front door. He had a woman to get back to. The sooner he got the door fixed and assured his family he was okay, the sooner he could finish what he and Eden had begun before they'd been so rudely interrupted.

That thought put a smile on his face even in the midst of all that was happening. And that proved to him how right it was for him to be with Eden. She truly was a ray of sunshine in a hell of a lot of darkness.

He'd been a fool once. Once was enough.

Chapter Twenty-Six

Eden's fear had quickly dissipated. But the fear had made her realize they weren't all that safe. Someone was after them, and they might not have a tomorrow. That thought made her want to be with Owen. It might be foolish, and she might get broken again, but she needed him. She needed him to make this pain and fear go away.

She cleaned up in the kitchen while she waited for him and his brothers to finish repairing the door. She'd been about to straddle Owen when Declan had literally smashed his way inside. She was glad they'd been interrupted, though, because it gave her time to realize this was exactly what she wanted to do.

She wasn't going to make love to him again because she was scared, or because her adrenaline was pumping out of control. She was doing it with a rational mind and a clear conscience. She was doing it because she'd thought she was about to die, and though she'd been scared, she'd been glad it was while she was in Owen's arms.

She cleaned up everything she could; then she made a cup of coffee and went into the living room and waited. The longer it took Owen and his brothers, the more calm she felt. Yes, there was a bit of panic, as she had no doubt she was still in love with Owen, but that didn't matter right now. All that mattered was they were alive. And they both needed to feel something that was good and pure and magical.

"You look stunning," Owen said from behind her.

Eden smiled as she turned to look at him. She'd felt him enter the room. It was odd how in sync the two of them had always been when they weren't angry or bitter. It would be so easy to fall back into a pattern of what had once been.

"Are you finished?" she asked.

He nodded. "My sister arrived, demanding to come inside, but I managed to calm her down and send her to my parents' place. Then Declan helped seal up the door he destroyed. It will do until tomorrow when I can get it replaced. They're all gone now." There was urgency in his eyes—the same urgency she knew was in hers.

Eden put her cup down and stood, then walked with purpose to Owen. She felt confident, something she hadn't felt in a long time. Her world had been spinning, and it was time to feel dizzy for an entirely good reason. She reached her arms around him, clung tightly as she saw passion flare in his eyes. It made her feel wanted . . . needed . . . appreciated.

She smoothed her fingers over the rough skin at the back of his neck, just stood there looking into his eyes. She wasn't scared. She felt content. This moment was right.

Maybe it was the fact that she didn't know if she had a tomorrow. Maybe it was because there was so much evil in the world, and maybe it was the realization that this man had always been her calm in the storm.

When he bent, bringing his lips deliciously closer, it wasn't a mad rush to fulfill their needs. It was a sweet tasting, a blending of their passion in the most delicate of ways. She sighed, their lips vibrating as he ran his tongue out, tasting her.

The kiss went on, and Eden pressed closer to him, loving how his hardness engulfed her softness, loving how perfectly their bodies fit together. He backed them up against the kitchen counter, and Eden pulled back, a chuckle escaping her. His expression was confused.

"What is it about your kitchen?" she said.

His confusion evaporated as he smiled. Then he swept her into his arms and quickly carried her through his large house. She kissed and licked his neck, loving the moans coming from him—loving that it was her making him lose control.

They made it to the bedroom and fell onto the bed together, his large body engulfing hers, making her squirm beneath him, hating the clothes keeping them separated. This time when he kissed her, the gentleness was gone. This kiss was full of heat and urgency. Playtime was over.

Owen broke away from the kiss, and Eden whimpered, then moaned as he trailed his lips down her chin and sucked the skin of her neck, continuing lower, making her quiver.

She loved him. She'd tried not falling back into that place, but it was impossible with his hands and lips caressing her body. She truly loved him, and being with him had always been magical. It had never been an act she'd grown complacent about.

He undid the buttons of her blouse, his lips following as he revealed more skin. She squirmed beneath him. Her movements aided him in removing her clothes as he sped up the process. His tongue lapped at her breasts, and she felt heat building in beautiful waves.

She tried helping him undress, but her trembling fingers weren't very helpful, so he threw off his clothes, the sound of ripping material hanging heavy in the air.

Then he lay against her, their skin scorching each other's as she felt his thickness resting between her thighs. Perfection. This moment was utter perfection. She felt as if they'd never been apart. They were made for each other.

He tried to break away from their kiss again, but she held on tightly. "I'm done with foreplay," she told him as she wrapped her legs tightly around his solid hips. "I need you to fill me."

The last word came out on a moan as he thrust inside her wet body. There was no resistance. She was more than ready for him—always ready. She clenched around him, holding him tight, not wanting this moment to ever end.

"Home. I'm home," he said as his lips caressed hers, his urgency growing as he began moving his hips, pulling almost fully out of her before thrusting back in, their bodies clashing together in perfect harmony.

"Yes," she cried out, unsure if she was agreeing with him or calling for more. Her orgasm was building, and she was greedy for the release. She felt him swell even more within her, filling her to completion. He moved faster and she met him, thrust after beautiful thrust.

Her body shook beneath him as she felt the imminent release. And then a cry of pleasure was torn from her as he echoed her yell, both of them shaking as they gave each other a beautiful release.

Owen collapsed against her, then tried to turn, but she kept her legs wrapped around him, held him tightly, feeling reassured by his heavy weight. She felt herself growing tired. She knew she shouldn't stay, knew she shouldn't let this be about more than sex. She also knew she was long past being able to think that way.

Her sleepiness made her weak, and Owen turned onto his back, pulling out of her, making her feel unbearably sad at the loss of them being connected as one. But he didn't let her go far as he pulled her into the cradle of his arms, her head resting on his chest where his heart was a steady rhythm of comfort.

"I should go," she said with a yawn.

"No." It was a simple word, spoken almost pleasantly, but there was steel in his voice. He didn't add anything as he reached down and pulled the covers over them. She didn't have the will to fight him. She snuggled in closer and fell asleep, feeling utterly peaceful.

This was home. This was where she'd always belonged. Maybe she'd simply accept it for as long as it would last.

Chapter Twenty-Seven

Eden opened her eyes before slamming them back shut. She tried again, this time opening them only to a slit. The curtains were open, and the sun was up too high in the sky for it to be early morning.

She was still wrapped around Owen, closer than she'd been when she'd fallen asleep, if that was even possible. She was practically on top of him. Her body shifted and she felt his arm tighten around her as he gripped her hips and pulled her over him.

She immediately felt his thickness between her legs, and her body heated and grew wet in response. She looked down at his alert expression and knew he'd been awake for quite some time.

"Mornin'," she mumbled, feeling self-conscious for some reason. She found herself wanting to cover her chest. As if he could read her thoughts, his hands traveled from her hips, up her stomach, then cupped her breasts, squeezing them, making her even wetter, making her wiggle against his hardness even while she told herself to get off him.

"You were snoring," he told her with a smile while his thumbs rubbed across her hard nipples. She had to bite her lip to keep from crying out.

"I don't snore," she said indignantly.

"Okay," he said with a smile, as if he knew so much more than she did. She tried to move off him, but he simply moved one hand back down to her hip, shifted her body, and thrust up into her, making her forget why she needed to go anywhere.

He was leisurely as he moved his hips in small thrusts while his fingers pinched her nipples and rubbed her breasts. She sighed as she looked at him. His eyes were flashing, but his face was serene.

"We should stop now," she said. There was no oomph to her words. The last thing she wanted to do was stop.

"We're doing what we should always be doing," he said, letting go of her breasts so he could hold both hips and thrust up a little harder into her. She clenched around him as more heat rose in her body. She began rotating her hips, making him groan as she sank down on him.

"We aren't a couple anymore, Owen," she said, her voice husky.

"If it makes you feel better to say that," he told her. "But you're mine."

The words were spoken with such possession that she felt more heat shift through her.

"Oh, no more talking," she gasped. She splayed her hands against his hard chest, pinching his nipple, making him cry out in surprise and maybe a bit of pain. That made her smile as she took over.

She rode him, her head thrust back, her body on fire. Then she cried out as she clenched around him, feeling his body tense as he released deep inside of her. As she once again collapsed against his hot skin, she realized there never had been any truth in her words of protest. She was exactly where she needed to be.

But . . .

"I can feel it whenever you get lost in your own head," Owen said as his hands ran up and down her flushed skin. "Quit trying to rationalize this. Quit trying to run away. We're adults, doing what we need to do. Enjoy the moment."

"I don't think I've ever just lived for the moment," Eden told him.

"I know. It's one more thing I've always loved about you. But sometimes we get so wrapped up in what we're supposed to be doing, and what others think we need to do, that we stop living. Let's agree to live and not feel guilty about it," he practically pleaded.

She processed his words and wondered if she could ever be that type of woman, the type of person who could live without worrying about consequences. She didn't think so. It seemed an almost impossible thought to even imagine.

"We're different, Owen. You live for a thrill. I enjoy organization," she said. "There's nothing wrong with either choice."

"And there's nothing wrong with adapting to different situations," he said.

She thought about that. "But isn't it wise to know when you're simply banging your head against the same brick wall?" she asked.

"If you're equating our relationship to a brick wall, I'm a bit disappointed," he told her with a chuckle. "I'd like to think you could come up with something better than that, like maybe beating a dead horse."

"Do you ever take anything seriously?" she asked. She tried pulling away from him, but he lifted her chin, making her look him in the eyes.

"I take us very seriously. We're too important not to. Once I was young and stupid, and because of that I risked losing you forever. But I see the look in your eyes. We're never over, Eden—never." The words were spoken with such conviction that she couldn't help but believe him.

"Sometimes in life we don't get what we want, and sometimes we think we want something but later realize it's a blessing we didn't get it," she told him. The words hurt to even say.

"And sometimes," he said softly, gently holding her chin. He kissed her lips so delicately she found tears forming. He still wouldn't allow her to look away, allow her to put her guard back up. "Sometimes we don't realize what's right in front of us, and we let it get away when it didn't want to be set free. I won't ever be that foolish again."

She couldn't answer. Her throat was too tight. Instead, she deepened the kiss. For this moment, she didn't want to be strong; she just wanted to be with him. He turned her and made love to her again. This time she didn't have the strength to guard her heart. She was his, just as he was hers.

She just didn't know what that meant.

Chapter Twenty-Eight

Owen dropped Eden at her car after a whole lot of protesting. He was still worried someone was after her. She'd had to point out that it was daytime, and she wasn't planning on going hiking through the woods anytime soon.

She wanted to do more investigating before she was pulled from this case. It was Tuesday morning, and she was sure someone would be in at any time to tell her to hand everything over. If she could have it all wrapped up by then, she'd be safe to do what she wanted when she wanted.

When this was settled, she realized her life would most likely go back to normal. She and Owen wouldn't be in this danger, and there'd be no need for them to stick so close to each other. That thought was far less pleasant than her other thoughts. But that was their reality. Even if they did love each other—and she could admit there was still love between them—that didn't mean it solved their problems. It didn't erase the past.

Needing caffeine before she did anything, Eden snuck into the kitchen at Roxie's place, hoping her friend was out. It wasn't that she didn't love her best friend, it was just that Roxie was going to be able to read her like a book, and she wasn't sure she could talk about what she was thinking, as she really didn't know what her plans were.

She was out of luck, though.

"You know, you can call when you're going to be out all night. I was worried sick until Kian got back and told me you were still with Owen," Roxie said, leaning in the doorway, tapping her foot but wearing a Cheshire-cat grin.

"News always travels fast in a small town," Eden said, surprised that heat was infusing her cheeks. If anyone knew of her history with Owen Forbes, it was Roxie. The two of them had been in love with the brothers from the time they knew what love was.

"I'm not going to force you to talk, but you were there for me when I was going through hell, even when I tried to push you and everyone else away. I realized that wasn't what I really wanted. You should know I'm here for you now," Roxie said. She moved over and poured herself a cup of coffee and sat at the kitchen island.

Eden was torn. She wanted to spill her guts to Roxie, but she also knew the words would come out in a jumbled twist. She didn't know what she was feeling. She knew there were many emotions, but she couldn't seem to sort them out.

"I don't think I'm ready yet," Eden finally said.

She looked at Roxie and was relieved when her friend didn't appear to be disappointed. She gave her a reassuring smile. "Why don't you fill me in on the investigation, instead?" Roxie asked. "Is my brother-in-law going to jail?"

She asked the question as if she was asking Eden to pass her a donut. It suddenly gave Eden the giggles. She couldn't hold them back after the first one escaped. Roxie smiled as she sipped her coffee, waiting for Eden's hysterics to be over.

"Yes, I know Owen isn't guilty. I called the investigators, and they're clearing him for duty," Eden finally said. "I don't know why I ever thought he could be a criminal. Maybe it was easier to feel that way than to admit he'd walked away from me, that I hadn't been good enough to keep him around." Suddenly the need to laugh was gone.

"You know that isn't what happened. There's always more to a story," Roxie said.

"Yes, there is, but it hurt so much when he left. Too many people leave me," Eden told her. "I don't know why it's so hard to stay." She had to fight to not fall apart. "My mother was the first, but she wasn't the last."

Roxie was quiet for several moments, as if trying to form her words carefully. Eden appreciated that. She didn't want her friend to spout empty words.

"I did the same to Kian. I walked away because I was dealing with demons I couldn't talk about. I hurt him." She winced as she said this. "But fate is a funny thing, and though I wish I could change how everything happened, I wouldn't change how it turned out—not for anything in the world."

"You guys were meant to be together," Eden said, feeling that to her very soul.

"Just as you and Owen are," Roxie pointed out.

"It's different with us," Eden tried to say.

"Hogwash. We say whatever we need to say in order to feel better about our actions. But at the end of the day, what's meant to be is gonna happen whether we want it to or not," Roxie assured her.

"I'm not a big fan of fate right now," Eden said, her eyes narrowing.

"Yeah, I get that. You've had it rough this year," Roxie said. She reached out and patted Eden's arm.

"I've decided no one's in charge of my destiny, that the decision is in my hands, and *only* my hands." She said this with such force, she knew she was trying to convince herself as much as her friend.

"Good. Woman power," Roxie said, holding out her closed fist for a bump. Eden tapped it lightly and smiled.

"Okay, okay, you can quit mocking me now," Eden told her.

"I would never," Roxie said with a chuckle.

"It's just that when things hit rock bottom, they really sink," Eden told her.

"Man, do I ever know that," Roxie said.

"Then don't you think that we can change all of that? Shouldn't we be allowed to define our own destinies?"

Roxie was quiet for a moment as she looked at her friend.

"No. I think we can take many paths, but at the end of the day, what's meant to be will be, and we're going to arrive at the same destination no matter what road we take to get there," Roxie told her.

"Well, that's not at all what I want to hear. You're being a terrible friend right now," Eden said, but the smile on her lips took away the sting of her words.

"I'm just trying to keep it real," Roxie assured her.

"I think I'd rather live in a fantasy world. I want to write my own story."

"We do write our stories," Roxie said, her smile growing. "That's what makes us unique. It's just that a few plot twists are thrown in along the way to keep us from getting writer's block."

The scary thing about this conversation was that Eden got it. She could completely see Roxie's point. Maybe her story had been written. Maybe it just needed one hell of a good editor to fix all that was wrong.

Again, this took her plans and burned them to ashes, but it also made her feel as if she wasn't continually messing up. It made her feel as if she was simply living her story. Someone else was in charge—someone else was responsible.

"It might be that Owen's not on my suspect list anymore, but there's something that's been nagging at me. I know it's stupid, but maybe if we talk about it, I can push it from my mind completely," Eden said when she'd worked up the courage.

Roxie smiled as if she had no worries in the world. "Don't tell me you think it's Kian," she said. "I'm not raising these kids on my own. He's not getting off that easy."

Eden sighed. "I know this is stupid. Really, I do," she said. But she might as well move forward. "What about Declan?" she asked.

Roxie's eyes widened in shock.

"Why in the world would you think it's Declan?" she asked. There wasn't judgment, just disbelief.

"Do any of us really know him?" Eden asked.

"Yes," Roxie said with assurance. "He's honorable. He'd never take a life without one hell of a good reason, and he certainly wouldn't risk the life of one of his siblings."

"I know . . ." Eden threw up her hands in frustration. She needed a bad guy, and Declan was scary. But it was so stupid that it wasn't even worth talking about, so she wasn't sure why she'd even brought it up.

"There's no buts in this," Roxie said. "I know you desperately need to find a bad guy, but I'd bet my life on this, Eden. It's not Declan. Don't waste your time investigating him. There's a real bad guy out there, and the sooner he's found, the easier it will be for all of us to sleep at night."

"I've known that all along. I just need to solve this, and he is pretty damn scary. You have to at least admit that," Eden said.

"I can fully agree on that," Roxie told her with a laugh before grabbing her hand. "And you definitely do what you need to do, but just know that in the end, you'll find that Declan is always the hero—never the villain."

Eden walked away knowing she already believed what Roxie was saying. She'd just had to get the thoughts out there for her friend to say what she needed to hear. She was also more frustrated than ever before.

One thing was for dang sure. Maybe it was time she started believing in fate again, because it seemed it was playing with her a hell of a lot.

Chapter Twenty-Nine

There wasn't a lot of fanfare when Owen was called into his chief's office and shown the paper releasing him back to work. He was officially off the suspect list. He should be glad about that. He was happy . . . but . . .

Eden was out there alone, and someone was after her. It seemed all he wanted to do was keep her safe. He had no idea who was coming after her, but it was killing him to be at the firehouse, suiting up with men he loved and respected, instead of ensuring her safety.

He had to remind himself there were plenty of people keeping an eye out for her, but there weren't nearly enough firefighters to get this damn blaze under control. If they didn't stop it, the fire would consume them all. He was keeping her safe by doing his job. It was just so odd for him for the first time in his life to want to run from the fire. And it wasn't fear for himself; it was a need to take care of her.

There hadn't once been a time in his career when any person had come above his job. Not even his best friend, the one he'd moved away for. Yes, he'd stayed away to help him, but the minute he'd been on the job, that had been his focus. Only Eden had ever been able to consume him—she was so much hotter than any flame he fought against.

If something happened to her . . .

Owen shook his head. He wasn't going to do her any good if he got himself killed, and if he didn't get his head in the game, that's exactly what he'd do. Having your head anywhere else but the current situation when dealing with an unpredictable fire was suicide.

Too many people had already been injured, and he didn't want to add to the burden he knew his chief was already carrying. Owen could prioritize, and right now he needed to be here with his crew, needed to be an asset to the team.

But no matter how much he tried to talk himself into being in the present, he couldn't seem to jump out of the past. He had left Eden behind when he'd gone to New York, and though they hadn't been together, she'd been with him the entire time he'd been there.

The first time he'd walked into that New York fire station, he'd been just a green nineteen-year-old kid. The chief had sized him up and smirked. Owen had looked him dead in the eyes and told him he was going to be the best damn firefighter he'd ever seen.

The chief had taken that as a challenge.

Owen had never worked so hard in his life. They'd put him through the paces, but he'd come out the other end stronger than he'd ever been and feeling proud of his accomplishments.

Time had passed in a blur while he'd been in New York, and he'd tried telling himself he was doing the right thing—the only thing he could do. He had to be away from his family to protect a friend and to become a man.

It hadn't taken Declan long to find him, and the fury in his brother's eyes when he'd faced him had made Owen realize why so many people feared Declan. Owen hadn't been afraid, of course, but he'd realized he'd hurt his family in his quest to help his friend and find himself.

He'd promised never to do that again.

And for the first year he'd been in New York, he'd thought he'd be able to put Eden from his mind. He knew he'd been a fool to leave without saying goodbye, but he'd also known if he had attempted to tell her he was leaving, one look from her would've stopped him dead in his tracks.

Love was a funny thing. It bound you so tightly to another that it was impossible to know where you ended and they began. He'd thought he'd get over her in time, but his feelings never disappeared.

He'd had moments where his heart hadn't ached so badly, but those had been few and far between. The only thing that had truly brought him happiness was when there was a hose in his hands and a scorching fire before him. But as soon as the adrenaline rush was over, he'd go back to his small apartment to find his friend there, and the ache would nearly consume him.

He couldn't seem to do anything without thoughts of Eden. He'd walk to his favorite coffeehouse and see a couple leaning across a table whispering intimately to each other and remember all the times he'd done the same with Eden. A walk in the park felt cold and empty. A woman's laughter would make him spin around, hoping to find Eden coming toward him.

Yes, the nostalgia had ebbed through the years, and that's why he'd waited so long to make his first visit back to Washington. But his feelings had never disappeared. And now he was home, and all he wanted was to have her in his life. He knew he'd messed up, knew he had to make it up to her.

She *would* trust him again. She would give him more than just her body. He'd prove he was worthy of standing beside her—not in front, not behind, but right at her side. They'd carry each other. He liked being a hero, but for her, he could admit he just might need rescuing.

When Owen realized how long he'd been sitting in his current fire station lamenting over the past, he shook his head with a rueful smile. Eden was always with him. She was his past, his present, and if he had anything to say about it, his future.

She might not believe in fate anymore, but he did, more than ever. They were meant to be. It was only a matter of time.

Taking a deep breath, he walked over to the men who looked exhausted but still wore determined expressions. He had so much respect for each one of them. He smiled, feeling slightly guilty that he'd had a few days off, that he'd been able to recharge his batteries.

"Damn, man, you in uniform is a beautiful sight," one of the guys called out.

"Someone has to carry the dead weight around here," Owen replied with a smile.

"Yeah, easy for you to say. Have you been sitting with your feet in the pool while drinking mimosas with your pinkie finger out?"

"Something like that," Owen said with a grin. "But I guess the powers that be actually believe I'm not guilty of lighting my town on fire."

"That was bullshit," another of the guys said.

"Yeah. Assholes," another added.

"They're just doing their job," Owen said, feeling generous. "Besides, if it was someone on our crew, we'd want to know they were doing their job right."

There were grumbles all around, as these men knew each other better than they knew their own families. The thought of any of them being responsible for something this destructive was too outrageous to even contemplate.

"The fire's nearing that ritzy new community. We've already had calls from the governor and mayor," Chief Eric said as he approached the group. "Let's see if we can save our city."

"Damn right we will," Owen told him.

The chief clapped his back as he turned and walked away. All joking was cast aside as the men decided on a plan of action. Hopefully no one was making any more cocktails to blow more of them up.

The next ten hours were hell. The fire pushed at them, and they pushed back. But at the end of the day, they won. Not a single house went up in flames, and they managed to shift the direction of the fire. It still wasn't contained, but it was taking a turn through the mountains instead of coming closer to their town.

Owen was oddly energized as he walked into the station, his face covered in black, his uniform the same. He guzzled down some water and chatted with some of the crew when the chief walked in. The expression on his face told them it wasn't good news. They all went silent.

"The hospital called," he said.

"Please, no," one of the men said.

"Trevor's family is going to terminate life support. It's time." The words were short and to the point. Owen felt numb. Trevor was just a kid, and his life was ending because someone had a vendetta. It was sick and unacceptable. And the person who had done this would pay. If it was the last thing Owen did, he knew he'd make the person pay.

Chapter Thirty

Owen walked into the hospital and found Eden standing there talking with one of the nurses. Several of the firefighters were coming and going. Trevor's family was letting them say goodbye before they did what needed to be done.

Though Owen wasn't a man to break down, he felt on the verge of doing just that. His eyes were burning as he neared Eden. He hadn't been expecting her there, but he was damn glad she was.

"I heard," she said, fear and sadness in her eyes.

"Will you come in with me?" he asked.

She nodded as a tear slipped down her cheek.

The two of them walked to the end of the hallway. Owen stopped and gave Katrina a hug. She and Trevor had been married less than six months, but they'd known each other since they were kids. She was losing her husband and best friend.

"I'm sorry, Katrina. I'm sorry I didn't get him out in time," he told her. He knew this rested on his shoulders. He should have kept Trevor from danger.

"He loved you so much, Owen," she said before she had to stop. He held her close as she shook in his arms. Eden stood next to him, her own tears streaming down her face. "And I know you loved him, too. Please don't blame yourself. He was doing what he loved, living the only life he could live. He would've died for you. I don't want to lose him, but I can't be selfish anymore. He needs us to let go."

Owen felt his control slipping as a solitary tear escaped before he could stop it. He hated feeling this weak.

"I should've saved him," he told her.

"You gave him all you had, and you were there to train him to be the best. This fire just doesn't give a crap about any of that, and it keeps on taking lives. It has no mercy. Don't you dare put this on your shoulders," Katrina told him.

She leaned back and placed her hands on his cheeks and gazed at his face. He was fighting desperately not to lose it.

"I know you don't need me to say it, but if there's anything you ever need, I'm here for you," he told her.

"I know that, and it matters more than you could ever imagine," she told him.

She stretched up on her tiptoes and kissed his cheek. Then she turned and looked at Eden. "Please take care of him," she said.

She let Owen go and walked over to her family. Her father pulled her into his arms and held her while she sobbed. Owen grabbed ahold of Eden's hand, and the two of them walked into Trevor's room.

The monitors were beeping, the only indication of any life in the room. Trevor's body was covered in gauze and blankets. He was utterly still. They approached his bedside, and Owen looked down, feeling pain unlike anything he'd ever felt before. This kid had been special to him.

"I should've done more," he whispered.

Eden squeezed his fingers but said nothing. She knew words wouldn't help him right now. Nothing but capturing these men would help.

When he finally did look at Eden, she was shaking as tears dripped from her chin. She couldn't seem to tear her gaze away from Trevor. Owen was barely holding on, and seeing her so broken was making it that much worse.

"Let's go," he told her. "He can't hear us, but I believe he can feel us."

"This could be you," Eden said, her words barely audible. "This has been my worst nightmare from the time I learned you chose to be a firefighter. This could be you. I couldn't handle it, Owen. I couldn't handle the pain—I couldn't bear to have you ripped away from me like this."

He didn't know what to say as he gazed into her anguished face.

"It's not me, Eden," he finally told her. He tried to pull her into his arms, but she backed away.

"You don't understand, Owen. Everyone leaves me. Everyone," she told him. "I can't take it. And if this was you, if you left me like this, it's forever. The job you do is necessary. It's heroic and beautiful. You save people, and I never want to take that from you," she insisted. She was stepping farther away from him. He wanted to go after her, but he knew she couldn't handle it.

"I love you, Eden," he said, not knowing what else to say.

"I know. I love you, too," she admitted. There was so much pain behind the words, though, that he knew she wasn't saying it to tell him they were going to be okay. She was saying it almost as an accusation. "But I can't . . . I just can't."

She turned and walked from the room, leaving him alone. He turned back and looked at his friend, at the broken body lying on the bed. Trevor's family was going through so much pain right now. Would Owen one day put all those he loved through the same? Was his need to save the world causing those he loved the most unbearable agony?

Was it time for him to accept help? Was it time to admit to himself there was only so much he could do? Maybe.

"Goodbye, my friend," he whispered as he looked at Trevor one final time. Then he turned and walked from the room. He needed to alter his life. He was going to start making those changes right now.

◆ ◆ ◆

He punched the wall, a satisfying crunch echoing through his house as a giant hole appeared in the drywall. His body was shaking in rage.

Three men stood before him, fear visible in their eyes and their shaking bodies. With a poise he was known for, he moved across his office and sat down at his desk before looking up with steely eyes.

"Why are they still alive?" he asked.

One of the men stepped forward, clearly the leader of the three of them. He was trying to be brave, but he was weak, just as most people were.

"We've been trying to kill them, sir. They are just a hell of a lot smarter than most people," the minion said.

He didn't blink as he pulled open a drawer, never taking his eyes off the man. He pulled out a gun and pointed it at the guy, watching for only a moment as the man's eyes widened.

He put a bullet in the center of the minion's forehead and watched him drop to the floor. He looked on as a satisfying red stain spread out across his wood floor. Only then did he look up at the other two men, who hadn't moved.

They were clearly terrified, but he had to give them props because they didn't try to run. *Good.* He hated wasting bullets on a man's back. It was much more satisfying to shoot them while they looked at you.

"That's how you kill someone," he said. "See how easy that was?"

Neither of the men said a word as he gripped his gun tightly, not even the smallest of tremors shifting his focus. He thought about what he wanted to do next. His temper had evaporated as quickly as it had arisen.

Exercising the swift arm of justice, he fired twice more, killing the other two men who were useless to him. Then he turned and looked at the man in the corner of the room. His eyes were cold, no fear showing in them.

"Clean up this mess, and get the job done. I'm sick of excuses," he said.

The man nodded.

He put away his gun, then stood and walked from the office.

All traces of his operation were being eliminated from this stupid town. Soon, it would be over, and he'd be gone. But not before he took care of a few of his worst pests. They weren't going to get to go on living their lives when they'd messed with the wrong person.

No. They'd pay for the trouble they'd caused him. They'd pay with their lives.

Chapter Thirty-One

It was getting late, and Eden found herself heading to the lake. She could see the glow of the wildfire lighting up the evening sky, and something drew her near it. With Owen back to work, Eden's world was beginning to crumble. She'd let him in again. She was a fool.

His job was deadly, and she didn't want to be that loved one on the other end of a phone call telling her he wasn't coming home. She didn't want to be the person who had to choose whether to pull the plug or not.

Something inside of her asked if it was worse to not get the phone call, though, to not know if he was okay. She wasn't sure which was worse. She knew whether she was with him or not, she'd hurt beyond repair if something happened to him. The pain would be unbearable if he was no longer in the world. It was all so damn confusing. She didn't know how to process it.

She pulled to a stop on the shore of the lake and stepped from her car. There was so much ash in the air. It covered her vehicle, the buildings, the trees, the land. It took all the color away. But there was an odd beauty to the glow from the flames against the lake. Nature had a way of starting fires to clean things up, just as it created waves and wind tunnels. No one could explain natural disasters, but at the end of the day when one happened, the survivors came together. That was the rainbow at the end of the storm.

But this hadn't been an accident. This fire had been deliberately set, and someone was up to no good. Someone was coming after her, after Owen, after the entire town. She wasn't sure why, hadn't come any closer to finding an answer. And she might not.

She looked out at the lake, at the glow from the fire, at how it reflected off the water. If the thing wasn't so deadly, it would be oddly serene. Maybe it was, and maybe she was simply losing her mind. She wasn't sure.

As she stood there, feeling the calm begin to settle over her, an idea hit Eden—an idea she knew Owen wouldn't like, wouldn't endorse. As a matter of fact, he'd lock her in a jail cell if he figured out the thoughts going through her mind.

But someone was after her. That much was obvious. They'd burned down her house, fired shots at her, and killed people she cared about. This was personal. She couldn't think of anyone she'd wronged, but somehow she'd done just that. Probably the only thing she could do at this point was make herself an open target. They needed to flush this person out, and she could be the bait.

She winced as she thought about how furious Owen would be. Hell, Roxie would be just as upset with her. But she smiled. Just a few short weeks ago, she'd thought she was completely alone in this world, had been at about the lowest place she could possibly be. And now she knew that if something were to happen to her, there were at least two people in this world who'd mourn her loss. That didn't mean she had a death wish. Just the opposite, in fact. But she was determined to catch a killer.

She had to not think about what Owen or Roxie would say. She just wasn't sure how to set the trap. If Owen would work with her, she knew she could pull this off. The problem was, she knew with absolute certainty he wouldn't. That meant she had to come up with a plan on her own.

She'd come up with something foolproof. That was for sure. When Eden made up her mind, she didn't allow anything to stop her. And one thing Eden knew for sure at this point was that she couldn't slow down. If she did, she was afraid the weight of her burdens was going to bury her.

Seeing Trevor on that bed, knowing he wasn't ever getting off it, had hit home in such a painful way that Eden had to focus on something else. She couldn't keep dwelling on what might happen. She had to do something to stop more deaths. She had to save Owen.

One more loss in her life might be the end of her.

Closing her eyes, she took in a breath, imagining it was just a normal day with no fire in the air.

"What do I do?" she asked out loud, needing her dad to help her.

You live your life unafraid. You remember who you are, that no one is better than you, and you're better than no one. You live each day as if it's your last, but you live each moment as if you have forever. Don't let fear bury you. Don't let yesterday define you, and don't let tomorrow scare you. Live your truth and share your light with the world. And then each night you can rest with a clear head and an open heart.

Tears rolled down Eden's cheeks as she remembered her father telling her this after Owen had left town. He'd held her as she cried and assured her she was stronger than she realized, assured her she'd be okay. She felt him so much in this moment that it took her breath away.

"I miss you, Dad. I miss you so much," she said.

I'm with you.

If she let her mind go enough, she could feel his arms around her, could almost believe he really was there with her.

It was *almost* enough.

Chapter Thirty-Two

Eden stayed at the lake until the sun sank below the horizon. She'd left Owen when he needed her most. She knew she had to turn around and go back to him. Fear had made her walk from that room, but love was making her turn around.

He needed to know Trevor's death wasn't on his hands. He'd lasted as long as he had, giving his family a chance to tell him goodbye because of Owen, because Owen and John had risked their lives carrying him down a mountain that had been trying to consume them all. He and John were heroes. And she'd walked from that hospital room with him thinking he was anything other than that. She was stronger than that.

He needed her. And she needed him. They'd take care of each other.

She climbed into her car and raced to his place, knowing that's where she'd find him. His family would want to surround him, take him in their arms, but he wouldn't want them to make him feel better, not when he felt responsible for Trevor's death. She wasn't allowing him to do that to himself, not after all he'd done for her these past few weeks. Not after she'd left him once today.

Though she'd known he'd be home, she was still grateful to see his truck parked crookedly in front of his place. He'd come here in a hurry. He shouldn't have been driving after that visit. Grief could wreak havoc with the body worse than alcohol.

She made her way to his front door. She knocked lightly, and silence greeted her. She tried again, louder this time. Again, all she heard was the sound of bullfrogs croaking beneath his deck.

She took a chance and tried his doorknob. She knew he was inside, and now wasn't the time to respect his privacy. He wouldn't have allowed her to wallow in grief on her own, not if she was the one in unbearable pain.

The doorknob twisted easily in her hand, and she pushed it open, stepping inside the dark entryway. She stopped, letting her eyes adjust. Then she moved forward, somehow knowing he'd be in the den.

That's where she found him.

The only light in the room came from the gas fireplace. Owen was sitting on the couch, a glass of what appeared to be scotch resting easily in his fingers. He looked up, his expression unreadable to most people.

But not to her.

She saw the anguish in his eyes, the firm lines of his mouth, the wrinkle in his brow. He was barely holding it together. There was a mixture of rage and sadness rolling through him, and she didn't know if she was the right person to help him. All she knew was she couldn't walk away again, not right now.

"I can't promise you nothing will ever happen to me," he said before taking another drink. His words were full of anguish, as if he knew it wasn't what she'd come to hear, as if he knew it would make her turn and leave.

She respected him so much more in that moment for being truthful with her, for sharing his pain with her—sharing his soul.

"I'm sorry, Owen, sorry you lost a friend, sorry we haven't caught the person responsible, sorry you were accused. I'm sorry I left," she whispered, moving closer to him, but not reaching out yet. She wasn't sure if that was what he wanted, and right now it was about his needs—not hers.

"It's not your fault. You're scared, too, and it's not your fault Trevor was killed," he told her, his voice low as if he was barely keeping it together.

"I've always hated when people say that," she told him. She took a chance and sat down close to him, still not touching. "When someone says they're sorry, they aren't taking the blame; they're saying they hurt for you. It's an empathy thing," she finished.

She was wondering how she'd gone from wanting to comfort him to lecturing him. She'd known she wasn't the best person for the job. She hadn't had a lot of people in her life she'd needed to carry the burden for. With her father and her, it had been her dad always carrying the burden. Her heart ached at that thought. She'd been selfish all her life, so selfish. She didn't want to be that person anymore.

"I'm just mad right now," he said after a few moments.

She reached out and set her hand on his knee, knowing that sometimes the simplest thing, like another person's touch, could be the only thing that kept a person grounded—it let you know you weren't alone in this vast universe.

"I know you are," she said. "You have every right to be mad. Just don't take the blame on your shoulders. You gave his family a chance to say goodbye. Without you, they wouldn't have been able to do that. So many people lose a loved one, their bodies never recovered. That's even worse than the death because they'll always wonder if they're still out there, always wonder if they've said goodbye too soon. You gave his family moments that are more precious than any other gift you can possibly give."

He was looking at her, and she could have sworn she saw a gleam of tears in his eyes, but he turned away. When he looked at her again, he'd managed to compose himself. She wanted to tell him he could trust her, that he could let go. But she wasn't sure if that was true. Yes, he could trust her right in this moment, but could he tomorrow? She just didn't know. She didn't think she was strong enough to be anyone's rock for very long.

"Thank you for that," he finally said. Then he set the glass down, the rest of the liquor untouched. The light in his eyes shifted, and there was a part of Eden that wanted to run, run fast and far. They were already growing too intimate.

But as he grabbed her, hauling her onto his lap, the thought evaporated. Tonight was about him. That's why she was there. And if he needed her to help him grieve, she'd be there for him in any way he wanted.

His arms engulfed her as he pulled her against his solid chest. Her breasts ached as she felt the heat of his body. It would always be this way between them. They could go twenty years without seeing each other, and the second they were in the same room, she'd feel herself awaken. There'd never been another like him, and she somehow knew there never would.

He cupped the back of her neck and pulled her forward, his lips taking hers in an angry kiss. He was trying to get lost in her, and she wanted to let him know there was a better way.

She kissed him back as she circled her hands behind his neck, then brought them to his cheeks and rested them there. She rubbed her thumbs against his temples in a slow arc. His urgent kiss gentled, his movements becoming less hurried.

The hand gripping her neck loosened, and the one on her lower back began rubbing up and down. She sighed into his mouth. She loved him. Damn, how she loved him.

He made love to her right there on the couch after slowly stripping them both. His lips trailed down her body and back up again. He caressed her, loved her, and got lost with her in a beautiful symphony that healed them both.

When they were finished, he lay against the soft cushions of the couch and cradled her back against his chest. She gazed into the flickering flames in his fireplace. It was still so odd to her how fire was so calming, so beautiful, so warm and comforting . . . and yet so deadly.

"Do you ever think about the fact that fire is essential to our very existence, yet in the blink of an eye, it can also take your life?" she asked.

He was rubbing his fingers along her hip, her stomach, her breasts. She didn't want to feel a response, just wanted to lie there in his arms and feel content. Of course, anytime he touched her, she responded. She decided to try to ignore the heat building again and hopefully get him speaking.

"I've never thought of it like that," he told her. She rubbed the one arm he had wrapped around her, the hand holding her breast.

"It came to me today. I was at the lake. The sun was setting, and the glow from the fire was creating a beautiful backdrop. The scene was something painters can only hope to capture. Fire is beautiful, but dangerous. It gives us warmth and comfort, and it can also destroy our lands and take our lives. I can't think of anything else that has two such extreme differences," she said. "Can you?"

He was quiet for a few moments as he continued rubbing her while he thought about her question.

"Water is beautiful and we need it, but it can be deadly as well," he said.

Now it was her turn to think. "Really, I guess the same can be said for all the natural elements—wind, water, fire, earth. But nothing is as extreme as fire."

"No, there's nothing quite like fire," he agreed.

They lay there in silence again. But it was comfortable, easy, just like it had been so many years before when she'd been happier than she'd ever been, when each day began with excitement.

"I let my grief last too long," she said before realizing she was going to say it. He tensed the slightest bit, then relaxed as he continued rubbing her.

"What do you mean?"

She could tell he hadn't wanted to ask, was most likely afraid to ask. She might as well continue now. "When you left, I hurt so badly—" she began.

"Eden, I'm sorry," he cut in.

"Please just let me say this?" she asked. She was glad her back was to him, but also glad he was holding her. It somehow made it that much easier.

"I was hurt, but we were young. I understand why you left, but you were wrong in how you did it," she told him.

"I know," he said, his voice filled with shame.

"I forgive you," she said, meaning it.

She felt him tense behind her, but this time he didn't say anything; she just felt his arm tighten around her middle as he squeezed her close to him. She'd needed to forgive him for a very long time.

"Then six months ago, I was with you when I lost my dad, and I blamed both you and myself. I thought if I'd have answered that phone call I could have saved him. Or I could have at least spoken to him one last time. It hurts my heart so much that I missed that chance, that I could've had my dad again for even a few minutes. I really thought he'd be here forever. I thought he'd never leave me. When you left me, I didn't feel safe; I felt as if anyone could walk away. My dad was my one anchor in the storm, the one person I knew would never leave. So him doing just that was the ultimate betrayal to me. I wasn't sure I could ever trust another person again. I still have doubts I can. I don't want to feel that way, but I'm scared," she said, stopping when her voice hitched.

"Eden . . . ," he began, and she squeezed his arm.

"I'm sorry, Owen. This night is about you, not me," she said on a hiccupping sob as tears fell down her cheeks.

He raised his hand and wiped them away before turning her so she was facing him. He leaned in and kissed her gently, his strong arms wrapped around her.

"When I'm with you, any pain I feel disappears," he told her. "I love you, Eden." She opened her mouth to beg him not to say that, but he held a finger over her lips. "I know you can't tell me that right now. I also see how you feel by the look in your eyes, by the acceptance of your body. It's okay. I'll build your trust again. Together, we can face anything. We're better with each other than apart."

She didn't want to lie to him, didn't want to deny what he'd just said. But she couldn't say the words she knew he wanted to hear, not right now, not when she was feeling this vulnerable, this open.

"You're a good man, Owen. I'm sorry I doubted that," she said instead.

He smiled before kissing her again. And then they stopped talking. There was one way she could show him she loved him without having to say the words. And that's exactly what she did.

Chapter Thirty-Three

Owen had woken in the middle of the night, his body warm, with Eden locked tightly in his embrace. This was right. It was perfect. It was exactly how they should wake up every single day.

He slowly extracted himself from her arms, enjoying the grumble she let out as she reached for him, her defenses down in her sleep. He knew it wouldn't take a whole lot longer before she realized the past truly was buried and that he wasn't that teenage boy anymore. She'd realize she could trust him, that she did, indeed, have one person on this earth who would carry her burdens. Just as he knew she'd carry his. She'd proved that a few hours earlier.

He lifted her, his heart thumping contentedly when she curled against his chest. He carried her to his bed, and as soon as he lay down next to her, she wrapped herself around him, let out another grumble as if telling him not to leave her again, and then silence filled the room.

Owen fell asleep. When he woke next, his body ached. Eden was wrapped around him, and though they'd made love so many times in the last few days that he'd think he'd be a little bit sated, it was as if he hadn't touched her in months. Maybe there was a fear that this was a dream, that he'd wake up to find her gone when all he wanted to do was have her beside him.

He took his time admiring her. She was so innocent in sleep, her face flushed, her lips turned up, her hair a mess. She was the most beautiful woman he'd ever known, inside and out. He'd truly been a fool to walk away from her, even if he'd done it out of loyalty for a friend he owed his life to.

Her eyes fluttered and his body stirred as if knowing she was waking, knowing he could flip her over and plunge deep within her hot folds. He forced himself to calm down. He craved making love to her, but he wanted her to know it was about so much more than sex. He couldn't prove that to her if he was climbing on top of her every five minutes.

Finally, her eyes opened and she looked at him sleepily, dreamily. She smiled, true joy showing in her expression. This moment right here was indescribable, this unguarded moment where there wasn't a care in the world, where she loved him and he loved her and there were no walls, there was no bitterness. He leaned down and gently ran his lips across hers, and she hummed her approval.

"Good morning," she muttered as she snuggled a little closer, making him pulse with need.

"It's better than good," he said, kissing her again.

She looked confused for a moment, then giggled as she threw her leg over him, obviously feeling as great a need as he did to have their skin touching in every possible place.

"Make love to me, Owen," she said, the words music to his ears.

He didn't even attempt to fight it as he gently pushed her over and began worshiping her body. He never would have enough of her, and he prayed she'd never get enough of him. They'd come out the other side of this together.

His heart thudded as he kissed her slowly, then trailed his lips down her throat, sucking on her skin, enjoying the little gasps she let out. The taste of her nipple took his breath away, and he sucked the pink skin deep in his mouth.

She clutched his head, holding him tight against her breast, and he sucked harder as he pressed his hips forward, trying to feel a bit of relief.

"You taste so good," he murmured against her chest before kissing his way across to the other side. He tasted and nibbled until she was pleading for mercy. She pulled on his hair, and he kissed his way back up her throat, finally bringing his lips back to hers.

His hunger grew as he devoured her mouth, capturing the moans escaping her. He wanted to taste all of her, though, so he trailed his lips back down her body, feeling the shake of her stomach as his tongue circled her belly button before his mouth descended.

He spread her legs wide and gazed at her beauty before leaning forward and tasting her, sweeping his tongue along her heat, the scent of her sending his body into a frenzy of need.

He plunged his tongue deep inside, making her body arch off the bed as she groaned. He moved his lips up and sucked her swollen flesh while pushing his fingers into her slick heat. She screamed as her body went rigid before it came apart, trembles racking her frame.

He slowed the sweep of his tongue along her flesh, and she shook in his arms. He was now ready to claim her as his. He moved back up her body, but she smiled at him, her skin flushed.

Then she pushed him over. "My turn," she whispered against his neck before her lips moved lower and she ran her tongue along his chest, flicking his hard nipples. It was his body arching off the bed now.

She dipped her tongue into his belly button while her hands whispered across his arousal, then swept underneath, her nails scraping along his flesh. Then she pulled him into her hot mouth and sucked hard.

He was on fire and trying desperately not to come, and she moved her head up and down, taking him deeper with each pass. She hummed against him as her hand gripped him and rubbed up and down, his erection slick with her spit.

He felt himself completely losing control.

"You win," he cried out as he reached down and pulled her off him, flipping her over and pressing her into the mattress with his body.

"What do I win?" she panted.

"You drive me crazy," he answered before stopping their conversation by plunging his tongue into her mouth as he surged forward, burying himself in her hot folds.

He didn't want to move slowly. He wanted to take her with as much passion as he felt for her every minute of the day. He gripped her hips and buried himself in her over and over again. She rose up, meeting him with each thrust as their mouths tangled and their bodies heated to unbearable levels.

Their bodies grew slick with sweat as they moved as one. He pulled back in time to see her eyes open when her orgasm ripped through her. She looked dazed as her mouth opened in pleasure.

He let go, releasing inside her, looking deep in her eyes. It was the most beautiful sight he'd ever witnessed.

"I'll never get enough of you," he promised her as the last of his pleasure ebbed from him.

He collapsed on the bed, holding her close to him as he gained control over his breathing.

"I'm afraid I won't ever have enough of you, either," she admitted. The words filled him with unbelievable joy.

When they could move again, he carried her to the bathroom, and they showered together, then took their time helping each other dry off. It took a while before they made their way downstairs to the kitchen. Eden's stomach rumbled, making Owen laugh.

"I guess we can't survive on sex alone," he said.

"I'm starving," she told him. Then her smile faded as she remembered what her father had always said to her when she'd say that. He'd always told her, *You're not starving; children in Africa are starving.* Instead of letting it make her sad, she felt a smile lift her lips. "I mean, I'm hungry."

"Are you okay?" Owen asked as he came to her side and pulled her into his arms.

"There are times I miss my dad so much I feel as if I can't breathe," she said. "He used to always get on me if I said I was starving, pointing out I had no clue what it was like to truly go hungry. Some days I forget he's gone. I mean, I know he's gone, but there are moments, even days, where I experience real joy, and then something will trigger the fact that he's gone, and it brings the pain right back to the surface. I don't know how people ever get over this."

He rubbed her back as he said a quick prayer that his parents were okay. He wasn't sure how he'd handle losing them, or any of his siblings . . . or Eden. He squeezed her a little tighter.

"I think people get through it because they don't lose everyone on the same day, so they always have someone to share their grief, and to keep leaning on. I think we also get through it knowing the loss isn't forever, that we get to see them again someday."

She let out a shaky sob before pulling herself together. He watched the strength come back into her expression. "What if there isn't another side?" she asked.

"I choose to believe there is," he answered. "Otherwise, what's the point of living? If we're only here for a short time, why should we love the way we love? Why should we trust? If losing someone is too painful to bear, we couldn't survive as a species. I'd much rather believe there's something after this earthly life."

"I just wish I knew for sure. I wish . . ." She trailed off and he held her.

"He's going to always be with you. In your memories, in your thoughts, in your prayers. And when you have kids, remember that a piece of him will be in them, too. They might have his eyes, or his hair, or his smile. They might have his laugh. You have the same nose as your dad, and when you roll your eyes, you're his spitting image."

She laughed as she pulled back, her eyes still sparkling with tears, but there was joy in them as well. She was more beautiful than she'd ever been.

"Thank you, Owen. I truly needed to hear that. It's the best thing anyone has said to me since I lost him," she said. She leaned in and kissed him. "Now I need to have a baby."

She turned away as she walked to the fridge, and Owen felt his heart thump so hard he was surprised it didn't rip right out of his chest. He wanted to grab her, haul her back to the bedroom, and tell her that her wish was his command. If she wanted a baby, he'd damn well be the person giving it to her.

He knew she'd just been making a joke. But maybe she hadn't. He had to force himself not to scare the living hell out of her by pursuing that line of thought. She turned from the fridge and looked at him in disgust, and he worried she'd been reading his mind.

"How do you live like this?" she asked.

He was confused. "What do you mean?" He slowly walked to her.

"You have a case of beer, a tub of expired butter, and a loaf of bread with mold growing on it."

He looked at the contents of his fridge and gave a shrug. "I don't like to cook. I either act pathetic enough for one of my siblings to feed me—or usually their wives, since my brothers don't care if I starve—or I go to the diner," he said, as if that was perfectly normal.

"People need to have the basics at home," she said.

He pointed to the door of the fridge. "I have coffee creamer. I'm not a heathen."

She laughed at that as she pulled the creamer out, double-checking the expiration date just to be sure he wasn't going to poison her. Of course he'd never do that—not intentionally, at least.

"I'll take you to breakfast," he said.

She looked pointedly down at his T-shirt that she was wearing. "I might get arrested if I go out like this."

"You definitely can't go out like that, or I'll be fighting off the entire town as all the men try to take you away from me."

She laughed again. "I'm going to snoop through your bookshelves while you run to the store and get groceries; then we can make breakfast like two normal human beings," she said.

He looked at her blankly for a moment. "You want me to go shopping?"

She laughed again, this time the sound definitely filled with joy. "You've been on your own a long time, and shopping is a necessity. How have you survived so far?"

"I just explained that," he told her. It was pretty simple. "I eat at other houses or diners."

"What about when you didn't live near your family?" For the first time, she said this without looking hurt, without adding "when you left me."

"Takeout and delivery," he said, as if that was no big deal.

"You're terrible," she told him with a laugh. "I like to eat at home. Now go and find us food, or there will be no more sleepovers." The main thing he got from those last sentences was that there would indeed be more sleepovers. He'd give her the moon if that's what it would take to keep her at his side.

"Yes, ma'am," he told her with a salute. He'd go to Antarctica if it ensured she would stay with him . . . forever. Her laughter followed him all the way up the stairs as he threw on a pair of sweats and his favorite raggedy jogging sweatshirt.

He was whistling as he slipped from the house.

Today was going to be a great day. And each new day would get better. As long as he knew he could come home to Eden, he knew he could face anything.

Owen got to the store with no clue what to buy. He sweet-talked a clerk into helping him and ended up with pastries, bread, eggs, sausage, lunch meat, and a variety of snack foods. He figured he'd have Eden help him out with the dinner items. He threw in a couple of bottles of whipped cream, planning on using that in the bedroom. He had to stop that train of thought immediately or risk embarrassing himself and the young clerk helping him.

Owen's drive back had him grinning just as widely as his drive there. The shopping had taken him longer than he'd wanted, and he was sure Eden was starving . . . um . . . *very* hungry right about now, but she'd sent a novice to do her bidding. Maybe she'd found some crackers or something to take the edge off her appetite until he got back. He had no idea if he had anything edible in the pantry, but he was sure he at least had some peanuts or pretzels, something that went well with beer.

As Owen turned off the main road toward his house, his gut clenched. He knew something was wrong—something was very wrong. He floored the gas pedal as he wound his way down the drive. He had a sudden urgency to get to Eden. How could he have forgotten for even a few minutes that someone was out to get her?

When he turned the final bend in the road, his heart nearly stopped in his chest. He slammed on his brakes, jumped from his truck, and circled his house, looking for a way inside.

His entire wraparound deck was engulfed in flames, the fire licking its way up the walls. And from the devastating circle of fire, he had no doubt this wasn't an accidental burn. This was arson.

"Eden!" he yelled at the top of his lungs, praying she was already outside of the house. He lapped the entire structure, his eyes going everywhere. He called it in while running in a circle. He hung up and called out her name over and over. He was about to jump through the flames when he heard her voice.

He looked around, then realized her voice was coming from up high. He arched his neck and found her on the roof of the house, her expression frightened and furious.

"Someone lit your house on fire!" she yelled. "I'm sorry."

He looked up at her incredulously, his heart completely stalled as he choked on fear. The flames were reaching for her, and he couldn't even put a ladder against the house. If he had a fire truck, he could save her, but he feared they weren't going to get there in time. He didn't even have a damn fire blanket so he could rush through the flames to get to her.

He was going to run through them, no matter what. He prepared to do just that. He had to find the best place possible so he didn't burn up and do her no good at all.

"Forget about my damn house," he called. "I'm going to get to you!" His voice was panicked, not assuring. He was normally good at his job. But this wasn't a job. This was the woman he loved, and her life was in mortal danger.

"I'm going to jump into your pool," she called down. "By the time I realized the place was on fire, it was surrounded. The air constantly smells like smoke with the wildfire going, so that didn't alert me. It was the heat. I was reading."

Owen had a hard time keeping up with her. How could she have a rational conversation with him when she was shouting from his damn roof? He wanted to kiss her and strangle her at the same time.

He looked over to his pool, which was only eight feet at the deep end. He then looked at the height she was jumping from. With his tall ceilings, she was the equivalent of three stories up. It was doable but risky. She had to jump just right. It might be her only chance.

"You're aging me right now, baby. You have to jump from the right side of the house, fling your body out, and aim for the middle of the pool." He tried to sound encouraging, but fear was choking him.

"I was on the swim team. I know how to jump into water," she said. He finally heard a trace of fear in her voice. She was desperately trying to hide it, for his sake. The fear encouraged him. She knew to be careful, knew this wasn't just a walk in the park.

A sudden loud bang sounded, and Owen watched in horror as his front porch collapsed. The fire was inside the house. This had to happen now.

"You need to jump, Eden. I'm right here," he said as he stood next to the pool. He couldn't remember ever having felt this much fear, this much helplessness, not even when flames were nipping at his feet, circling him, surrounding him from every direction. That was his life. This was hers.

"I got this," she said with a slight wobble to her voice. She stepped back out of his view for a moment. Then he watched as she launched herself from the roof. He didn't take a single breath as she headed toward the pool feetfirst. For one moment it looked as if she wasn't going to make it, as if she'd land on the pavement. He quickly moved, holding out his arms to do his best to catch her. He'd take the impact to save her.

But she did make it, flying over the top of him, making a perfect arrow into the pool. Another loud crash happened as his roof began collapsing. He didn't care. He dove into the pool and swam to her, pulling her into his arms as she emerged from the water, coughing.

"Are you okay? Does anything feel broken?" he asked as he rubbed his hands along her entire body while dragging them to the shallow end of the pool. Thank goodness he had cement separating the house from the pool, or they'd be surrounded in this thing, too.

"I'm cold but fine," she told him, her teeth chattering.

He walked to the steps, lifting her in his arms as he carried her out. He took her to his truck and set her inside, giving her body another examination.

"I'm fine, Owen. I promise." She turned and looked at his house. "But your house . . ." Tears fell down her face.

"The house doesn't matter. It's just wood and plaster. We'll build a new one together," he told her. He jumped up in the cab with her and pulled her close as they heard the sound of sirens in the distance.

Whoever had come close to taking her life had seriously screwed up this time. They'd come for her too many times. Owen wouldn't sleep until they were behind bars.

Chapter Thirty-Four

The next few hours were an utter blur for Eden. The fire department came, and she sat back as she watched Owen help his crew put out the flames engulfing his house. There was about as much left as there'd been of her own place. It was heartbreaking.

Yes, she'd been terrified as she'd made her way onto the roof of his house, knowing it was her only chance of getting free. But she'd also been grateful Owen wasn't trapped in there with her. To watch him die would be unbearable.

But she was okay, and he was okay. She tried telling herself it was just a house. But both of them had lost everything within a week. Who could be this savage? Who wanted them dead this badly? Would they ever figure it out?

By the time it was over, all Eden wanted to do was be alone, go somewhere and have a little bit of time to think. She wasn't sure anything could make it better, but she needed some time.

Owen came to check on her, and the worry in his eyes wasn't helping her stay calm. She shivered in fear. He pulled her close.

"I'm sorry," he said for the hundredth time.

"This isn't your fault. Please quit apologizing, and please don't worry about me," she said. She kissed him to take any sting from her words. He didn't seem appeased. "I'm going to town. I want to change and look over my papers," she added.

"I'll come with you," he told her.

She smiled as she cupped his cheek. "No. You stay here. We'll meet up in a couple of hours." He looked as if he was going to argue with her. "Please. I need this."

At those words he looked utterly defeated. "Only a couple of hours?" he questioned.

"Only a couple of hours," she promised.

He walked her to her car, and she kept her composure as she started it and drove away, looking back at him; he looked like a lost puppy while he watched her leave. She didn't allow herself to so much as tremble until she was around the corner.

That's when she pulled her car over and took some deep breaths. She was a strong person, but she just wasn't sure how much more of this she was going to be able to manage. She shook her head as she pushed away that thought. She'd take whatever she needed to, because she wouldn't let this person get the best of her.

Somehow she found herself driving toward the airport where she'd met Sherman what felt like forever ago. She was trying to remember when she'd taken her flight with him, but she couldn't quite pinpoint it. Maybe a week ago. Heck, maybe a day ago. She was so fried she had no idea. But that had been a great day.

She liked the privacy of the airport, and maybe Sherman would be there. He was easy to talk to. And though she wanted to be alone, he was someone who seemed safe to her.

There were no cars parked there when she arrived. She was relieved. She should have headed back to Roxie's, but she didn't want to try to keep her composure anymore. She wanted to have a good cry without having to explain why.

She moved to the back of the hangar and looked out at the hills beyond. The fire was moving closer to this place. She hoped it didn't consume the hangar, this haven. She hoped it didn't consume the entire town.

She heard the crunch of boots rounding the back of the hangar, and her heart started pounding before she forced herself to calm down. This was a private hangar, a private runway. Only those who had planes came here. It was most likely Sherman looking for her, since he'd seen her car parked out front.

She turned, forcing a smile she didn't feel. The person turned the corner, but it wasn't Sherman. She hoped she was hiding her disappointment as he drew closer.

"Hi, Chaz," she said as he sidled up beside her.

"Hey, Eden. What are you doing here?" he asked before looking her over in a way that made her just the slightest bit uncomfortable. "And why are you all wet?"

She'd completely forgotten that her clothes were still wet. They weren't dripping, since she'd had a couple of hours in the heat of Owen's truck, but they definitely had seen better days, and she'd be throwing them out as soon as she could peel them from her body. She was just glad she'd changed before the fire had started, or she'd have been having a wet-T-shirt contest in front of the entire Edmonds Fire Department—and Chaz.

"It's a long story," she said with a wave of her hand. "I came out here to get away from the noise of the city," she added.

Chaz smiled, an expression that didn't quite reach his eyes. And in that moment, everything seemed to click into place. Eden's stomach sank as she looked at the man who seemed to be enjoying the dawning horror of her look.

"Is there something wrong?" he asked, moving a little closer.

"No, nothing," she said, instinctively moving away from him. "It's just that Owen will be here any minute, so I should wait at my car." She really hoped her bluff would work.

"I don't think so, Eden. He's fighting a fire right now," Chaz said. He wasn't even going to try to pretend to be the good guy any longer.

Eden was in trouble. She was in big trouble, and she knew it. Chaz's smile widened.

Chapter Thirty-Five

Eden knew she had two choices. She could run screaming—not getting very far. Or she could play dumb and hope Chaz didn't realize she now knew at least one of the players in this deadly game.

What she didn't understand was why. She had a slight history with Chaz, but nothing that made any sense of why he'd want to kill her. She vaguely remembered he'd asked her out on a date once. She hadn't wanted to date, hadn't been interested in anyone. It was hard to be interested when Owen came in and out of her life.

But she'd accepted Chaz's friendship, had gone to lunch with him several times, had even taken some walks with him on her breaks at work. This made no sense at all. He was successful, charming, and wealthy. Why would he throw all of that away?

"I'm glad you're here, Chaz," she said with what she hoped passed as a friendly smile. "It's kind of eerie out here all by myself."

She saw that her words confused him, that he was trying to decide what to do next. That was a positive in her favor. She found her hand in her pocket as she searched for anything to defend herself with. There was nothing.

"Yeah, this place is private. I like it," he said as he moved a step closer. She desperately wanted to retreat.

"Have you seen Sherman? I went flying with him a few days ago. It was a lot more fun than I imagined it would be. I can see why you became a pilot," she said, hoping the stroke to his ego would afford her some mercy. She shouldn't have come out here when she'd known someone was after her.

"Sherman isn't really out here much. No one is," he said, his smile becoming even broader. He took another step closer. Eden turned as she looked out at the mountain, stepping away from him as if she was enamored with the view. She was really looking around for anything that could be a weapon. Pebbles just weren't going to do it.

"That's too bad. Once a person retires, they should be able to do whatever they want." This small talk was killing her.

"How are things going with you and Owen?" he asked, his smile fading.

"They are the same as always," she told him. There was no way she was getting into a discussion of her and Owen with this man.

"Yeah, you guys are together a heck of a lot. It's difficult to find you alone," Chaz said, not even trying to hide his pleasure at finding her so defenseless now. He moved closer. She was on the verge of panic.

"He's been a friend for a long time, and there's a lot going on right now," she said, knowing she was running out of time.

"I had a crush on you once, you know," Chaz said, a look of humor in his eyes.

"I didn't know that," she told him with a laugh she didn't feel.

"Business gets in the way of me pursuing relationships, though."

"Yes, you're gone a lot with your real estate deals," she said. She had nowhere to run.

"That's just a side business. It's not where I make all my money," he told her.

"Oh, that's nice," she said. She wasn't going to ask him for information. He just might let her go if he figured she didn't know anything, if he didn't deem her a threat. She somehow knew it was far too late for that, though.

"Aren't you going to ask me what my business is?" he asked, sidling a bit closer. She was stepping away from him, not wanting him to grab her. There was no way for her to fight him off. Her only chance was if someone else showed up. Silence greeted that thought.

"It's none of my business what you do," she told him.

He smiled. "That's where you're wrong, Eden. It's very much your business, since you and your friends have been messing with it, have cost me far too much money."

Utter silence greeted these words. She stared at him, not knowing what she should say to that.

"Please don't do this, Chaz," she said. She couldn't keep pretending he wasn't being hostile when he was saying these sorts of things to her, advancing on her, cornering her.

"Do what, Eden? What do you think's happening here?" he asked.

"I don't know," she said.

He moved closer and Eden tried to pull out her cell phone, but his eyes latched onto it. He grabbed it before she could stop him, throwing it against the wall of the hangar, the screen shattering. She was in worse trouble than she'd imagined.

"Taking you out wasn't part of the plan, but then you started investigating this case, and my boss has no tolerance for anyone who messes with us," Chaz told her.

"Chaz, you don't want to do this. It will ruin your life," she warned him.

He laughed for a long moment, the sound containing zero humor. "My life is already ruined. You and your buddies have seen to that. Our entire operation has been destroyed. We had to burn it all down—the factory, the buildings, all of it. But it's been a pretty burn, hasn't it?" he asked as he looked out at the smoke-filled landscape.

"Why?" she asked. She was going to die. He'd just admitted to being part of this disaster. He wouldn't leave her as a witness.

"We've been making money hand over fist for years, no one the wiser. Then that fool of a vice principal got caught with a hell of a lot of our merchandise, and the damn Forbes family got involved. Declan's been hot on our case ever since. They nearly discovered our factory, so it had to go. We lit it up. We've almost covered all our tracks, but you've gotten too close, so you have to go, too," he said, a laugh escaping him. "And I've never liked Owen, so I wanted to take him out just for the fun of it. He was supposed to die up on that hill, but he sacrificed his buddy instead."

She glared at him.

"He tried to save him," she said.

Chaz's smile fell away as he glared back at her. "You're going to defend him to the end, aren't you? Disgusting, considering he left you as if you meant no more to him than stale bread."

"You know nothing," she said, hating how scared she was, hating the tears that wanted to fall.

"I know enough to kill you," he told her.

He advanced on her, his intent clear.

Eden wouldn't just stand there. She turned to flee, her heart racing. She only made it a few steps before his fingers fisted in her hair, stopping her dead in her tracks as he bruised her scalp and threw her to the ground. The air rushed from her as she scraped her back and elbow. She felt dizzy as he loomed over her.

Chaz pulled out a revolver and pointed it at her. Eden's heart thumped. She wasn't ready to die, wasn't ready to let go of her life.

"Please don't do this, Chaz. I'm sorry. I won't tell anyone," she said, hating it when a tear fell down her cheek. She didn't want to be this weak, didn't want to plead for her life.

There was a boom behind them, and Eden turned her head. Something in the woods had exploded. She looked back at Chaz, who was gazing in the same direction, his eyes fascinated. Eden knew this was her last chance.

She jumped to her feet and ran as if her life depended on it. Of course, her life *did* depend on escaping. It was foolish to run toward the fire, but maybe she could hide in the trees, maybe lose him in the smoke. She was amazed when she entered the thick grove of trees. Her throat was burning as her mouth filled with the hot taste of ash.

She almost smiled as she turned and ran through the bushes, looking for a place to hide. Maybe she'd done it. Maybe he'd been so enamored with the disaster his actions had created, he hadn't noticed her sprint to safety. She was feeling hope. That was until her arm was practically ripped from its socket, and she was thrown to the ground again. Her head spun as it slammed down against a rock.

The world went black.

Chapter Thirty-Six

Owen stood back as the rest of his house collapsed. He should feel more anger, feel something other than relief. He certainly wasn't relieved his house and everything he owned were gone. He was relieved the woman he loved was safe.

But just as he had that thought, a chill ran through him. He didn't know what it was, but he was suddenly uncomfortable, as if something was wrong. He stepped away from the noise as firefighters continued checking the perimeter of his house, making sure the fire didn't spread. The last thing they needed was another point of origin for the wildfire to grow.

He picked up his cell phone and dialed her number. It went straight to voice mail. He tried again and it was the same thing. He tried to tamp down the panic that wanted to stir in his gut. But something was wrong. He could feel it. He dialed Kian's house. Roxie picked up on the second ring.

"Has Eden made it back yet?" he asked without a greeting.

"I haven't seen her," she said, her voice concerned as she recognized the tenseness in his words. "Is everything okay?"

"I don't know. I have this feeling," he said, restless. He needed to find her. "Some asshole burned down my house, and she said she needed time alone." Why had he let her go?

"Let me make some calls," Roxie said, her voice now as tense as his.

They hung up and Owen made a few of his own calls, all without getting anything satisfactory. No one had seen her. Then his phone rang. It was Roxie.

"Owen, someone said they passed her car on the road leading to the private airstrip. You know, where Sherman keeps his plane. Would there be a reason she'd be out there?" Roxie asked, her voice puzzled.

"She wanted to be alone," he said, trying to feel relief. At least he had an idea of where she was. The knowledge that something was wrong wouldn't leave him, though.

"I'll head out there," she told him.

"Not alone. Bring Kian, and call Declan and Arden. I'm on my way there," he said.

"Get there fast," Roxie told him. She trusted him, trusted that he knew something was wrong. They hung up and Owen rushed to his truck.

He didn't say a word to anyone, didn't explain his urgency. He didn't notice the puzzled looks from his men as he peeled off down the driveway. His property was being taken care of. All he cared about right now was getting to Eden. Something was wrong and he feared he was going to get to her too late.

He pressed his foot down on the gas pedal and picked up speed. If a cop spotted him, good. He could lead him to the airport and have more backup. Owen feared he was going to need it.

He was a fool. If he hadn't been in such shock over finding her on the roof of his burning house, he wouldn't have let her drive off by herself. It wasn't a matter of trying to control her; it was a matter of knowing the enemy was stepping up their game.

He drove a little faster. Time was running out. He didn't know how he knew that. He just knew.

Chapter Thirty-Seven

Eden woke with a splitting headache. She tried to lift a hand to assess the damage done to her head, and that's when she realized her hands were bound. Panic seized her as she realized she was tied up.

Opening her eyes, it took a moment for her vision to clear. The smoke seemed heavier, and she wondered how close she was to the flames. She wondered if Chaz had left her there to die a slow, tortured death. If so, she could only hope the smoke would take her before the flames did. Tears tracked down her cheeks.

"It took you long enough to wake up. I was worried for a while that you might have killed yourself," Chaz said, almost conversationally.

She turned her head and found him sitting close by, a large knife in his hands, his fingers tracing the shiny silver blade as if mesmerized. Another dark shiver raced down her spine.

"What comes next?" she asked. She'd rather know. This fear was more than she could take.

"I'm going to kill you," he said simply. "You know too much, and you have to die." He paused as his horrible eyes traced her entire body, filling her with disgust. "But I figure we have a little time. I might as well get a taste of you first. Let's call it payment for the trouble you've caused."

"Don't you dare touch me, you disgusting pig!" she shouted. She'd rather die than have this man's hands on her, to have her last moments tainted by him.

His eyes narrowed, but he didn't move. She had a decision to make. She knew she wasn't getting out of this alive. He'd bound her. She'd tried to make her escape and had failed. The only thing she could hope for was that her body was found so Owen and Roxie could have closure.

"Owen's next, you know. I want that to be your dying thought. I want you to know he won't make it another few days. I might not have been able to get him yet, but he will die." The eerie way he spoke so calmly was almost worse than if he were yelling. At least then she'd feel that she could enrage him, do anything that would make her death swift instead of drawn out. She wasn't sure she could shake this zombie of a man, though.

"I'm not surprised you've lost everything, Chaz. You're disgusting and stupid. You have no sense at all. You'll continue to lose everything in your life, including any so-called friendships you have. And that boss you speak of will dispose of you because you're a loose end for him, just as I am for you."

His eyes narrowed, but he shook his head, and an evil smile appeared on his lips. He stood up and moved toward her, slow and deliberate, as he held out the knife. Worst of all, his other hand shifted, rubbing over the front of his jeans, and she was horrified to see the bulge in his pants. Her stomach rolled.

"I know you're trying to piss me off. It might have worked on someone else, but not on me. I finally have you right where I want you, and I'm going to savor every moment of it. No one's coming to your rescue. I can play with you for hours if I like," he said.

He loomed over her as he clasped the knife in one hand and undid the top button of his jeans with the other. Eden twisted and pulled against the ties that bound her arms behind her back.

Chaz kneeled in front of her, grabbing her hair and lifting her painfully off the ground so she was forced to her knees. She twisted her head and spit at him. Her mouth was so dry there was barely any moisture. Chaz laughed as he leaned in toward her, licking her lips.

She tried to hold it back, but a sob ripped from her, and this made him laugh. He still held the knife in his other hand, and he lifted it, the tip resting against her neck as he ran his tongue along her jaw. She was trembling.

The blade nicked her throat, and Eden prayed he'd screw up, that he'd gouge her before he could rape her. Death was so much better than what he had planned for her. She was going to die, anyway. She'd rather it happen before this man took from her everything that was good.

"You're a very pretty woman. It'll be a shame to kill you," he said, a husky murmur in his voice that made her stomach roll again. She wished she could puke all over him. Maybe that would disgust him too much to continue. But there was nothing in her stomach.

"I hate you," she said, her voice filled with revulsion.

"That's okay. I don't care. Fight me. It'll make this so much more fun," he said. He set the knife down, and much to her horror, he gripped her head, then bent and lapped up the blood on her neck. Her stomach turned again, but nothing came out.

"You're going to suck me, and if I feel anything from your teeth, I'll rip them out, and we'll do it again," he said with glee. He let her go and backed up a few paces as he began undoing his pants.

"If you put anything in my mouth, there won't be anything left of it," she warned. Her body had grown cold. She wasn't going to be able to stop this.

Chaz looked at her and smiled again. She knew at this point that he was completely out of his mind. He stopped undoing his pants, and suddenly there were flashes of lights all around her as his fist connected with her jaw. Pain seared through her head. She wondered if he'd broken her teeth like he'd threatened. She didn't care anymore.

"Be a good girl," he said.

Eden opened her mouth and screamed. The sound echoed around them, and Chaz laughed even harder as he reached for his pants again.

"Go ahead and scream all you want!" he yelled. "No one can hear you."

He finished unbuttoning his pants and was beginning to pull them down when there was a noise behind them. Chaz turned, but not fast enough. Owen came flying out of nowhere, rage unlike anything she'd seen before masking his face. He smashed into Chaz, the two of them soaring through the air before landing on the ground. Chaz's head crashed down hard enough that it should have knocked the man out. Owen gripped it, pulling his head up and smashing it down again.

"You son of a bitch!" Owen roared. Eden had never seen that sort of look on him before. It was enough to send another shiver through her. He was furious. Chaz didn't have time to react.

"You're both going to die," Chaz said, but his voice was weak. Owen had his hands around the man's neck, and Eden feared he was going to kill him. No, she had no sympathy for Chaz. He'd been about to rape her, and he'd have killed her with zero remorse. But she didn't want Owen to live with the reality of taking the life of another person. He was too kind, too good of a man, and it would haunt him.

"I'll kill you for touching her," Owen hissed, his fingers white as he pushed them harder against Chaz's throat.

Eden was trying to find her voice, trying to tell him to stop. She began coughing, and Owen's fingers eased the slightest bit as he looked at her, allowing a small amount of air to get into Chaz's deprived lungs.

"Owen, you have to stop. You can't do this. Let the law have him. Let the victims of the families see him in court," Eden said. Her voice was weak. The smoke was growing thicker. It was getting harder to breathe.

"What?" Owen said, looking as if he were in a daze. "I can't let him go," he told her.

"No, don't let him go. Tie him up. Let's bring him down the mountain," she said. Then she began choking again. She was having a hard time breathing. "Owen, please," she said, her eyes watering.

"Did he hurt you?" Owen asked, his hands still against Chaz's neck, but not pressing so tightly.

"No," she lied. "You found me in time." She smiled at him as best she could, trying to assure him she was fine. But his eyes narrowed as he looked at her jaw. She was sure there was a hell of a bruise forming.

A spark flew through the air, and Eden looked to her left and saw a bush light on fire. She turned back to Owen with panic.

"Please untie me. We have to go," she said. The bush crackled, and it was only a matter of time before they were circled by a ring of death.

Owen realized the same thing. He let go of Chaz, who didn't appear as if he'd be going anywhere anytime soon. Owen rushed to Eden's side and began undoing the knots on her hands. She shook with terror and relief as the knots loosened.

Owen hauled her into his arms, and she wept. They didn't have time for this, but she needed to be in the comfort of his arms more than anything else. Both of them had temporarily forgotten about Chaz.

Another spark landed about three feet from them, and fire exploded. Owen pulled away from her, and they both turned to where Chaz had been. A sound to their left caught their attention, and they saw him running up the hill.

"We can't let him go," Eden said, panic in her voice.

"He's running into the fire. He's not going anywhere," Owen said. He seemed relieved.

"But what if he gets away? What if he causes more damage?"

"He can't make it out of this in that direction, Eden. We have to go now." There was urgency in his voice, and the smoke was growing thicker. She nodded, and the two of them began running in the opposite direction of Chaz. They needed to get the hell out of there before they were consumed.

The two of them never looked back as they made their way down the hill. She realized Chaz must have carried her farther up the mountain from where she'd fallen when it took them longer than expected to escape. She was glad Owen was there, or she never would've found her way down.

But as they descended, the air got a little clearer, and she found her lungs weren't burning nearly as badly. Her entire throat felt as if it had been scorched, but she was alive, and Owen was with her.

"How did you find me?" she asked as they continued moving down the hill.

"Someone saw you driving out here," he told her. "I saw your car, then walked to the back and saw blood on the ground. It was the worst moment of my life." A shudder went through him. "Then there was more blood. I followed it. I heard you scream, and blind rage took over."

As much as her head was killing her, she was grateful for the injury. Without it, Owen would never have found her. There was no way he could have. That injury had ultimately saved her life.

The two of them broke through the trees, and only then did Owen stop and turn her, pulling her into his arms again as he ran his hands up and down her back, her arms, the tops of her legs.

"Where are you hurt?" he asked, as if the words gave him great pain.

"I don't know. I know I hit my head, but I'm lucky, Owen. You came just in time. He didn't get to hurt me," she assured him.

"I should've killed the bastard," Owen said as he leaned back and looked at her with such pain in his eyes it was heartbreaking.

"No, you shouldn't have. You're not a killer, and it would've haunted you. You're a good man, Owen, and he'll be caught, or he'll die in the fire. Either way, he'll pay for what he's done," she told him.

There were sirens, making both of them turn. Coming down the road was what appeared to be a fleet of emergency vehicles. Eden looked at him in surprise.

"Did you call the National Guard?" she asked, amazed she could find any humor in this situation.

"When I saw that blood . . ." He stopped as he cleared his throat. "When I saw that, I didn't know what to think. I called Declan and told him to get the damn marines here," he said.

"It looks like he might have." Several vehicles rushed around the back of the building as they saw the two of them. An ambulance was next.

Owen squeezed her, then gave her a quick kiss before they were intercepted, the two of them pulled apart as questions were fired at them, and she was placed on a gurney. She tried telling everyone she was fine. No one seemed to hear her. She just continued to stare at Owen, who kept his hand in hers as he told the men about Chaz and his last known location.

"If he's not dead already, he'll pay," a man said.

They'd found the arsonist. At least that much good had come out of all of this. Eden closed her eyes as an oxygen mask was placed over her mouth. She might need to take a little nap.

She was relieved when the world once again went black.

Chapter Thirty-Eight

There was a quiet hum of voices when Eden regained consciousness. She kept her eyes closed, not quite ready to wake. Instead, she listened, trying to figure out where she was and who she was hearing. It didn't take long to recognize Owen's voice, and then Roxie's.

She smiled, unable to help herself. Just a few short weeks ago, she'd been cursing the heavens, the entire universe. She'd been so angry with everything in this world. And now she felt more love than she'd thought she'd ever feel again after the loss of her father.

Her eyes opened.

It wasn't just Owen and Roxie in her room, but what appeared to be Owen's entire family. The room was bigger than some hotel suites she'd once cleaned to earn a paycheck. There was a seating area in the corner where Owen was speaking to his family.

As if he could feel her looking at him, he turned, his lips going up as their gazes locked. Eden loved him so much. But even knowing that, she wasn't sure what it meant. Was love enough? Their love had nearly destroyed each other time and time again. It had been wonderful on some occasions, and heart-wrenching on others.

Was love enough?

"I've been worried," Owen said. He'd stopped speaking in the middle of a sentence and was now by her side. Roxie quickly approached on the other side of the bed. Eden looked from her to Owen and back again.

"How long have I been out?" she asked. She was surprised by the sound of her voice. It sounded nothing like her. She cleared her throat and realized she had the mother of all sore throats. That was the worst, in her opinion. The flu was gone within twenty-four hours, and a cold was irritating, but a few pills usually took the worst of it away. But a sore throat made it impossible to eat anything, and doing something as simple as swallowing your own spit sent arrows of pain all the way down to what felt like your stomach.

"Two hours, fifteen minutes," Owen replied as he looked at the clock.

"He's been tracking it, annoying the nursing staff every five minutes when you didn't wake," Roxie said. "To be honest, I might have yelled a time or two," she added sheepishly.

"I'm okay," Eden said, though her body felt as if it had been run over by a dump truck, then scooped inside and tossed down a hill.

"You're not okay, but you will be," Owen said. He sat down next to her so he could bring his head closer. "I'm sorry it took me so long to get to you. I'm sorry that man got his hands on you."

"I'm just glad you came when you did. My stubbornness and refusal to believe I was really in danger put all of us at risk. That's unacceptable. I need to be more conscious of what's happening around me. I had no idea Chaz was part of the drug ring. I didn't know this fire was a part of that circle. I thought we'd gotten through the worst of it when Ethan was found out. If I would've been a better investigator, maybe our homes would still be standing."

"Our homes don't matter," he told her. "All that matters is you're okay. And you did a good enough job that you scared the hell out of the criminals. They wouldn't have come after you so hard had you not," he pointed out.

"Was Chaz caught?" she asked.

He shook his head. "Not yet, but there's a manhunt the Texas Rangers would be proud of going on right now. We're going to catch him . . . and make him talk."

"Good. I won't feel at ease until he's caught," she admitted.

"You won't be alone. You're safe," he said, fierceness in his eyes.

"I should call this in. They were pulling me from this case, anyway, and I think I might want to gloat just the tiniest bit that I solved it," she said, making Roxie laugh. "Even if it was really more of me stumbling into it and coming close to dying." The laughter stopped.

"The investigators have already been notified," Owen said. "You don't need to worry about any of that." She opened her mouth to speak, but he continued. "And you received credit for solving the mystery of how the fire got started."

"I don't need credit. I just wanted them to know I wasn't as biased as they thought. I thought I wanted it to be you who was guilty because maybe that would help me not love you anymore. But I knew all along you weren't capable. If the arson investigators had done their job right, they'd have known it, too."

Owen was silent for a few moments as he looked down at her. She couldn't really read his expression, which surprised her. He was normally an open book.

"We've been through a lot in a short time," he said.

"We've been through a lot our entire lives," she responded, chuckling a bit, which sent pain shooting down her throat. She accepted the ice water Roxie handed her and took a sip.

"I've messed up so many times, but I do love you, Eden. I want to be there for you the rest of our lives," he said. It could've been just the two of them in the room. Eden didn't see or hear anyone else. She was quiet as he waited for her response.

"We *have* been through a lot, and our adrenaline is pumping fast and steady right now. I think we need to have this discussion later."

She was surprised to see hope bloom in his eyes. "I can do that," he told her, his lips turning up in a wide smile. "Because I have no doubt about the way I feel about you, and I know you love me, too."

He leaned down and gently kissed her. There was a low whistle from the other side of the room, and Eden found her cheeks flushing as she looked over to where his brothers wore wide grins.

"I'm not promising you anything," she said, hating that they had an audience.

"That's okay, because I'll promise you the world," he offered.

She couldn't look over at his family, couldn't tear her gaze away from Owen. She was so confused right now. She'd been confused for what felt like forever. She turned to Roxie, who now seemed a bit uncomfortable witnessing this intimate moment.

"Tell me what the cops have on Chaz," she practically begged, needing to have a subject change. Roxie was more than eager to share.

"They went to his house, and, man, did they get a lot of information," Roxie said. "They are most likely still going through it all."

"Like what?" Eden asked.

"He had a crapload of drugs in there, and a file with a lot of addresses. I really think he was so pompous he didn't think they'd ever suspect him. There were also all sorts of newspaper articles plastered on his wall of the damage the fire was doing, on the fire department's activities, and on all the Forbes men. This investigation is busted wide open now."

"What about a ringleader?" Eden asked with hope.

Declan stepped up. "There's nothing yet, but he's got to be feeling boxed in. We've ruined his operation, and the noose is closing around his neck. He's mine." There was such ferocity in Declan's face that a shiver ran through Eden. She wouldn't want to be this man when Declan caught up to him.

"What if Chaz got away? What if he comes back to finish what he started?" she asked, looking once more at Owen.

He squeezed her hand, and she realized how much she trusted him. It was odd how easy it was to fall back into a pattern of relying on this man. She wanted to not need him, but now wasn't the time to even think about that.

"We'll get him, dead or alive," Owen assured her.

"Let the authorities get him. I don't want you anywhere near the man," she said. His gaze drifted from hers, as if he didn't want to lie to her but wasn't going to stop personally looking for the guy who meant her harm. "Promise me right now, Owen, that you'll let the cops go after him."

Owen's eyes came back to hers. "Eden," he said, the sound almost a whine. That made her smile.

"You're not five years old and being put in time-out, Owen. I want to save your soul," she said. She wouldn't allow him to look away. Finally, he nodded.

"I'll do anything for you," he said. "But I don't like it." He grumbled so low he probably thought she couldn't hear him. She just smiled as she turned back to Roxie.

"Thank you for being here and for filling me in." She took another drink of water. Her body hurt all over, but there were no casts, and she had no doubt they'd run every test they possibly could on her. She looked over to the large Forbes clan and spotted Kian in his doctor's gear.

"When do I get to leave?" she asked.

Kian stepped up with a smile. "I'd like you to stay at least twenty-four hours, possibly forty-eight. We'll see how you feel tomorrow. You hit your head hard and have a slight concussion," he told her. "You're also lucky your jaw isn't broken."

"Did I lose any teeth? Just be straight with me," she said with a wince. Her jaw really hurt, probably worse than her head.

He smiled. "Not one loose tooth," he assured her as he squeezed her hand.

She let out a sigh of relief. "I don't feel all that bad, and I really hate being in these places. They're too sterile," she said before looking around the room. "But this is more like a hotel suite than a hospital room. I'd almost be fooled if it weren't for these dang beeping monitors."

Kian laughed as he held tightly to her hand. "This is the VIP room," he said with a wink.

"I guess knowing you mooned the middle-school audience during intermission in seventh grade gives me blackmail material, so you upgraded me," she said with glee.

Roxie joined in on the laughter. "I can't believe I forgot about that," she said.

Kian smiled big. "I wasn't the only one who did that," he pointed out. "And it's a good thing my parents aren't here right now. My poor mother would most likely have a heart attack if she found out that incident involved two of her four sons."

"Your secret's safe with me," she assured him.

"Not with me. I have permanent blackmail to always get my way," Roxie said, still chuckling.

"You already do," Kian said, adoration in his eyes. The two of them kissed, and Eden realized she'd been totally forgotten for the moment.

"I'll stay here with you the entire time," Owen told her.

She smiled. "No, you won't. You're going to go out there and kick this fire's ass so I have a place to go when I get out of here. This fire has caused enough damage. I need to find a new home, so make sure the town I love is safe and sound," she insisted.

He looked as if he wanted to argue, but finally his shoulders drooped. "I'll go if that's what you really want." He was obviously hoping she'd change her mind.

"It's what I need," she told him. She wanted to think.

Everyone came up and wished her well; then finally Eden was alone. She didn't know what would come next. But for now she'd give her body a little bit of time to heal, and perhaps that would clear her mind and heart as well.

Maybe then she'd get answers as to what would come next in her life.

Chapter Thirty-Nine

Chaz had come down the mountain covered in soot and burns, all his hair gone, while there was still a search team looking for him. He'd raised his gun and basically initiated a suicide-by-cop. He wouldn't be a threat to anyone ever again. He also wouldn't be giving them any answers as to whom he'd been reporting.

Many people wondered how someone who had seemed so successful, who seemed to have his entire life together, could commit such a monstrous act. They never would get their answers. Owen figured it all came down to drugs. They drew a person in, and they never let go. It was tragic.

He wiped sweat from his brow. There was still danger out there, but it was growing weaker. They were on the winning team, and they'd get their town back soon.

It had been two weeks since that day in the hospital, two excruciatingly long weeks. Eden had been released, then told him she needed to take care of some things. She'd left town. He'd gotten only a few text messages from her the entire time. But Roxie assured him he needed to give her space to figure things out on her own. He'd taken ten years to pull his life together. The least he could do was give Eden a couple of weeks.

Even if his love life was a disaster right now, his work life was going a lot better. The winds had died down, and they'd gotten a couple of strong rainstorms, and now the fire was 98 percent contained. They'd finally gotten it under control, and even though Edmonds had a new view in many directions, the town was safe, and the air was beginning to clear.

Nature had a way of cleaning itself up. He had no doubt the phoenix was going to be rising from the ashes all over the Cascade Range. This time next year, new trees would be peppering the hills, and grass would be a soft carpet for visitors. This was why he loved fighting fires, to save the land and people's property. It was hard work, but he was always awed and humbled by the end result.

Owen had to force his mind back to his current situation. Even though the fire was contained, there was still a lot of work to be done, and all the men were exhausted. There were other things going on in his town as well that scared the hell out of Owen.

Chaz had been a lunatic, a man out for vengeance, but the evidence they'd found in his place had shown the scope of this ring he'd been a part of. That drug cartel had taken the lives of good men, had nearly taken the life of his sister-in-law, Keera, had nearly taken the life of the woman he loved, and had destroyed the land he'd grown up on. His brother Declan was more uptight than usual because he'd yet to catch the ringleader and put a stop to the mess.

They'd get the bad guy. It was only a matter of time, but right now Owen couldn't focus on that. By the end of each night, he barely managed to stumble back to the station, where he crashed on one of the cots.

He had to figure out if he was going to build a new home or buy one. He loved his land, though, and most likely would build. That just meant he didn't know where he was going to go in the meantime. That decision rested a lot on Eden. He didn't care where he was as long as she was with him.

On this particular night, he decided to visit Declan. His brother was in his den when Owen arrived. The two sat for a while in silence as they drank a cold beer and watched the flickering flames in Declan's fireplace.

It was odd, because he should have been sick to death of fire, but a contained one in a hearth was soothing.

"When are you going to propose to the girl?" Declan asked after they'd sat in silence for a while.

"I'd do it right this minute if she'd come home," Owen told him.

Declan let out a sound that some might have thought was a groan but that Owen knew was a chuckle. It was almost a scary sound, but Owen and the rest of the family were getting used to it.

"Throw her over your shoulder, and don't take no for an answer," Declan told him.

This time it was Owen who was laughing. "Aren't you FBI?" he asked.

"So?" Declan said.

"Isn't that considered kidnapping?" he pointed out.

Declan waved his hand. "Only if the girl doesn't want to be captured," he assured him.

"I'm pretty sure she wants to be caught," Owen said.

"You two have been in love for as long as I can remember. It seems all of you guys are falling in love. I'm going to be the only bachelor," Declan said. Owen was surprised by the note of bitterness in his brother's words.

"You don't have to be," Owen told him. "I'm pretty sure I've seen some sparks between you and Angela."

Declan glared at him. "She's a mom, and she has no business with someone like me."

"What's that supposed to mean?" Owen asked, slightly irritated. "I think you're far too hard on yourself. She'd be lucky to have you." He didn't like it when anyone put down a member of his family, even if the one slinging the insults was a member of his family speaking about himself.

"I've got too many skeletons in my closet," Declan told him. There suddenly seemed to be a sadness to his brother he'd never seen before.

"I hope you'll tell us about it someday. I think it would help," Owen said.

"I will," Declan told him. Owen wasn't surprised. Declan would talk when the time came.

They chatted for a while longer, then Declan stood. "Use the guesthouse on the back of the property. You'll have privacy, and you can stay until you build your new place."

"That sounds just about perfect," Owen said, feeling relieved. He hadn't thought of that, but it was a good idea. It was a place he could bring Eden where she'd feel comfortable.

Declan threw him a key, then left the room. Owen now had nothing to do but wait. He hoped it wouldn't be for too long.

◆ ◆ ◆

They think they've won.

Fury rushed through the man's body in waves so intense he found his heart thundering and his veins burning. They'd taken everything from him, and he wasn't sure how to strike back at them. Everything he'd tried so far had failed.

Looking through his high-powered lens, he watched as Declan approached the maid Arden Forbes employed. She had her child with her and was standing in front of the café she worked at part-time. Declan stood close to her—protectively close. A person walked by the three of them and nearly bumped into the kid, and Declan quickly swooped the boy up in his arms, cradling him close to his chest.

The maid looked at Declan as if he was her hero.

The man on the hill above the town smiled. His fury dissipated as a plan began forming in his mind.

Declan had a weak point.

And he had a way in. They all thought he'd died long ago. But he was a man not easily killed. He was a man used to hiding in the shadows. And he had history with Declan's love interest . . . history with her and with the boy. He had more history than any of them could possibly imagine. It was about to all come around in one beautiful circle.

A smile replaced the scowl the man had been wearing. He knew how to get his revenge. He knew exactly where to strike to make the entire Forbes family bleed.

"I'm Mario Vasquez, and I take no prisoners," he said aloud. It was time to finish what he'd begun.

Chapter Forty

Eden found herself smiling as she came back to town. She didn't know why it had taken her three weeks to realize the heart knows what the heart wants. The past didn't matter anymore. It was all about the future. And her future wouldn't be complete without Owen Forbes as a part of it.

She sent him a short text as she rolled into town, telling him to meet her at the dock. She had no doubt he'd be there. She should've called him, should've told him more, especially after making him wait what had to feel like an eternity. But she'd had to do that. She didn't want him to think she was only staying with him because of the situation they'd been in together.

A lot of relationships that began in highly intense situations fizzled out when the adrenaline was gone and the people realized they had nothing to sustain them. But what Eden had failed to realize was that she and Owen had something so much deeper than one moment. They had years. Not all of that time had been good, but no matter what, she'd loved him, and she knew he'd always loved her. That would be enough. Love truly would get them through a lifetime together.

Her passenger gave a yelp of excitement, and Eden turned, smiling as she reached out and scratched the four-year-old black-and-white boxer's scruffy head. She didn't have a home, didn't know what tomorrow would bring, but on her journey of finding herself, she'd managed to walk into a shelter. The moment she'd looked into Scooter's eyes, she'd known they belonged together.

"We're almost home, Scooter," she told him.

His tongue flopped from his mouth as he looked at her with total adoration. They'd found each other, and she had no regrets.

She reached her property, glad she was the first to arrive. She didn't have to put a leash on Scooter, as he didn't let her more than a few feet out of his sight, so she let him out of the car, and the two of them walked down to her dock and looked out at the peaceful view of the water. The smoke was gone, the winds taking the final tendrils that had been hanging around far away. The smell of burning trees still hung in the air, but that was fading, too. Soon, no one would even know there'd been a deadly fire there, threatening their town.

Soon life could get back to normal.

Rolling up her pant legs and tossing her shoes aside, Eden sat on the dock, immediately feeling at peace as she stuck her feet in the refreshing water. Once Scooter was assured she wasn't going anywhere, he explored the water's edge and began marking as many places as possible. They were both relieved to be out of the car.

She was tuned in to the sound of Owen's arrival and knew the minute he'd parked his truck. Her heart began thumping. There wasn't a single doubt in her mind he'd accept what she was offering, but she still found herself nervous. It was silly and irrational, but so were a lot of things in life.

She felt him before she saw him. Turning her gaze from the beautiful view of the sun beginning to set over the water, Eden watched as Owen made his way down the trail to her dock. At the sight of a new person, Scooter rushed to her side and sat there, definitely trying to decide if this man was friend or foe.

Her heart stopped for a few moments, before it started beating like a sledgehammer. She'd missed him so much. There was no way she could go endless amounts of time without being with him, not when she knew he wanted her. Those days were behind them. It was time to grow up, stop playing games neither of them knew they were playing, and open their hearts. She could do that. She knew he could, as well.

She loved him. It really was as simple as that.

Love. What a tiny word for such a massive emotion with so many facets to it. Not even the brightest of the bright would ever figure out why or how love happened. At the end of the day, it was something a person had to take a leap of faith on. She guessed she was back to believing in fate.

Owen drew closer, and each step he took made her feel as if she was becoming a little bit more whole by the second. He truly was her other half, and without him she never quite felt right, never felt complete.

"Looks like you found a friend," Owen said as he looked down at Scooter, who looked as if he hadn't made a decision about Owen yet.

"This is Scooter. I've adopted him," she said, laying a protective hand on him.

"I like him," Owen said with a smile. She let out a relieved breath. Scooter seemed to do the same, as he relaxed. She didn't have a chance to say anything else before Owen continued speaking. "I've missed you." His words were quiet and intense at the same time.

And just like that, Eden couldn't stand not to touch him. She stood and rushed to him, throwing her arms around his neck, nearly knocking them both over. It was a good thing Owen was so strong, or they probably would've ended up in the lake. Scooter chased after her and whined at their feet, unsure of this new development.

Owen didn't hesitate as his lips met hers, the kiss so hot it nearly burned them both. It was several moments before she was able to break away, her skin tingling, and his eyes burning with a light that made her want to forget all about talking.

She reached up and caressed his cheek, loving the feel of his five-o'clock shadow, loving how strong his jaw was, but loving the light in his eyes above anything else. How could she ever doubt her emotions for this man? She'd been a fool.

"I missed you, too," she said, then giggled. "Obviously."

"Are you back to stay?" he asked. She loved that he was trying to hold back, that he was trying to give her the space she'd asked for. It made her love him that much more.

"I'm not going anywhere," she promised, and saw relief in his eyes.

"I love you, Eden." He spoke the words almost defiantly, as if daring her to tell him not to say it. She had before. She never would again.

"I love you too, Owen," she said with ease.

His arms tightened around her, and his lips crashed against hers as his hands molded to her back. It was a very long time before he stopped, leaving them both out of breath and about to be in trouble for indecent exposure if they continued. She pulled back, her thumb rubbing over his bottom lip, which was swollen and red from her teeth.

"I carried the past as armor for too long. We were just kids. We're all grown up now, and I love you and trust you," she said.

He looked at her with such adoration, she knew she'd made the right decision. There was no longer anything that could keep the two of them apart. It made her happier than she'd ever been.

"If I hadn't hurt you, you wouldn't have had anything to fear. I won't bring it up again, but this final time I'll tell you I'm sorry. You're the most important person in my life, have always been. I want to give you the world, give you those babies you want, and be by your side when we're old and gray," he said.

She sighed as she reached up and kissed his jaw. He suddenly picked her up, and she let out a giggle, forgetting all about her shoes as he carried her up the trail. Scooter was running circles around his legs, and Owen spoke softly to the dog, assuring him everything would be okay. Scooter seemed to understand him and calmed down as he stayed right on his heels. Eden was confused when they reached his truck and she found a chair sitting beside it.

He set her in it, then dropped to his knee and reached into his pocket. Tears instantly filled her eyes. Scooter's head twisted back and forth between them.

"I've carried this around for years," he admitted, and she believed him, as half the velvet had been rubbed off the box. That only made it that much more beautiful to her. When he opened the lid, she couldn't stop her gasp. The box might have been damaged, but the diamond inside sparkled as the setting sun hit it.

"I'll spend the rest of my life cherishing you, loving you, and being your equal partner. I can't promise we'll never argue, but I can assure you you'll always win. There's nothing I'm not willing to do for you, and I know you feel the same. Let's start over right here, right now. And let's ride off into eternity together. Marry me," he said.

She could barely see through her tears. She could barely speak as she watched him tremble before her. But she knew this was the most perfect moment of her life. She knew this was right.

"Oh, Owen, it will be my honor to marry you, to carry your name, to be your wife and the mother of your kids," she said, amazed she was able to get the words out.

The sun sank below the horizon as he slipped the ring on her finger; then she jumped into his arms, knocking them both over. Scooter joined in, and Eden realized her life was so beautifully good. They had to put Scooter up in the truck after a while because they didn't want any interference. They made love right there in the shadow of his truck, with the stars twinkling down on them.

When they were finished, Eden looked up and made a wish, knowing without a doubt it would come true. Fate had a funny way of working, but she was discovering it truly did always get its way.

Chapter Forty-One

There was never a more perfect time than the end of summer in Washington State. The breeze cooled the air just enough to make the sun's hot rays feel good on the skin, and the water was finally warm enough to touch. It wouldn't last long, but it was enough to make any ills fade away.

Eden was trying to figure out what her next step in life was going to be. There was no way she could go back and sit in a stuffy office five days a week, not after spending time investigating the arson and feeling what it was like to have freedom and responsibility.

She had loved her job for a while, but now she knew it was time for a new adventure. She just wasn't sure what that would be. Even knowing it was time to move on, she found she had a difficult time saying goodbye to Sal, her boss. A few tears might have been shed—and they weren't just hers.

Eden stepped outside, her bag hung over her shoulder, and when she looked up, she was stopped dead in her tracks. She blinked a couple of times and found herself grinning as she faced Owen in his worn blue jeans, black T-shirt, and baseball cap . . . leaning against a shiny black Lamborghini Reventón, Scooter happily sitting at his feet.

She approached slowly, afraid to even touch the $1.4 million car. Apparently Owen didn't have the same problem, since he was leaning against it, unafraid that his raggedy jeans might scratch it.

"What in the world are you doing?" she asked, unable to take her eyes away from the beautiful car.

"Picking up my fiancée," he told her, not moving an inch.

"In a ridiculously priced car?" she said. She wanted to touch it.

"Weren't you making fun of me because I don't act like a billionaire?" he asked with a laugh.

"Yes, I was, but it's something I love about you," she told him. "But dang, this car is pretty," she added with a sigh. "Now take it back before it gets damaged."

"Sorry, I can't return it. It's an engagement gift," he said.

Her eyes snapped to his face, and she looked at him with horror.

"You didn't actually buy this, did you?" she asked, her tone hushed. She looked around, thinking there might be cameras somewhere.

"I sure did," he told her. He finally moved and opened the driver's-side door. He pulled it open and held out his hand. "My lady," he said.

She didn't move an inch as she gazed at the interior of the car. It was pristine and unbelievable. She wouldn't dare get in. But . . . oh . . . she was tempted.

"It's yours," he said, his smile fading. "To do with as you please."

He grabbed hold of her and gave her a little tug and a little push until she was sitting in the driver's seat. Then he shut the door, and he and Scooter went around to the passenger side. She sat there in awed silence as her fingers caressed the wheel.

"Let's go for a drive," he said. She couldn't help but smile as she watched this perfect man next to her utterly comfortable with Scooter sitting in his lap, both of their expressions seeming to say, *Hurry up.*

"Maybe just a little drive," she told him.

And then it was all over. The engine purred to life, and the second she put her foot on the gas pedal, the car owned her. The three of them flew down side roads until they hit an open place on the freeway, and Eden laughed with joy as she shifted gears and marveled at how well the car handled.

Owen didn't say a word, just sat back, acting as if he didn't have a care in the world. When she finally turned back toward Edmonds, he asked her to stop at the docks.

"We can't keep this car, Owen. It's ridiculous to pay this much for a vehicle," she said, already dreading giving it back.

"You can't return a gift. It's unladylike," he told her.

"You're wearing ratty clothes, and I'm jobless at the moment. It's so excessive," she said, but she was caving. She didn't want to let go of the car.

"As you've pointed out, I'm a billionaire," he said with a laugh. Then his face grew serious. "And I don't flaunt it; I have a job I love that I do because I can help people, and I will die for those I love. I don't feel guilty about buying my future bride a gift."

Her tears didn't fall until she was parked at the docks. He climbed from the car, then came around and helped her out. She pulled him against her, wrapping her arms around him. Scooter was now used to this and stood by patiently, waiting for the mushiness to finish.

"I want it," she said. Then she kissed him hard. "But don't think I need it," she added.

"I wanted to give it to you because you'd be just as happy if I got you a ten-dollar picture frame," he told her.

"I love everything you've ever given me," she said.

"Well, then, you'll really love this," he told her with a grin.

He grabbed her hand, and they walked down the docks, just as they had so many years before. She looked back a few times at her beautiful car, afraid of someone hurting it. Scooter looked up at her with a grin. She was certain her dog could read her mind.

"The parking lot's secure. Your car will be fine," Owen assured her with a laugh. She turned to face forward.

"We've been waiting all night for you to get here. I told you not to give her the car until tomorrow."

Eden looked up and saw Dakota and Ace, Kian and Roxie, Arden and Keera, and Declan on board a massive yacht.

"Are we going for a ride?" she asked with delight.

"We sure are," he said. Then he pointed to the back of the boat. Eden gasped again.

In bold black letters on the back, it said, LIVE, LAUGH, DANCE, DREAM. OUR FATE IS WRITTEN IN THE STARS. EDEN & OWEN.

"Is this yours?" she asked.

"It's ours. And tonight we're taking her on her maiden voyage with the people we love."

She was silent for several moments; then she found herself kissing him again until they were both breathless, and his brothers were catcalling from above. Finally, she pulled away.

"I guess we've come right back to where we started," she told him.

"We took a while to get here, but I want to keep every promise I've ever made to you and make sure every dream you've ever had comes true," he said.

"You already have," she assured him.

He held out his hand, and the two of them walked on board the ship with Scooter happily following. Declan and Kian cast them off, and Arden piloted the boat as they made their way out to the water.

Eden laughed delightedly when Scooter walked up to Max and circled the large German shepherd. This was their normal routine. Max looked down at the small dog with indulgence before flopping to the floor and letting Scooter strut. They were quickly becoming best friends. And Max had no problem letting Scooter think he was the big dog in town.

Eden sat back with her future sisters-in-law, realizing it wasn't possible to feel any happier than she felt at this particular moment. She watched as Owen stood with Declan by the side of the boat, drinking a beer and talking intensely about something.

"Heads up," Kian called. A ball went flying through the air, and Owen jumped back to avoid being hit in the temple. He tripped, and Eden felt her heart stop as he tumbled over the side of the ship. She jumped to her feet, but she was too late.

Declan reached out, grabbing his brother's hand before he could hit the water. The words he spoke next made her realize everything would be okay.

"I've got you, little brother," Declan told him.

"No worries. I can climb back up," Owen said, trying to pull his hand free.

Declan tightened his grip as he smiled down at Owen. "It's okay to allow others to help you once in a while. You don't always need to be the hero. Trust me."

Owen grinned at his brother as he reached up and grabbed Declan's other hand and took the help being offered, leaving his fate in his brother's hands. When he was safely back on the deck, he gave Declan a hug.

"I think I honestly do realize that now, Dec," he told him. "Together, there isn't anything we won't accomplish."

They were right. They were a family, and Eden knew beyond a doubt she was a part of it. She always had been; it had just taken her a very long time to realize it. She was home, right where she belonged.

Epilogue

Though Owen had wanted to rush Eden off to the nearest justice of the peace and make their union legal, she refused. His sisters-in-law had emphatically refused as well, leaving him outnumbered.

As Eden stood gazing into the full-length mirror before her, she was glad she'd stood her ground. There was a part of her that was broken that her father wasn't there in person on her wedding day, but there was another part of her that had no doubt he was with her in spirit.

She couldn't think these thoughts because she'd become a weeping mess before her wedding. Instead, she took a few deep breaths and appreciated having a few moments alone after all the chaos of the morning and afternoon while she'd gotten ready.

It was time, sooner than she was ready, and when there was a tap on the door, she turned and smiled as Roxie walked in. She beamed at Eden.

"Are you ready?" Roxie asked.

"I've been ready since I was a blushing teen," Eden told her.

"Then let's get you down that aisle," Roxie said.

Eden had wanted to keep the ceremony simple. When she and Roxie stepped to the top of the aisle, she was pleased. Delicate flowers adorned the intimate room. There were about a hundred people in the small church. It was exactly how she'd envisioned her wedding so many years before, when she'd been sure she and Owen would marry.

Roxie put her arm through Eden's, and together they walked down the aisle. There was no way Eden could've handled another person stepping into her father's place on this magical day, so she'd asked Roxie to walk side by side with her instead of in front of her as her matron of honor. Her friend had tearily agreed.

The ceremony was beautiful, and Eden wasn't able to hold back tears as Owen promised to be hers for all time and eternity. They made it through the ceremony, and it felt mystical when they were pronounced man and wife.

The reception was intimate as well, though a lot more people came. They ate, gave toasts, cut the cake, and tossed the bouquet. Then the music began, and Owen pulled her into his arms, the safest place on earth for her.

"Thank you," she told him. "Thank you for giving me the perfect wedding."

He leaned down and kissed her gently. "There's nothing I won't do for you. I hope you truly know that," he replied.

"I do. I feel the same about you."

"And now for the father-daughter dance," the DJ announced.

Eden's smile fell away as tears instantly came to her eyes, and she froze in the middle of the dance floor, feeling faint.

"I thought I told him not to do that," she said, her voice barely above a whisper.

"I did it for you," he told her. He turned her, and huge screens had been moved into place across the dance floor while Declan and Kian wheeled out a table. On the table was a teddy bear wearing her father's favorite shirt and pants, which had been altered to fit the bear. His cane rested there, as well as his favorite books and his eyeglasses. There was a plate with rice and beans, and a cup of coffee next to it.

The screens lit up as "Dance with My Father" by Luther Vandross began playing. Eden was mesmerized as pictures of her and her father played, beginning from the time she was a baby all the way to a month before he'd passed. The last image was of her and her dad, arm in arm, both of them smiling, the love between them clear for all to see.

"You were the person he loved most in this world, and I know he's here with you. I wanted to give you your moment with him," Owen told her. "I'm so sorry you can't be held by him. I just want you to know my arms are strong enough to carry your burdens, and though I don't ever want to replace him, I'll love you as much as he loved you, and I'll keep his memory alive for you."

She turned around and wrapped her arms around his neck, crying in his arms while the music continued. Her heart was broken and healing at the same time.

It took a while for her to be able to speak again, but when she could, she looked into Owen's beautiful face and rested her fingers against his cheek. "Thank you. It's the best gift you could have given me," she told him.

He leaned down and kissed her, then pulled her back into his arms and held her tight as she thanked the fates for not giving up on her. She had no doubt, as she felt the whisper of lips against her cheek, that it was her dad letting her know she was where she needed to be—and that she was strong enough to be happy and not feel guilty about it.

She'd found her forever, and it was only just beginning . . .

ACKNOWLEDGMENTS

No matter how many books I finish, I will never, ever forget that I don't do it alone. As authors, there are times we live a very solitary life. My favorite writing place is my back porch, looking out over the fields and mountains in my small town. I recently moved about a mile from my old house, and now my view is even more peaceful and wonderful. And though I may write these stories alone, I don't come up with them by myself, and I certainly don't polish them on my own. Without a team of people supporting me, I never would have come this far in my journey as an author.

First and foremost, thank you to my fans. I couldn't do the job I do without you. You stay with me through thick and thin. You stay with me as I try new genres or get a whim. I love you and appreciate you so much for that! I thank you for allowing me to do this job. You are the reason I get to live my dreams. I'll never forget that! You tell me your stories of pain and triumph, and I'm so grateful. There are no authors without readers. There's no inspiration without you. I can't ever say thank you enough times.

I also need to say thank you to my best friend, Stephanie. I was with her as she was taking a nursing class, and she worked through so many issues in this book with me. She's a nurse practitioner, which is about the coolest job ever. She's a total stud. ☺ She helps me with all of my medical scenes in every book I write. Also, she was the first person on my doorstep when my dad died, and she was there to work through painful scenes in this book. I have used many, many, many ideas in my books from our conversations.

I need to thank Lauren, who's my editor at Montlake. She's been with me from the beginning with them, and we click so dang well. I value her advice, opinions, and input. She has forced me to be a better writer, to challenge myself, and to not settle on mediocre but to reach for great. I know that when I turn in a first draft of a book, it's crap. I also don't worry because I know we're going to sit there for two hours if we need to, and we'll work it all out. I also just like her. I'm one of those people who can't work with people I don't like. It's impossible for me to separate business from personal. My work is personal, and I've never been able to do it. I decided I don't care. It's just who I am, and I don't want to change that. I don't want to compromise my integrity in the name of work.

I have a new editor at Montlake now who's been added to my team. At first I was a little worried, since I've loved working solo with Lauren so much. But then the edits came in, and I was instantly in love. Lindsey is fantastic! She has an eye for detail, doesn't mind going over issues again and again, and gives me new challenges to face. If I ever hear authors say they don't need help, that they are fine as they are, I cringe. We are never fine as we are. We get stagnant without asking for help. We need new voices. I'm so grateful for Lindsey and her new voice and her perspective. She's helped so much with this book.

I know this has been long, but this book has been a journey for me. Every book I write is an adventure, but this book was more so than any other. As usual, there isn't enough space to thank everyone who helps me. But I am grateful for all of you. I adore publishing with Montlake. I love all the people who work there so dang hard without getting a lot of praise. I love the people who fight for me and my books and who keep me doing what I do. I found a fit with Montlake, and I know it's where I'm supposed to be. Thank you all!

AUTHOR'S NOTE

I think *Owen* has to be my favorite story I've ever written. When I began this book, I had originally had the heroine's father die, as that was part of her journey. I've killed off countless characters in many books, and I always say that I use and abuse characters according to my own whims. But then tragedy struck me, and my own father unexpectedly died with zero warning. My world crashed hard. Anyone who knows me knows I'm a daddy's girl through and through. My dad raised me, and I'm so grateful for the years I got with him, for the lessons in life he taught me, and for the memories that will carry me through this pain that seems to never end from missing him.

I couldn't write for a while. I was a mess. And then I opened up this book again, and I felt blessed. There are so many people out there who go through tragedies, and they don't get to take time off; they don't get to grieve the way they need to. But because of this beautiful job I have, I can grieve through my work. I don't need journals; my journals are my books, and I share them with you, and your words help me get through even the toughest of situations.

Eden's father in this book is my dad to a T. My father was a man of nature, larger than life and willing to give the shirt off his back to a stranger. He loved being outdoors and was simple in what he wanted. He raised me with love and compassion and didn't judge others. The pain Eden goes through and the things she says are a huge reflection of my own journey in losing my dad. I've been sad and angry and happy. I got so much more time with my father than most people get. But I'm selfish and needy, and I want more. I want him here now. There's a line in the book where Owen tells Eden that her father lives on through her and through future generations. I sobbed as I wrote that scene, but it also gave me some peace, because as I look at my twenty-one-year-old son, I realize those words are true. He is so much like his grandfather in looks and demeanor. He even loves to debate, which his grandfather was famous for. My son does things that take my breath away. We get to talk about my dad and heal together. I have my dad's ratty old guitar, and I ask him daily to strum it so I know he's here with me. So far he hasn't, but I'm not giving up. ☺

I took a hard journey, and I've gone through every emotion known to man. I've been mad at my dad for leaving me. I've told people forever that you don't have children to be loved, because children are inevitably selfish. It's how we have to be to survive. What I've realized is that it doesn't matter how old we get; we are still selfish when it comes to our parents. We still want them to always be there for us, no matter what. Yes, our children love us, but they grow older and get their own lives. That's the circle of life. But as parents, we know that our door is always open. My dad's door was never closed to me. I knew what I meant to my dad. I also know that he had no doubt how much I love him. There was nothing left unresolved. And now you get to know this wonderful man a little bit through this book and into the next story, as Eden shows up a few times to slowly heal from her loss.

I asked my publisher if I could have the last pic my dad and I took together as my author photo for this book. My dad was a giant, standing at six-foot-five inches, and he was a hippie through and through. This photo was taken in the summer of 2017. My dad passed in January 2018. I love this picture so much. I love that content look on my dad's face. I love how much he loved me, no matter what. I love that he was proud of me. When I was a kid, I allowed people to make me think there was something wrong with the way he chose to live. But then I grew up and realized that I am who I am because of him. I am so thankful he didn't hand me everything, but that he taught me to work for what I want. I'm so thankful for all the lessons in life that he taught me. I love that you get to know my dad a little bit through this book and through the years of my posts on social media. Thank you for that. Thank you for helping me grieve. This book will forever be special to me. I will read it over and over again myself and think of my dad. I won't ever stop missing him, but I will forever be grateful for the influence he's had, and has, over me.

ABOUT THE AUTHOR

Melody Anne is a *New York Times* and *USA Today* bestselling author whose popular series include Undercover Billionaire, Billionaire Bachelors, Surrender, Baby for the Billionaire, and Billionaire Aviators, along with a young adult series and other romance novels. She loves to write about strong, powerful businessmen and the corporate world.

Since finding her true calling, she has been an Amazon top 100 bestselling author for three years in a row. When not writing, Melody spends time with family, friends, and her many pets. A country girl at heart, she loves her small town and is involved in many community projects. For more information and updates about Melody Anne, visit her at www.MelodyAnne.com or follow her on Twitter @authmelodyanne and Facebook @melodyanneauthor.